BOOK 1

ElevenSeventeen

Middle School,
A Storm is Gathering

PHILIP J. MACK

Print ISBN: 979-8-35091-040-7
eBook ISBN: 979-8-35091-041-4

To God:

You have been, are, and will be the Hero on every page of my life!

To my Wife:

Thank you for putting up with all the late nights and bouts with writer's block!

You are the BEST gift in the world and I thank God for you!

Kyrie Eleison

CONTENTS

CHAPTER 0:
ACKNOWLEDGMENTS

FIRST, A DISCLAIMER...

Any similarity to living or deceased people or events, real or imagined, is coincidental. Basically, it's like this: If you weren't involved in any of this stuff then I don't know you and it's not about you. If you were involved and I do know you, I'm just telling my side of the story in the manner I feel is best.

TO ALL THOSE **MYSFITS** OUT THERE:

Keep being your unbelievably cool selves!

TO YOU KNOW WHO YOU REALLY ARE:

I wanted to take a moment to address you. We have not seen each other since that night when we were seventeen and I'd like to think that we've moved on. Congratulations on your career. Given the fact that your resources both financial and legal are vast to say the least, please consider the following. I have never mentioned you until this writing and even now I have done so in the abstract and with respect. Also, the experiences we shared are just that, shared. I have the same rights to them as you do. I have merely written my perspective. Should you wish to do the same, please do so... it is after all, your right.

CHAPTER 1:
MUSE

The sun was sitting just above the treetops to the west. Its warm rays were spread out in lines across the large porch as they strained through the banister poles onto the grayish weather-resistant paint floor. It had been a perfect day, a wonderful Friday afternoon at home with my family. It had been an unusual day in that for November in Maryland, 83 degrees is an anomaly. Promise, my five-year-old was playing on the porch, an afro-puff on either side of her head. Her hair was parted perfectly down the middle which spoke to her mother's meticulous care in making sure our child was always presentable. I couldn't help but get lost in the moment, thinking of what it was like to be five, and thinking of what it meant to be a father.

Promise, dressed rather smartly in a dark blue denim suit of sorts and tennis shoes, hopped up into my lap and smiled. We shared a special understanding, she and I. With a smile or a wink, we could communicate a simple, uncomplicated love. A love so basic yet so profound; the paradox that is the parent's heart. I knew she felt safe. Her eyes examined my face, softly moving back and forth as if examining some painting of a grand landscape. Soft giggles as I made faces at her. Let's face it, this little manipulator had me wrapped around her little finger and even at 5 years she knew it all too well. I was doomed... and I wanted to be.

Promise glanced about. She followed a bird until it landed on the banister. She smiled at it and if I could see through her eyes, I would surely be able to see it smile back at her. My right arm was wrapped around her and she fixed her gaze on my high school class ring just as a ray of sunshine shown through the faux ruby set atop the large silver and black Towson Christian Academy ring. She paused for a moment and ran her fingers across the stone. "Pretty." she said with that sense of wonder only a child can supply. My wife, Tempest, emerged from the house with a pitcher of southern sweet tea and cups. She sat next to us on the swinging white bench from which we'd seen many good times since building the house a year ago. "What's pretty, baby?" she asked with that softness mothers reserve for their children. "This diamond." she replied. "Ruby, baby, it's a ruby." Tempest said. "Your daddy and his friends met each other in high school and that means a lot to them. Except for them, you didn't really like that school too much, did you dear?"

"Not really but… you know, they were some of the best days of my life… and the worst."

"I know, that's what you keep saying. You'll tell me the whole story one of these days I guess."

We'd been waiting for my best friend Gene Tucker and his wife to arrive. They and their son were coming over for dinner, something we make a point of doing at least once a month. Out of the corner of my eye I caught his black SUV as it turned onto my driveway. I watched with antic- ipation as it slowly crept up the long driveway and came to a stop in front of the garage. This feeling… This feeling takes me back to when we used to hang out when we were teenagers – the anticipation of good times and cherished memories.

Gene stepped out wearing his usual black t-shirt, showing off his obvious athleticism. Khaki slacks and black Nikes rounded out his outfit. For as long as I've known him, Gene has always dressed well. He let his son, Ethan, out of the back and approached the house. "Uncle Gene! Ethan!" my daughter exclaimed as she dropped from my lap, bounded down the steps, and wrapped her arms around the six-year-old who was equally happy to see her.

I crossed the porch to the top of the steps to assume a position of judgmental dominance as I said condemningly, "Late, I see…"

"Oh, come on, you know it takes a few extra minutes now that you guys moved out here to Daniels."

"Yeah, I guess. Come here!"

I put out my hand and we went through our special handshake that ends in an embrace. I loved this man like he was my own brother.

"Just us tonight, short-staffed at the hospital."

"I understand. No problem, we'll see her next time." Gene's wife is a head-nurse and when they get short-staffed, which happens all too often if you ask me, she has to go to work.

"Aww, I was hoping to get some girl time." Tempest said as she gave Gene a hug.

"She wanted that too, believe me."

"Daddy's ring… Daddy's ring!" the five-year old blurted when she saw Gene's class ring.

"This one's mine but you know…"

"Mommy said it means something." she interrupted.

Just then Ethan tagged Promise and the two kids were running around in the front yard. Without a word, the three of us got lost in the show that was our children carelessly and effortlessly enjoying themselves. Their laughter comprised a melody the likes of which sets men to dream, to dare to become better men if only to keep the laughter going.

Leave it to my stomach to break the mood. "Was that your stomach?" Tempest asked. "Yeah, I guess it wants some of that mac and cheese you made."

5

"Well, let's go to the deck, I've already set the table." Tempest suggested.

Gene agreed and we called the kids and started into the house. We'd just received the last bits of furniture that finally made this house feel like a home rather than an empty shell devoid of any sense of life or relationship.

"I love it!" Gene commented. "This place has really come along!"

"Yeah, we couldn't make up our minds on furniture until this month. Things just fell into place." Tempest replied.

"I'm so glad writing is working out for you, Joe. That book deal was a real blessing." Gene said.

"Thank you. You know I'm not quitting my day job. I'm still a geek at heart."

"Me too. Once a geek always a geek I guess." Gene opined.

The picnic table on the deck was adorned with the clichéic red and white checker pattern tablecloth. A spread of food ranging from fried chicken to macaroni and cheese to salad was laid out on the table. The back of the house overlooks a wooded preserve and the full orb of the setting sun was visible through the screens that kept the deck bug-free in the Summer. A couple of large plants, products of my wife's gardening hobby sat in the corners. The children found their places and giggled among themselves over some secret amusement they shared. "Let's ask the blessing." I said. I gave thanks to God for all present and absent and for all that He'd done and continues to do. After that we dug in.

During the feast Tempest commented on the weather and how unusual it was for a November day in Maryland to be so mild and that she had to take advantage of it and have dinner outside. "It's supposed to be nice all weekend and Promise and I were talking about going to the Inner Harbor. You guys could come too, Gene, it would be fun. Thought we could sit on Federal Hill and have a picnic or something." she said as she continued to eat. Gene and I both grunted in agreement as we stared into our respective plates. For a moment, our eyes met and then we looked down again. Both of us displayed a little nervous fidgeting.

"I know you so well Mr. Mack, spill it…" Tempest said sternly, the gentle hint of her southern accent becoming more pronounced.

I glanced at Gene who surreptitiously shook his head to say, "No." "Um, it's just that the Harbor you know, been there, done that, touristy and all…" My words trailed off as I glanced back at Gene hoping to get some nod of approval – I got none.

"After all this group has been through, you two keep your secrets?" Tempest, annoyed, asked.

Shrugging at Gene as if to say, "What do you want me to do?" I said, "You know Gene and I have known each other for a long time, over thirty years now. We've been through some stuff and some of it we just don't talk about."

Gene gave me an incredulous look and interjected, "We've just got history is all… and history should stay in the past." He was looking at me as he said that last part and I knew it was a polite "shut up!"

"I see, well if it's *that* important I guess I should back off." Tempest said.

"Exactly!" Gene exclaimed. "Oh, I didn't mean… I mean, could you? Um please?"

"Don't worry, I get it." Tempest flatly replied.

"Can we have dessert, Mommy?" the little girl with the manipulative look asked.

"Sure, baby." said the adult with the sarcastic glances at Gene and me.

"None for me please, I've got to save up for Thanksgiving." Gene said.

"None for you, you need to eat better." my food warden decreed, looking at me.

"May Gene and I be excused to the office?" I asked.

"Sure, leave the wife in the dark and keep secrets." Tempest said with a wry smile on her face denoting the return of the playful nature on the list of things about her that led me to fall in love.

"Thank you, baby!" To the chorus of two children exclaiming "Ewwww" we kissed.

Gene and I went into the house as she said, "Run along and play nice now."

In stark contrast to the rest of the house, my office is intentionally spartan so as to decrease distraction when I'm writing. My wife would say that I'm attention deficit. I disagree, I just need to focus when I need to focus. A burgundy couch lines the far wall while a small flat panel television sits atop an entertainment unit that I made years ago – the only distraction I will allow at times. Three monitors, a keyboard, and mouse decorate my desk along with a picture of my family and another of three high school aged kids showing off their class rings by holding out their fists toward the camera.

"Next Friday is the seventeenth you know." I stated.

"I guess that's why I'm a little on edge." he responded.

"Look, Gene, maybe she's right. Maybe it has been long enough."

"The statute of limitations never expires on stuff like that." he quipped.

"I know, but why don't you let me write about it?"

"You're kidding right! I mean if you let that story fly... All I'm saying is I spent hours in interrogation; you spent four yourself. Do you really think we won't land right back there if what happened that night came out?" he argued.

I sat on the edge of the couch and looked up at him. "This might help us resolve some of that for ourselves. It could be cathartic." I offered.

"You mean to get Tempest off your back. You know I'm good with keeping it to ourselves... obviously." Gene stated.

"Tempest has nothing to do with this. I know you're good with it like it is but we, because of our pact, have never spoken with anyone about that night, not even our wives. Without that night we're not the men we are now and you know it." I fixed my gaze right on him, right into his eyes and said, "We need this."

"It can't be done without messing <expletive> up, so no!" he quipped.

There it was, profanity. He'd gotten MUCH better over the years but when he gets agitated a few of them will slip out. That's how I knew I had him on the ropes.

"What if I told the truth about that night but couched it in some fiction and obscured the facts so that no one would ever be able to tell exactly what happened? That way we get the closure we need and nothing gets stirred up." I volunteered.

"Why write the book at all? I mean if talking about it is all we need to do?"

"Good question. I think we need to get the story off our collective chest and besides it would give us something to offer the curious when asked. Also, I'll just say it, I need another book idea and I think this is a good one. Ghostwriting has been good for me but they're not *my* stories. Depending on the contract, ghostwriters can't even talk about what they wrote or seek any credit at all. The thought of giving voice to somebody else's stories was appealing for a while but now… well, it's time to tell my own, you know?"

He stared off into space for a minute and returned to earth with, "OK, say I was onboard – not that I am, how would something like this work?"

"Well, because this is based on real events, I would need to interview you. Since we want to muddy the waters a bit so that we don't stir up stuff, we would need to decide what goes in, what stays out, and what needs to be altered."

He looked at me. I could see in his face that he agreed on some level. I even dared to anticipate his agreeing to the idea. Just then he said, "I'll think about it." and nodded his head one time quickly. There it was, the end of the conversation. I knew with that nod that no other evidence was to be allowed in this court. It was up to the jury now and I just had to wait. Sure enough the topic shifted to football and Baltimore's schedule.

The next day was brutal because I couldn't sleep that night since my mind was spinning over how the story of our secret could come to life and whether or not Gene would give me his consent to write it. Breakfast that morning consisted of grits, eggs and bacon. I rather enjoyed the fact that my southern bride was in full effect. Tempest said, "So when are we going down to the Harbor!" This was followed with a squealing "Yay!" from the little lady with the key to my heart. How could I resist? The truth is that I wanted to resist because of all the memories that place stirred up. So, a few hours later we loaded up Tempest's SUV and headed up I-95. There is a point on I-95 north between mile markers 50 and 51 where the city of Baltimore is displayed before you like a feature in a pop-up storybook. Seeing the city in that way caused my mind to race through the many memories about which I wanted to write.

The weather was gorgeous which was why we had to contend with the literal bazillion people who each woke up that morning and chirped "Let's go to the Harbor." to their spouses. Eventually, after circling the Harbor and the "put my kid through college" expensive parking lots like a bird of prey, we found a rather decent parking space just off of Pratt Street.

We spent the day going through the Pratt and Light Street Pavilions and looking at boats all while navigating the throngs of like-minded Marylanders trying to enjoy an unscheduled Spring day. I was pretty much able to avoid thoughts of the past by experiencing the things we saw through the eyes of my daughter as if the world was new. That was working well until my wife said, "Let's go sit on Federal Hill." "Oh Joy!" I thought to myself sarcastically. Federal Hill was specifically where I did not want to be but my wife was taking me there as if she knew where to go. On the walk over there I kept thinking about how much I really did need to bring closure to that night. I would have to find another way if Gene was not willing.

The sun was setting on the city. The view was simply dazzling just as I remembered. It had been years since I last sat atop Federal Hill overlooking Baltimore. We sat there for an hour enjoying Promise's wonderment while the sun's rays became increasingly orange as they fell on the skyscrapers. That was just the right time to be there in the afternoon. So many memories flooded my head as I recounted the times I'd been there when I was younger – especially that last time.

We packed ourselves up and began the long trek to the car. It was an hour or so before we made it back to the car having stopped to observe a number of street performances. I suppose the juggler beguiled my daughter the most as her eyes lit up with glee when he juggled the balls of fire. I knew I was supposed to be in that moment with them but my mind was still on Federal Hill and how I just had to write the story. I've had this feeling before and there is no other way to explain it other than to say it is the closest I could feel to being nine months pregnant. You have this thing with a life of its own inside of you and you simply must let it out.

Later that night, after putting Promise to bed, Tempest and I sat up in the bed to talk and pray as we do as often as we get the chance. "What is it, baby?" she inquired.

"What do you mean? Nothing's wrong."

"I know you, remember? It's like the *Princess and the Pea* with you, I can tell when the slightest thing is wrong and you've been weird all day. Time to come clean." she stated.

"Yeah, come clean." I echoed. "It's this baby." I said while pointing to the class ring on my right hand.

"What, that – whatever it is – you and Gene are carrying around?" she blurted.

"Yeah, Gene is considering letting me write about it. The more I think about it, the more I *need* to write about it."

"I get that." she insisted, "but what does that have to with you're being all weird today? I don't understand how your process works." she admitted, "but I am trying."

I told her that I appreciated her willingness to learn and reminded her that I was trying my best to honor Gene's request to keep things under wraps although I was finding it difficult right then.

"I love you and that works for me." she concluded.

"I love you too."

I reached to turn off the light just as the phone rang. It took a moment for the caller ID to display "Gene Tucker" in the window.

"Hello?" I answered. "Hi Gene, what's... oh really, well... that's great! Can I see you tomorrow? OK then, goodnight." I put down the receiver.

"What was that all about?" Tempest asked.

"Gene said they were sitting up apparently having the same conversation as us."

"And..." she prodded.

"He's in."

CHAPTER 2:
ARCHAEOLOGY

The next morning, we got up for Church. Unfortunately for my wife and daughter, it was my turn to make breakfast. My wife jumped in after I burned some eggs and sausage while producing what could be best described as hockey pucks rather than biscuits from the oven. She salvaged what she could and served what we had. A child's face is one of the purest reflections of the truth we will ever see in a person. I did not need the expression on her face to know how bad I'd messed up.

"Sorry about breakfast this morning." I apologized, "It's just that I'm distracted, preoccupied with this story and all."

"I understand. I know you get this way." Tempest assured.

"I'll have my act together for lunch. I'm sure that'll be better."

"I know it will be better. I'm not letting you in the kitchen until your mind is back on earth." she wore the half-joking expression I knew all too well as she dumped the "hockey pucks".

"Where is Daddy's mind?" the cute kid inquired.

"I don't know baby but he's gonna find it real soon, OK?" she said as she hugged Promise.

Only the wasted food bothered me. I knew my family was in my corner and that was all I needed from them in that moment.

"So, are you inviting Gene over here or are you going over there?"

"It would be best if we talked here in my office."

"Yea! Ethan!" exclaimed the little girl with sunshine for a smile.

Disappointing the kid, my wife said, "No, baby, Uncle Gene and Daddy have work to do."

"Awww…"

As soon as we got back from Church, I went down to my office to prepare. I'd called Gene after the service ended. He told me to expect him around one. This was the perfect Sunday for this because Baltimore had a bye week. Football is one of my guilty pleasures; I wanted to use a purple theme in Promise's room but someone else prevailed making brighter colors the order of the day.

"Joe, do you need snacks or anything?"

"I think I'll run out and get a pizza, if that's OK."

"Fine by me, I haven't started lunch yet."

I called the number for the nearest *Pizza Baltimore*, a cheap pizza franchise in the area, and ordered an extra-large "*Baltimorioni*". This was our favorite, a twice-baked pizza with two types of cheese and twice the pepperoni. We used to get pizza from them and wile the night away playing video games. I played a playlist of our favorite music from those years and walked over to the mini-fridge to retrieve two bottles of *Peach Vanilla Mystic*. There were only six left when I opened the fridge. We only drank these on special occasions, the last being when Promise was born. These have been discontinued for well over a decade. I'm a nostalgic person and I thought all of this would help us recall facts and nuances we may have lost over the years.

Gene showed up sometime around one as promised. I could tell he was somewhat skeptical even though he was willing to give it a try. We exchanged pleasantries as we walked down the steps.

"How is this going to work?" he asked as we stopped at the door to my office.

"I think this will be the first of several sessions. I've prepared some basic questions; they will be like seeds and hopefully detailed conversations will grow from them. All of this will be recorded and will serve as my notes from which I'll try to build the story. Each of the questions should help us dig deeper and hopefully we'll find what we're looking for."

"That *sounds* OK, but what if I, or we get to a point where we don't want to continue?" he questioned.

"This is the story from our perspective, it takes the two of us to tell it – or at least to tell it right. So if we stop, we stop, but I don't think that'll happen."

"Oh yeah?"

"You remember Tempest wanted to go down to the Harbor yesterday? While we were there she wanted to sit on Federal Hill. I thought it was too ironic but it turned out to drive me to want to do this. I think something like that will happen to you."

"Well, I guess we'll see… Won't we."

I agreed as I opened the door. The smell we both knew so very well hit us in the face like a boxer with nothing to lose.

"You are one nostalgic son of a gun, aren't you?" he spouted, "Peach Vanilla Mystics too?"

"Yeah, that's me." I admitted.

"OK, you know I'll do anything for you, so I'll play along. But you need to know that if I need you to leave something out or change something, I'm trusting you to do it." he advised, one finger in the air.

"The readers will never know and I'll never tell them what actually happened and what didn't. The story will stand on its own." I pledged.

"And one more thing, we're just going through high school, right?" he asked.

"Just high school." I promised.

He gave that one quick nod and sat down to eat at the card table I'd set up for the occasion.

We were half-way through the *Baltimorioni* when he said, "OK, shoot!" I pulled a small digital recorder out of my pocket and pressed the record button. A soft tone emanated from the device and I set it on the table between us.

"This is interview conversation #1 for an as of yet untitled story, Gene Tucker and P. Joseph Mack present. It is Sunday, November 12, 2017." I would go on to mark every recording in this fashion. "That's about as formal as any of these conversations will be. Let's just talk and let the recorder take the notes. It has memory for hours on end so no worries."

"Um, OK..." he replied somewhat trepidatiously.

"When did we first meet?"

CHAPTER 3:
SALUTATIONS

From across the room the alarm clock bleated its cruel electronic beeps like an electric sheep from some android's dream. This was the electronic rooster's cry, the impersonal and unrelenting reveille that I knew all too well as my wake-up call for non-summer months. It was the first day of school. Furthermore, it was the first day of middle school. A new school in fact, Towson Christian Academy – a combined middle and high school. I'd attended a Christian school for elementary and this would be no different in that I knew what to expect. My brother graduated from this school the year before so I already knew the campus and at least some of the players on the faculty. Not unlike a prisoner assigned anew to a different facility, I knew the game, the rules, and that if I played my cards right, I could find a pretty good position in this new social order of things.

I shook my head in a vain attempt to clear it and accelerate my wakefulness. Motionless, I stared at the alarm clock across the room on the radiator and for a brief moment I hated myself for intentionally putting it that far from the bed. Struggling to push myself out of bed my feet found the floor. I drifted across the room and, silencing that retched alarm, allowed the silence of the pre-dawn bedroom to momentarily tempt me to go back to bed. Those red digital numbers, 5:30, bore themselves into a mind that had yet to shift from "Summer mode". I yawned and shook my head in disbelief. My attempt to convince myself that I was in some terrible dream was interrupted by a knock at the door and the voice of someone oblivious to the time.

"Time to get up! Big, big day!" chirped my morning person mother.

"OK... OK!" I grunted.

My father would have been boarding a subway in DC on his way to work by this time of the morning having left more than an hour earlier. My brother was in college in Delaware so for the first time in my life I had the room to myself. Bathroom time was divided between my mother and me. Since she insisted on getting up so early it was like I had it all to myself, a luxury I had not known.

"You don't want to be late on your first day. Time to move!" she lectured through the door.

"I'm moving, I' moving..."

I realized a week earlier that since I would have the room to myself, it would serve as my sanctuary throughout my high school years. With this in mind I did something for which my parents could have had me committed, I cleaned. I got the room just the way I wanted it. It took all week but it was worth it. Against the wall to the left as you enter was my elevated single bed. On the far wall was my new desk that I got for my birthday. On either side of the desk were the room's two windows. The radiator with its white grill housing was situated under the right window. It was here that my sadistic brain decided to put that alarm clock. Next to the radiator on the right wall stood another desk with a computer and a TV. To the right of that was a wall-mounted mirror under which stood a chest of drawers. The floor was covered with a red and blue carpet that endured the years of torture that only boys can supply. On my work desk sat a light-blue binder that would serve as the journal. The word "diary" didn't sit well with me, girls had diaries. I thought "journal" was a better term. It was an old binder inscribed with the word "French" that my brother used for that class at some point. In it I would chronicle my journey through high school. I'd envisioned a book filled with the ups and downs that go along with the thrill of dating an endless supply of cute ladies in the coming years. With this I figured I could capture details I was sure to forget. This way I would never forget important facts that I may need... like a cute girl's birthday or something. Though I had yet to write in it, I prepared it earlier that week by inserting about fifty blank pages. I even had the perfect hiding place for it, a large cavity in the wall exposed by a window sill that could be removed.

After dressing, I brought myself downstairs to the dinette. Putting a plate together for me she asked, "So are you excited?" Somehow "excitement" was not the word I would have used to describe the jumbled mass of nerves that grew in my stomach as the time to leave neared. I managed to push out an uninspiring "Uh, I guess..."

"You guess?" she said as she put the plate in front of me. "When I was your age, I couldn't wait for the start of the school year!"

"I don't know Mom, I guess I'm a bit nervous about the new school."

"You know Towson, your brother just graduated from there."

"I know, but that was him and his time there. I have to make my own way, my own place."

"I suppose I can't argue with that." she resigned. "You're growing up so fast – middle school already!"

It didn't seem so fast to me. In fact, it had taken a lifetime for me to get to that point. My twelve-year-old brain couldn't see the reason for her amazement. The parent's perspective is something I would not understand until much later in life.

With a smile I offered a "Yeah... looks like it" in an attempt to draw a close to this part of the conversation.

Breakfast that morning consisted of my favorites, French toast and scrambled eggs. Mom and I talked about expectations, hers and mine. She gave me what must be the standard lecture about how good grades impact the future and then, it was time. I was expected to be at the bus stop by 7:00 and seated in homeroom at 8:15. I'd ridden a school bus before so this part wasn't new, it was the gallery of new faces and parade of new personalities that intimidated me. Sure, there were going to be some people from my elementary school but I barely related to them as it was.

My mom and I enjoyed an extra-long hug. I grabbed my bag and was out the door. As I stood on the porch I took a deep breath of the early September air. Baltimore is notoriously humid that time of year so the air was thick and smelled as only Baltimore does on a summer morning, that special mix of humidity and car exhaust. No matter the composition, to me it was the unmistakable fragrance of a brand-new day. I started my trek to the bus stop being careful to take it all in, the light of the rising sun on the trees, the houses of good neighbors I knew well, and the lawns on which I spent what seemed to be a million summer days playing with friends. I got to the end of my block and turned right just in time to see a cat lunge from a bush in an attempt to catch a watchful squirrel off-guard. The cat surprised me but not the squirrel which was now regarding the cat from a safe position among the leaves of an oak tree. I thought of the day I was about to have and how I had to be stealthy like the cat in order to get by. I made my way down 40th Street to University Parkway and crossed it to get to the bus stop. Being just a few blocks down from Johns Hopkins University I could see the early sunlight illuminate some of the buildings, the beautiful display of colors and architecture were part of the backdrop of the neighborhood I called home all of my life.

As I approached the bus stop, I could see several kids already assembled. There were cars along the side street each with one or two adults inside. No doubt these were parents who chose to see their children off on their first day. Still walking, I began to examine the others, how they were dressed, if they were talking to anyone, if they were sizing me up, etc. I noticed that, for the most part, they were keeping to themselves. I thought this was a smart move, better to see how people carry themselves before striking up a conversation.

In all there were about ten of us at bus stop by the time the bus came. I got a chance to examine everybody and determined as best I could the type of people they were, at least all but one. There was this one girl, maybe a bit taller than me, who I thought was absolutely gorgeous. Her hair was done in that style typical among black girls in the eighties where extended bangs mostly covered one eye. She had these light brown hazel eyes. "How exotic!" I thought. Her clothes could not have been better chosen if she were a model. She had an air about her, not of superiority, but as if she had an awareness – some type of clarity. She noticed my lingering gaze and shot me the softest grin. It was intoxicating. I wasn't even a teenager yet and I was smitten. The surge of emotion, or attraction, or, or whatever you call it was strong, something for which I was not prepared. I had to pull myself together!

The long yellow bus pulled into the side street next to where we were gathered. I noticed a bunch of kids of varying ages already aboard. We lined up when the bus came to a stop. I made a point of lining up behind this girl that seemed to make me forget all about school. One by one we filed up the three greenish rubberized steps, greeted the driver and turned left. The first dreaded social task was to find a seat on the bus next to someone without being rejected. Luckily, the bus was large enough to accommodate us without having to share seats. I was now in the position of rejecting someone if I wanted though I wouldn't. Being in this position did offer some comfort. The driver was an older white woman, maybe in her fifties, with deep wrinkles who had what I would later find was some kind of love affair with cigarettes. The sign posted above her head read, "Ms. Lucy".

Two stops later I was given the chance to reject someone. Before I could and not that I would have, he sat down next to me and looked me dead in the eyes. "Wales, Tommy Wales!" he said enthusiastically as he offered his hand to shake, "but call me Wales!" This kid was blowing all of the social conventions I'd cooked up. I was dazed by his obvious lack of shyness. "Uh… Joe." I muttered. "Joe Mack!" I said with more authority as I gripped his hand. He grinned this rather toothy smile. Tommy was an interesting character; you could tell by looking at him. He was a thin white guy who, in my opinion, was overdressed. He wore black dress shoes with gray dress slacks, a pinstriped shirt with one of those thin black ties common to the eighties. On his head he wore his signature article of clothing that tied everything together, a gray tweed fedora. The hat had a short brim and if I were to be honest it looked good on him. This oddball pulled me off my game of "sit back and observe" as we talked, or rather he talked, the rest of the way to school. His dizzying verbal avalanche began with this opening salvo...

"So, what do you know about this school? I mean we're new to the area. We're originally from Connecticut. I have a younger brother and if things work out here for me, he'll probably go here too. Have you checked out the girls on this bus? Get a load of that guy over there, what's up with him? You think the other kids will be nice here? Do you think the teachers will be nice? The teachers weren't all nice at my last school."

"Tommy." I said with my eyes closed to prevent them from glazing over any further.

He tried to continue his assault on my ears with, "Do you know many people here? If not we could sit together at lunch..."

"Tommy!" I interrupted, "I need you to slow down and focus, you're killing me."

"Oh, OK, I get it. My mom told me that I need to listen more and talk less but when I'm nervous or excited I kind of talk too much and not let other people talk..."

Interrupting again, "Wales!" I said.

"Oh yeah..."

"So you're nervous? I can relate, let's talk about it... both of us."

From that point I think Wales and I hit it off. For some reason I understood where he was coming from with his insecurity and he understood my wanting to take my time and do some people-watching. In truth both of us were insecure, we just had different ways of dealing with it.

The bus pulled into the parking lot of Towson Christian Academy and parked in the bus lane behind two other buses. The doors swung open and Wales and I gathered our bags and joined the line forming down the aisle. Wales looked back at me and said, "You know, last year we were the oldest and biggest kids in our schools, now we're the youngest and smallest. Welcome to kindergarten all over again." I let that thought settle in for a bit as we shuffled down the aisle to the front of the bus. I suppose I was oblivious to the fact that so many people boarded the bus while Wales and I talked. One by one they stepped out of the bus but there was one in the line off of whom I could not take my eyes. The mysterious girl a number of people ahead of me elegantly departed the bus. So captivated was I that I had no idea that Wales had been talking the whole time.

"Earth to Joe… You read me?

"Uh… yeah." I uttered.

"No way man! You ain't even set foot on the campus and you got eyes for that girl?" he half-whispered.

"Uh…"

"Be honest!" he interrupted.

"So what of it? She's cute!" I whispered.

"Cute? Dude, she's freakin gorgeous!" he exclaimed with a bit more enthusiasm than I would have liked.

He was facing me now, walking backwards towards the front. It was his turn now so I motioned to him to turn around and step down.

The school grounds included a large open field on which kids could congregate before going into either of the two two-story buildings. The buildings were connected by Kraft Hall, a one-story building which I knew housed the music and fine arts departments. The building on the right, mine, the junior high building, housed the middle school lockers while the high school lockers could be found in the one on the left, the senior high building. The campus also included several undeveloped acres of woods on the left and was bordered by a residential street on the right. I could hear the cacophony of the throng of students' conversations, birds in the woods, buses and cars in the lot, and Wales sputtering some nonsense about meeting the mystery girl.

Wales continued whatever he was saying as we made our way up the sidewalk to the junior high building. Once again, he was walking backwards in order to bestow his wisdom concerning women upon me. I'd just about had enough when just then he backed into some kid.

"Hey, watch it you jerk!" the kid shouted.

"I didn't mean to..."

"Shut up, preppy!" the kid shouted as he pushed Wales so hard that he stumbled back.

"Hey wait a minute! He didn't mean to walk into you!" I shouted in defense of my, I guess, friend.

"This don't concern you, midnight!" he shouted.

Everyone within earshot of him seemed to hush and began to form a circle around the area that was to be the battlefield. I quickly scanned the crowd to see what I was dealing with – if he had any friends there or not. As my eyes surveyed what was to be the audience, I saw the mystery girl's beautiful light eyes looking on with great interest. Her brow was furled as was that of every other black kid in the crowd. They were offended and I was to be their champion as though I'd stepped onto the arena of the Roman Coliseum to face some gladiator. I had to do something.

"What you gonna do, midnight?" he chuckled.

Now I was known in my neighborhood as that kid you did not mess with when it came to "doing the dozens". My insult senses went full throttle and I began to size him up to take him down verbally. I noticed his shoes – obvious Adidas knock-offs. I noticed the fact that his pants and shirt seemed to disagree on the color blue. I noticed the gap in his teeth that invited comment. I noticed the fact that he seemed to be in the process of growing the "rat tail" hair style. I also noticed the lean in his voice that indicated perhaps a rural background. All of these factors came together quickly like pieces of a puzzle and I had a clear picture of who I thought I was facing. What came next was instinct, pure nerve...

My right index finger went up in the air and I said, "Look here Appalachia, take your busted Adidas wannabe shoes and climb your buck-toothed, rat-tail growing, color-clashing behind back onto the Appalachian trail and hike back to the Ozarks because I think I hear your mother-cousin calling!" I didn't have to be accurate, the Ozarks aren't anywhere near the Appalachians, I had to be funny. The crowd erupted in loud "ooo's", "Oh's", and laughter. He spun around to look at the crowd as if he was going to get some help. He turned and looked at me with tears welling in his eyes, the hallmark of a well-directed insult attack. "Direct hit." I thought to myself. Now all I had to do since he was not firing back was to finish him off. My second attack rhymed so well it was almost lyrical...

"So look, I get it, jitters of the first day.

You had your chance - you don't know what to say.

What else to tell you?

Cause surely I can smell you?

What more can I say but financial aid is that way!"

As I ended my verbal assault I pointed to the administrative offices in the Senior-High building. The crowd lost – their – minds! It was another direct hit and I increased the distance between us by a few feet because I knew what comes next in cases like this. His brain told him to hit me because that would make up for what I said and save face. He swung, I moved – more laughter. He loaded up to charge me like some kind of bull. I knew at this point I would need to get more involved. Just as he lunged a black guy from the crowd intercepted him and wrapped the kid up in his arms. "It's over! You lost!" my defender yelled. He let the kid go after a few seconds and the kid ran through the crowd to parts unknown.

"Thanks! I was gonna have to get into it if you hadn't done that." I said with gratitude as the crowd dispersed. "I'm Joe, Joe Mack." I added as I extended my right hand.

He took it and said, "I'm Gene Tucker. I guess some people just can't take a joke."

"I guess not."

"That was amazing!" Wales interjected.

I threw in "Gene, this is Wales…" knowing that I might not get the chance if Wales had a lot to say.

"Nice to meet you." said Gene as he checked out Wales' particular style of dress. "Nice hat!"

"Thanks, you know, that's the first time anybody's ever stood up for me." Wales announced.

"That's what friends do, right?" I questioned.

Wales nodded in the affirmative and for the first time that morning he had nothing to say.

"Not even here ten minutes and I've already made an enemy!" I lamented. This was not the way I wanted to start off at this school.

"You've also made two friends, so that's something." Wales mentioned.

"Yeah, I guess that's something at least." Gene added.

As we continued up the walkway, I noticed people were looking at the three of us and either smiling, nodding, or giving us the single upwards head nod as the black kids were doing – even upperclassmen. Could it be that we accomplished in ten minutes what some people don't in years of high school, establishment? Before I could voice that idea Gene got there first.

"I think we got points for that."

"This could work for us." Wales replied in low tones.

How we must have looked walking up that walkway three wide. It was like we were doing that hero walk from *The Right Stuff* in slow motion. Wales, the preppy dresser in the hat, was on one side, I was on the other and Gene was in the middle. He was the tallest by about three inches and it was obvious that he was into something athletic. He wore all-black sneakers, black pants, and a Khaki button-down shirt with the top two buttons undone.

"We don't know if that kid has any friends, we should probably stick together." I cautioned.

At that we stopped and faced each other.

"Yeah…" Wales agreed.

Gene looked at Wales and then to me. He agreed with one quick nod.

A quick note about myself. Being one of the few black kids in my elementary school kind of frustrated me because I never really felt accepted there. To vent that frustration, I became a bit of a bully, more so in my neighborhood where I would win verbal battles than at school. I thought those days were behind me but this kid just brought it out of me with what he said. I'd never faced bigotry like that before so I reacted more out of instinct rather than reason. In many ways it's easier to destroy someone verbally, words doing more damage than fists ever could. Like the Bible says, "Life and death are in the power of the tongue…" At least this was self-defense and not just being a bully. I liked being on the right side of this but I didn't like what I did… I'm not proud of it.

CHAPTER 4:
ANTHROPOLOGY

Walking up the steps and through the large orange double doors of the junior high building, we stepped into a wide hallway lined on either side with salmon-colored lockers. Doors to classrooms could be found every so often amidst the lockers on either side. Kids crowded the hallway, new kids looking lost and eighth-graders caught up in conversation with people they hadn't seen for a few months. Thankfully we'd been assigned to the same homeroom. We had two minutes to get there so we figured we would get to our lockers after that. As a unit we walked down the hall and turned left. Another locker-line hallway and classrooms on the right. Our homeroom was the second door on the right.

We found seats near the windows on the far side of the room. This was good because it gave me a chance to check people out as they entered the room. In front of this rather typical classroom sat an overhead projector, a teacher's desk to the left of the large blackboard, and a world map on the opposite wall with an American flag on a wall-mounted pole. In the back of the room stood a table upon which sat a stack of textbooks. A man in his thirties was sitting behind the desk who I knew, because of my brother, to have taught at this school for a number of years. This was Mr. Philmore, a white man of somewhat average stature and gold-rimmed glasses. He was one my brother's favorites. He was reviewing and organizing some papers as he allowed a few extra minutes for people to file into the room. I searched his face for that look of exhaustion that often haunts teachers on the first day of school when they realize they have nine long months ahead of them – again. Refreshingly, he appeared to be well-rested and even enthusiastic about the prospect of a new year.

"Good morning!" he bellowed as he rose from his chair. The class responded with an unorganized muttering of the two words in reply. "Good morning!" he again filled the room expecting a more rousing response from the class. The class delivered as expected and he responded with a hearty, "Now that's better!"

Sitting behind me Gene leaned forward and said, "I like this guy already."

"Me too." I declared.

Wales had a smile on his face as he glanced over at us and then back to the front.

"My name is Douglas Philmore." he stated as he wrote his name on the board. "You will be tempted, like a lot, to spell my name with an 'F' rather than 'PH'. Trust me, I get it, but don't do that – fight the urge." Mr. Philmore carried an inviting open grin on his face that said, "We're gonna have fun this year, if you want." I knew somewhere in the back of my head was some story my brother told about how you did not want to cross this guy. He's fair and he wants to enjoy his work but he has no tolerance for kids who hinder either him or his students.

Before he did the roll call, he surveyed the class. When his eyes fell on our side of the room he called out, "Hey, you in the hat…" looking at Wales.

"Uh… Yes sir?" offered Wales nervously.

"Agh, don't call me 'sir.'"

"OK, Mr. Philmore." Wales revised with a little more confidence.

"Listen…" the teacher said, "I'll make you a deal. As we get to know each other if that hat fits your personality, I'll let you wear it in class but for today, can you please take it off?"

"Uh… sure Mr. Philmore, sure." Wales agreed as he took the hat from his head. His dark hair, well-molded to the inside of his hat, was now free to breath.

"OK, let me open us in prayer and then we'll pledge allegiance.

We rose and Mr. Philmore offered what I thought was one of the most sincere prayers I'd heard in years. He confessed his shortcomings and asked God to give him what he needed to effectively teach the students entrusted to him – this part stood out to me for some reason. He then asked God to bless us with the best year of our scholastic careers. After this we pledged allegiance to the flag and sat down.

Roll call was an opportunity for me to put some names to the faces around me. Mystery girl was not in this class so that wasn't helpful but what I did get was better. He got to my name in the roll.

"Philip Mack?"

"Here, Mr. Philmore, and uh… 'Joe', please." I announced.

He asked, "You have brother that graduated from here last year?"

"Yes." I replied. My brother had been an athlete with rather impressive mathematical skills and grades to boot.

"You don't have to live up to his reputation. You might think you do but you don't." he stated and without pausing he went on to the next name on the list. It's funny how the small gestures are the things that often have the greatest impact on someone's life – the things they remember. I actually felt free as though a burden had been lifted from my shoulders. With one off-the-cuff statement he changed my whole middle and high school experience for the better. My mind really wasn't on the roll call after what he'd said. Sure, my ears perked up when Wales' and Gene's names were called but I was still readjusting. A few more names and the roll call was done.

"OK, since this is a history class, let's start with the history of this place. Towson Christian Academy was founded in the 1960's, it is now 1984. OK, now that we've covered that, everyone go to the back of the room and pick up a book – in an orderly fashion please." There was some laughter and then the scraping of numerous chairs as people began to make their way to the back table.

After class, the three of us compared schedules and found that with the exception of History there were no classes shared by all three of us. We went from class to class throughout the morning running into each other in the hallways. So far, we found Mr. Philmore to be an exception, a rare gem among a pile of somewhat uninteresting rocks. To be sure, there were good teachers and I'd venture to say that all of them may have fallen into that category. However, that enthusiastic spark behind the eyes that leads a kid to the joy of learning was not to be found in every teacher.

At last, the lunch break came. We could finally sit and really talk for a while. We gathered at Gene's locker which was on the way to the lunch room. We walked outside and to the right toward the Christian Activities Building, CAB for short. There was a well-manicured courtyard between the buildings. The walkways were covered with metal green and maroon awnings, great for the rain. In the center of the grassy courtyard were several picnic tables situated around a large water fountain. The gurgling sound of the water promoted a sense of calm as we headed toward the CAB. The CAB had two gymnasiums, one large gym and a smaller one both on the lower floor. The junior and senior-high lunch rooms were situated over the small and large gyms respectively and shared a kitchen. On the way down I got the impression that people who'd seen us earlier that morning during the incident may have thought we'd known each other for years. It started to feel that way. Once again, we were walking three-wide as though we were comfortably at home.

The lobby of the CAB was a tall open space with a beige linoleum floor. Three wide floor-to-ceiling windows perforated the wall to the right.

To the left were large wooden double doors which led to the lunchroom. To the right of those was an impressive looking trophy cabinet whose latest addition was for a basketball championship earned by my brother's team the year before. To the right of the cabinet were another set of double doors that concealed the stairwell leading down to the gym. On the far wall, straight ahead as you walk into the building, a mural of the school logo consisting of a maroon bordered shield indicating the founding year along with icons representing Christianity and the school's mascot, the Guardian. Under the logo were the words in bold, "Home of the Guardians!" To the left of the mural stood another set of large double doors that led to the senior-high lunchroom. After a moment of observation, we turned left and walked into the junior-high lunchroom. The smell of food from the kitchen wafted lazily through the air of the lunchroom as students filed in and found seats at the tables. The three of us stood there for a moment, Gene and I were discussing where to sit because the room was filling up.

"I've got this, follow me…" Wales insisted.

Gene and I looked at each other and with puzzled looks on our faces followed Wales to a table in the back corner with two orange cones in front of it. The metal chairs were folded and leaned against the table.

"Um… Wales. What are you doing, man?" Gene asked.

"Hang on…" Wales replied while looking around for a bit and then gesturing with his hand. A few moments later the janitor arrived at the table. The janitor was an older black man who wore a blue-grayish mechanic's jumpsuit. He carried himself with pride and a gracious attitude. I liked him immediately and didn't even know him. "Guys, this is Mr. Murphy, the janitor. We can call him 'Murph.'" Wales said introducing Mr. Murphy.

"Hi, I'm Gene." he said with a handshake.

"Mr. Murphy, I'm Joe." I added, shaking his hand.

"No, my friends call me 'Murph', please."

"Ok, Murph…" I responded.

"Let me get those for you." Murph picked up the cones and set chairs around the table and then motioned for us to have a seat. "Thanks, Murph! We REALLY appreciate all of this!" said Wales with gratitude.

"Anytime Wales, and by the way, thanks for the advice!"

"Sure Murph! You know you're welcome!"

We sat there for a few seconds, mouths agape, staring at Wales. "You know him from somewhere?" I asked with all manner of curiosity.

"Yeah, from this morning between second and third periods." Wales said as though that was perfectly normal.

"That was ten minutes, man!" Gene exclaimed.

"Look, there's something you guys should know about me. I'm an organizer, I kind of pull people together. It takes time to build a network but I knew I had to hit the ground running. Janitors are among the best people to know and we're lucky we have such a kind man in Murph. He needed some advice about a car repair I'd overheard him say something about and I hooked him up with a mechanic friend of mine who'll probably do it for half the price."

Gene and I just shook our heads and agreed that we were glad to know him. Wales smiled and suggested we get some food.

Leaving our book bags at the table we got in line and waited to be served. Lunch that day consisted of fried chicken, mashed potatoes, and vegetables with corn bread. Wales wasn't kidding when he said he hits the ground running. One of the ladies behind the counter mentioned that she liked his hat and that sparked a quick conversation and a promise from Wales to come by later. We each grabbed a bottle of iced tea as we headed back to the table.

When we got back to the table, we found that three other seventh-graders joined us in our absence. The one girl spoke up, "We couldn't find any seats together because we came kind of late, do you mind?" Gene said, "Not at all!" and we sat down. The one girl introduced herself as Leigh

Adams. Leigh was a rather cute white girl about my height with a round-ish face and black glasses. "Bookworm." I thought to myself. The others introduced themselves as Wes Moon and Bruce Edwards. Wes was a white guy also about my height and a little more fit than me. Bruce was black guy similar in build to Wales. He was a bit more reserved but I figured he would open up as he got more comfortable with us. As lunch went on, the six of us really hit it off. We said that we would try to sit together at lunch whenever we could.

"Oh, I almost forgot, Saundra Wallace!" Wales proclaimed.

"OK…" I bated him for more.

"That's the mystery girl!" he said.

"What's so mysterious? What about her?" Gene interjected.

"You know her?" I asked.

"Sure, we went to school together. She's cool but her family is kind of weird. What about her?"

"It just that uh… I saw… um…" I stammered.

"Joe's trying to say that she's gorgeous and he wants those digits!" Wales blurted

Though he was right, I didn't want all my cards out on the table like that.

"She *is* gorgeous but I think Joe probably wants to approach her in his own time." Gene said, coming to my rescue.

"OK, cool." Wales conceded, "She's in my second-period math class, keep that in mind if you need it."

"I… I will, thanks!"

"By the way, that kid we tangled with this morning…" Wales said with a more serious look on his face, "His name is Jake Thompkins. He's a sev-enth-grader like us and is not connected but I hear that with his particular views he won't have trouble finding like-minded people – if you know what I mean."

"Thanks, Wales, I'll keep that in mind." I said contemplatively as I turned to Gene. "Can you believe we come to a Christian school and have to deal with racism out in the open like that? This is new to me."

"I look at it like this; at least we know where he stands. I'd rather have this stuff out in the open." Gene argued.

Leigh piped up, "I was there this morning, and I agree with Gene. If you're gonna be like that, identify yourself. It's like having florescent dog crap on a lawn at night – at least you know where not to step!"

I surrendered to their point of view with, "I guess I agree. It's just new to me is all."

Gene and I had PE next in the gym. It was a Tuesday and Thursday class and this being the first day it was only an orientation session. Gene and I left the lunchroom and turned left to go to the gym stairwell. The stairway was well-lit with a few pictures adorning the walls as we made our descent. I'd been to many basketball games in this gym but I never got used to how everything smelled fine at the top but as soon as you got halfway down, it was like you were breathing through a sweaty sock. As we reached the landing, Gene took note of the locker rooms, male and female, on either side of the stairwell.

The main gym had a grand vaulted ceiling over the regulation sized basketball court. The floor was made of some sort of rubber material which was the subject of not a few signs on the walls warning people of the danger of spilling soda on it. Across the gym floor were several sets of retractable bleachers. They had been retracted to the wall to maximize floor space. A group of high school students were gathered on the far end for what must have been their gym class. We were to meet in the smaller gym.

Walking through the door on the near side of the gym that led to the smaller gym we found a group of seventh-graders already assembled. Some of the students I recognized, others were new to me. One stood out above all, leaning up against the wall by himself, Jake Thompkins. His face was red and his eyes were locked on me with furious intent. I dared to meet his gaze for a few moments and then shifted my attention elsewhere. When I did so I quietly said two words to Gene, "You see?" In a testament to the depth of wavelength the two of us share, even back then on day one of our friendship, he replied, "I got him, he ain't gonna do nothing." I began to notice that whenever Gene shifted into "action mode", his vernacular changed a bit. This is one of those cues you learn as you get to know somebody. Cues like that are useful in that they help you figure out their mood.

The class was as we thought, a discussion of what we should expect followed by a discussion on hygiene as it relates to PE. The teacher, a petite muscular blond in a black and blue sweat suit named Eunice Rosenhoff, took the time to learn each of our names. As it turns out, only our last names were of interest to her as that is what she would use when talking to us throughout the year. It was the kind of thing you see in a prison drama with the guards firing off last names at inmates. We didn't mind, she turned out to be a fair, if not direct, lady.

After class, as Gene and I began to walk to our Religion class, we discussed what it would mean if Jake Thompkins found a few like-minded friends. We went back and forth and simply decided to wait and see what happens. Reaching the Junior High building by the time we finished that discussion, we found our class was the third door on the left.

Entering the room, we found most of the students seated, waiting for class to start. We acknowledged Leigh and Bruce on our way to the last group of open seats in the front of the room. The classroom windows were on the western wall so the sun beamed through them with such an intensity that one could debate the necessity of the overhead lights. The chalkboard was situated between the two windows. Beneath the right-most window stood a desk at which a man sat. Unlike Mr. Philmore in history class, who was focused on papers and administrative minutia prior to his class, this teacher intently scanned the faces of his students. I knew this look and the accompanying thought process. "What is he looking for?" I asked myself. His gaze fell upon me and it was as though he were looking into my soul. So rarely am I ever on the receiving end of this probing that my instincts kicked in beyond my better judgment. I matched his inquisitive gaze with one worthy of his own. There we sat for what felt like an hour but was perhaps in reality no more than ten seconds. He was picking apart any visual cues my possessions or expression could offer. I did the same seeing a man in what was probably his late thirties with premature salt and pepper hair and a stern face. His somewhat heavyset frame was leaned back in his chair but was in no way relaxed – this man was on a mission. I was convinced he knew something important that I did not. There he sat with both hands pressed together at the fingertips just in front of his mouth, staring at me. This was weird. Just then our "duel" was interrupted by a student sitting down next to me and dropping a book as they did so. I leaned down to pick it up and handed it to a grateful Saundra Wallace. My interest shifted from the teacher.

"Oh hi, Saundra." I said accidentally.

"Um... have we met?" she replied, busting me.

I could see Gene out of the corner of my eye shake his head as he stared at the ceiling as if to say, "real smooth!"

My mind was already racing because of the teacher and so it was already in a place to try to deal with this crisis. "Excuse me!" I retorted, "Pick-up lines like that have no place in the classroom!" With that I turned away, my head facing the chalkboard and waited for it. It took a few seconds, a few seconds in which I began to doubt my tactic but then there it was, a sweet, soft, chuckling laugh. I shot her a glance and a smirk just as the teacher began the class.

"Good afternoon!" the teacher spouted with a voice that seemed bigger than him. The class responded satisfactorily and he continued, "My name is Max O'Leary." "Oh yeah." I thought to myself remembering that my brother mentioned him a few times. As I recalled, he had not been there too long and he's really smart, nothing gets by him. He went on to tell us what we could expect in the class and about quizzes and exams, the same kind of mundane information with which we were bombarded in each period other than lunch.

After Religion class I endured a rather boring English class and then it was finally time to go home. I went to my locker which was not too far from Gene's, got what I thought I would need for the night and proceeded to walk down to the bus area with Gene and Wales. Gene rode a different bus so we parted ways and boarded our respective buses. As Wales and I boarded our bus, Saundra was already seated in the front. She acknowledged me with a smile as we walked by and sat somewhere in the middle.

"I saw that, I think she's into you!" Wales declared in hushed tones.

"I don't think so. I had to get her to laugh to keep from having to explain how I knew her name in Religion class. She's probably remembering that." I reasoned.

"Anyway, what a day huh?" he asked.

"Yeah, what a day."

Wales sat back in the seat, sighed, and asked if he could tell me something in confidence.

"Sure, of course… We go way back you and me so you can trust me." I joked.

He laughed and said, "for real though… I'm only good at networking with adults. When it comes to kids my age, I mess up every time. My little brother, Ben, he's the opposite. He's in first grade and when we moved here, he had no trouble making friends.

"Wow. Wales, no matter what problems you have with it, you have a real gift."

"You know what else?" he pondered, "This is the first time, like in my life, that I feel like I belong. Pathetic isn't it… I mean it's only been one day."

He sat there with a melancholy look on his face as he stared out the window.

The order of stops for the bus was reversed on the ride home so Wales' stop was before mine. His stop was next and we sat in uncharacteristic silence until he got off the bus. I told him that I'd see him tomorrow which earned me a slight nod.

Saundra and I got off the bus and I began to walk towards home.

"Wait up!" she spouted.

"Look, I know you're into me! I don't want any trouble. I just want to go to school in peace." I jested. This was one of my coping methods, I couldn't say what I wanted because I was too scared but if I couched it in a joke, I could say almost anything.

"Please!" she said wryly, "That was a good dodge back there in class. You're funny. Let's make it official, I'm Saundra Wallace."

"I'm Joe Mack."

We shook hands and bid each other a good night.

On the walk home I'd like to report that my mind was on my chores at home and schoolwork but it wasn't. I was in teenage mind prison, that state of mind where you deconstruct every word or action someone says or does to try to determine what they meant. I wasn't even a teenager yet and I had to deal with this.

I let myself into the house and disarmed the alarm system. My parents wouldn't be home for a few hours so I went to my room, sat down at my desk, and dumped the entire contents of the day into entry number one in the binder I used for a journal. I would follow the same routine of writing an entry at the end of each day, being careful to hide the journal in the wall cavity. The journal was my sounding board and I was committed to chronicling daily events as best I remembered them.

THE RALLY:

That Wednesday we learned that the classes would be shortened to make time for the New School Year Rally. I vaguely remembered my brother talking about these. It was kind of neat learning the traditions of the school, it made us feel like we were a part of something bigger. The Rally was held on the main athletic field between second and third periods and was apparently a big to-do. As the school body migrated up the steps to the field and toward the bleachers, we noticed Leigh ahead of us with Wes. She was making sure we would all sit together.

Sitting in the bleachers with the others, waiting for the event to start, I did what came easy to me… observe. I looked around just to get the feel of people. "People-watching" was a tool in my "introvert's toolbox" that I could not do without. I noticed Jake Thompkins sitting together with some other kids, laughing about something mean no doubt. Before long, my eyes fell on Saundra. Boy was she um… impressive. This was the first time I really noticed her smile. It was the kind of smile that made me want to smile too. I had a crush on her and until that moment I didn't really know what that felt like. She was talking to her friend Meghan. Meghan was really cute but weird. The weirdness wasn't because of any one thing, it was more of a feeling than anything else. Besides that, the two of them were something to see, Saundra with her perfect smile and Meghan with her shoulder-length blonde hair that seemed to be professionally-done and flattering.

"Earth to Joe..." Wales interrupted. "What are you looking at? Oh… pretty girls, I get it… carry on."

"Wales I was just..." I began to say when we heard the band start to play and the crowd erupt in cheer.

The cheerleaders came up the stairs first in two columns dressed in the signature green and maroon color scheme. They were twirling batons as they marched in unison. The band followed in the same two-column formation. Cheers went up when we saw the band and then more cheering when we all realized that two more sets of band members were streaming down from the upper field behind us. They met in the center of the field and organized into several rows with the cheerleaders in front. The band was playing some kind of rousing victorious theme while marching as though battle-hardened warriors would follow them onto the field.

After a few moments of playing, the music and activity stopped. The crowd cheered again and went silent as we noticed the performers stopped moving. They were frozen like mannequins, even their facial expressions were locked in place, the cheerleaders smiling, the band with furrowed brows looking determined. Just before the silence became awkward the school mascot, a man in armor with a helmet and shield, walked onto the field with two people in a large horse costume. Other than the "horse" being comically uncoordinated, it all looked really cool. The "Guardian" made his way onto a small stand in front of the assembled band and cheerleaders. He took out a conductor's baton and began to lead the band. They sounded horrible. Heads turned in the bleachers and the sound of murmuring students began to rise. Just then the back half of the "horse" tore away to reveal Lyle Tidewater, the Band teacher. The crowd exploded into laughter. We'd all assumed he was the guy with the helmet on the stand. He humorously stumbled onto the stand as the other guy jumped off. He turned to the crowd and grinned, really hamming it up. He then led the band into several rounds of truly beautiful music ending with the school's anthem. After some words from the Principal, Wayne McIntyre, we were dismissed.

Mr. Tidewater was an exceptional music teacher. His personality was vibrant. He would light up the hallway as he walked through, making sure to interact with as many students as possible. He would remember names and was truly interested in students' lives. He was really funny and flat out loved by students and teachers alike. In fact, Mr. Tidewater was so good that some students enrolled in the school just to be taught by him.

A FRIDAY FOR THE AGES:

On Friday, Wales got on the bus wearing a burgundy tweed fedora, a maroon shirt with black pinstripes, black pants and dress shoes. His light-gray tie peeked just right from behind the black sweater-vest. I shook my head as I asked, "What's the occasion?"

"Joe, my friend, most people will say you should dress down on Friday. My philosophy is that you upsell on Fridays. It sets you apart and besides, I always have something happening on Friday nights."

"But, but you're twelve!" I emoted incredulously.

"Yeah, in three weeks."

"What could you possibly have going on tonight?"

"The manager of the insurance company my mom works at is trying to get his writing career off the ground and his first book just got picked up or something. I met him over the weekend when I was getting my hair cut and he invited my mom and me to a party at his place tonight."

"Oh, OK." I said dismissing it somewhat. The author turned out to be Tom Clancy and the book, *The Hunt for Red October*. The kid had a gift for being in the right place at the right time.

Changing the subject Wales disclosed, "I've got some things to talk about at lunch. One of them is my birthday."

"Oh? When is it?"

"September 28th. That's a Friday but I was hoping maybe a few of you could hang out with me on that Saturday?"

"That sounds like something we might do. I've never really hung out with people from school. What would we do?" I questioned.

"I really don't know either but I'll figure something out." he assured.

We spent the rest of the ride discussing men's fashion and how everyone needs to pick a signature style and commit to it. He stressed that commitment was the key to successfully marketing oneself.

When we arrived at the school, we could tell that something was wrong. There was a police car parked in the administration driveway along with another car of the same design but no police logo. A group of arriving students began to congregate on the portion of the lawn near the police cars but was kept from getting any closer.

"Well, it looks like this is going to be quite a day." I sighed.

The sun bathed the campus in the kind of golden hues that would set your mind afloat upon a river of inviting memories. There was a bit of a chill in the air that morning that made Wales' sweater-vest look even better. The morning dew that settled on the expansive lawn added an iridescent quality that seemed to increase the mysterious feel already in the air. The stark juxtaposition between the golden sunlight in the east and the dark navy-blue clouds, remnants of an overnight storm, in the west cast a foreboding pall over the campus.

Wales and I joined the crowd next to Gene who'd been there for some time. "What's going on?" Wales inquired.

"We don't know, we just want to catch a glimpse of something maybe." Gene answered.

I pulled Wales and Gene aside. "Do you think you can…"

"Already there…" Wales interrupted. "I'll see if the janitors know anything about it."

"You know you've got mad skills, right?" Gene added.

"Well, we'll see…" Wales conceded.

After pondering the situation for a little while we were on our way to homeroom. On the way we noticed members of the staff and faculty seemed to be together in small numbers in the hallways talking among themselves. Whatever this was it seemed worse than I may have thought. Each of us carried a puzzled expression into the classroom and took our seats. Mr. Philmore seemed a bit distracted that morning, almost nervous. For the days I'd known him, he'd been rather stable so now my interest was truly piqued. He picked up a light-blue sheet of paper and began to read whatever was printed.

Wales, sitting at the desk between Gene and me, pulled out his book, placed it on the desk and took off his fedora. He brushed it with his hand and placed it on top of the book. This is the routine he settled upon since Mr. Philmore asked him to remove his hat on the first day. It interested me because he did this with such precision that I challenged myself to see if he would accidentally skip a step or change the order.

"Mr. Wales." the teacher said clearing his throat while still looking at the light-blue paper.

"Yes, Mr. Philmore?" Wales responded.

"Put the hat back on please. It fits." he said without ever looking up from the page in reference to the deal he'd made with Wales on the first day.

"Thank you, Mr. Philmore."

Wales picked up the hat, regarded it for a moment, and placed it in a professional manner atop his head.

"You see? Commitment!" Wales reminded me as he leaned in my direction.

The next two periods were not unbearable for the first Friday of the school year. The material actually seemed interesting. I learned that Leigh is a very good student and probably someone from whom we could pick up some good study habits. Next up was lunch and for some reason I was pretty hungry that day. The three of us and Leigh met up in the hallway before heading to the CAB to eat.

"Hey Wales, did you get a chance to talk to Murph and the janitors?" Gene asked.

"I almost wish I hadn't! I'll tell you guys after we eat." Wales declared.

The four of us entered the lunchroom and did the same thing we'd done all week. We stood there for a moment as if we had no idea where to sit and then walked to the far-right corner. Each day, Murph invented some reason to reserve a table for us. Yesterday, something had been spilled on the table requiring it to be cleaned just as we came in. The day before, there were no chairs around it until we arrived. Today, there was no table! Just as we started towards the corner, Murph and Jim, another janitor, pulled a table from the closet and set it up in the corner. We continued to be amazed. During the week I learned that Murph and Wales started a real mentoring relationship of sorts and I was glad because Murph is the kind of person you'd want in your son's life at this age. Murph was a good influence on us all, especially Wales. You see, Wales' father passed away when he was seven. Though his uncle loved them very much and was there for them, owning a big-time accounting firm in Baltimore meant he didn't have much time.

We all thanked Murph and Jim but weren't too loud about it. We knew people would catch on sooner or later but we didn't want to make it obvious. Bruce and Wes came in together and stood at the head of the table.

"Ready?" Wes asked.

We made our way to the line as a unit and engaged in small talk until we were served. Lunch was made up of pepperoni pizza, vegetables, and some kind of chocolate brownie. Weird but it worked well for me.

While we ate, Wales piped up, "So my birthday is the 28th and I was thinking maybe we could all hang out that Saturday."

Some quick head turns to each other and then everyone voiced their agreement. Bruce, who rarely addresses the group, spoke up, "What are we gonna do?"

"I'm thinking we all could hang out at the mall for a few hours and maybe catch a movie. I think I got an angle on some pretty good pizza and cake."

"You know who has the best pizza?" asked Gene.

"*Pizza Baltimore?*" Wes answered questioning him back.

"Yup!" Gene yelped, "That *Baltimorioni* is just incredible!"

"My little brother is friends with the son of the guy who owns the one near me. Maybe we can work something out. I'll let you know." Wales said, pondering a connection before adding, "Also, I wanted to lay this on you guys. I did some digging and did this like map of the cliques here."

"Come again?" Gene said acting as if he didn't hear him.

"How... you know what, never mind, just show us what you got!" I stated.

"OK, after watching people, hearing things, and making friends with the staff in the administrative office, this is the way I see it... You see those girls in the corner over there?"

He indicated a table of black girls who dressed to accentuate "certain qualities".

"I call them *The Fly Girls* - Lisa, Angela, Pamela, and Renee. What you see is what you get, brand names, big hair, jewelry, all of it. Yeah..." Wales said, his eyes lingering a bit.

"OK, see that second table from the right over there? Those are *The Punks* – Greg, David, Chris, Kevin, and Al. Punk rock and skateboards is where it's at for them."

"We knew this was probably going to happen. That table next to the *Punks*? *The Country Boys*. Our friend Jake Thompkins made some friends - Terry Elsmore, Al Stonebridge, Parker Wilson, and Milton Edwards."

Gene and I exchanged a meaningful glance.

"That table over there on the far left, *The Sidity Committee,* Ashley A, Jasmine C, Makayla T, Imani K, and Nicole G. Believe it or not, they actualy like to go by their first names and the first letter of their last names. Weird. The table two down from them with the one guy standing up is *The God squad.* Wendy Jackson, Henry Allen, Zachary Epstein, Nathaniel Price, and Petra Taylor. They have a Bible Study group."

I chimed in, "I know Petra, we went to elementary school together. She's cool."

"Finally, the table second-row center. I don't have a name for them because I can't figure them out. Saundra Wallace, Olympia Dupree, Meghan O'Neil, Destiny Daniels, and Ivanah Dvorak. One thing I know for sure and confirmed it two different ways, they all come from different places but they all know each other."

"Your right, that *is* weird." Gene agreed, "But where Saundra is involved, I'm not too surprised."

"That's the second time you've said something like that." I mentioned.

"We'll talk." Gene replied.

"Wait a minute, what do you call us?" asked Bruce with the others nodding their agreement afterwards.

"I was thinking 'Misfits' with a 'Y'." Wales answered to a group of blank stares. "Think about it over the weekend, trust me."

Leigh was the first of us, after an awkward pause, to thank Wales for his hard work. We all did the same after her and began to leave for next period.

Pulling Gene and me aside, Wales asked if he could talk to us alone. We agreed and found a secluded spot just outside the CAB.

"OK, lay it on us." Gene sighed.

"This doesn't leave the three of us – cool?" Wales insisted.

Gene and I agreed.

"I spoke to Murph and Jim this morning and all the janitors are spooked. OK, I got no other way to say it so I'll just say it. Somebody burned something on top of the logo on the upper field. They also dumped something on the front lawn. Some people think it was some kind of ritual. That's why the faculty and staff were on edge this morning."

CHAPTER 5:
MYSFITS

Knowing the sensitivity of the information Wales just dropped on us, Gene and I carried ourselves to English Literature class, the off-day replacement for PE. The teacher, Janet Warding, a squat brunette with a pink headband, was going on about something Shakespeare wrote. All the while my mind was locked onto the mystery of the upper field. "Who would do that and why? Was it a student?" For some reason I couldn't let it go. I glanced over at Gene and I could tell his mind was nowhere near Shakespeare. He caught me looking at him and shook his head in a cautionary manner as if to say, "This school's got real problems."

Before she let us go, she informed us that she would be, "…going off script for a bit so please bear with me." She gave us the assignment to read *The Screwtape Letters* by C.S. Lewis over the next month. I was not familiar with this book at the time so I dismissed it as another assignment among the many that were piling up.

Afterwards, as we were on our way to Religion class, Gene indicated that we should be careful to not give O'Leary any reason to think we knew what happened.

"You picked up on that too, huh?" I responded.

"How could I not! That guy could burn a hole through someone with that stare!"

"I know!"

"You guys headed to Religion?" Leigh asked, joining us along the way.

"Yeah, what class are you coming from?" Gene questioned.

"Um… Geometry 2." Leigh answered with some hesitation.

Gene squinted pensively, "Isn't that a high school class?"

"Yeah, I'm kinda good at math." she said with a bit of nervous laughter.

"Look Leigh, be yourself! Don't fear that! It's what the Mysfits are all about, right?" I added.

"Yeah, it's cool to be smart!" Gene insisted.

Stopping in the middle of the hallway she purposefully looked into our eyes as if trying to determine our sincerity. After a few silent seconds, the intense look on her face broke into a grin. She seemed almost relieved.

"OK, yeah!" she said, her voice punctuated with laughter. "So, what do you think about this whole 'Mysfits' thing anyway?"

"Look at us, we're a group that would never hang out with each other if things had been different. But look how well we fit together. It's like God wanted it or something." Gene opined.

At the time, Gene didn't talk a lot about God but acknowledged Him whenever something would happen that was bigger than he was. In this case, the unlikely circumstances that brought together this weird group of people that fit so well could, in his mind, only be attributed to God – and he was right.

"I totally agree!" I said, looking at Leigh as we started walking again.

We didn't say another word on the way to class. I think we knew the gravity of the few ideas we'd just exchanged. In our minds we each came to the same conclusion which did not need to be voiced because we each felt it, we were really friends and members of an appropriately named tribe – the *Mysfits*.

Taking our seats in class Gene and I noticed that Mr. O'Leary was observing the class from the back of the room. In my mind I imagined he wanted to see which kids would talk to each other without the distraction of his watching them. Smart.

His discussion that day was obviously informed by what happened on the upper field the night before. He focused on passages of the Bible that had to do with the work of Satan in the world. He was careful to show, in every case, that God prevailed. This was, without a doubt, the coolest class I'd attended in a very long time. Some of the other kids were digging it while others seemed to have checked out. Saundra seemed interested enough.

After this thoroughly entertaining class, English was up next. It was not thoroughly entertaining. Without having seen it for myself I would not have been able to tell you how to spend a whole class period discussing the particulars of diagramming sentences pertaining to the conjunction "and". Somehow Brian Osbourne, the English Teacher, found a way. Though his delivery of the material was slow and dry, I was still awake by the end and left with a sense of triumph.

On the bus ride home that day, excitement for the weekend was in the air. The driver, Ms. Lucy, was rocking back and forth in her seat to an upbeat station as she made stop after stop. Kids were laughing and playing pranks on each other. Even Saundra, who is normally aloof on the bus rides, found at least one person with whom she cracked a smile.

"I've been thinking about 'the park' all day and how I want to go." Wales said raising his eyebrows.

"OK, but I don't know if you'll get anything out of it." I replied, knowing he intended "the park" to be code for the upper field.

"There's only one way to find out."

"I don't think there will be any more picnics; the weather's getting bad." I argued, suggesting this would be a one-time isolated act of vandalism because everybody's on high-alert. "If you go and they see you they may think you're trying to have a picnic."

"Yeah, you're probably right." he conceded.

"I think the name 'Mysfits' will wind up working out. It fits us pretty well." I said, changing the topic.

"I think so too."

"Gene and I ran into Leigh in the hallway coming out of her math class, did you know she was in advanced math?" I asked.

"No, she does seem pretty smart though. I'm looking forward to hanging out with all you guys. I think we'll get to know a lot about each other."

I nodded, "I agree, I think there's a lot to this group and we just need some time together. I must admit it sounded weird at first, probably because I never really got along with people at school, but I think this will be good."

"Why didn't you get along with people at school? Were you bullied or something?" Wales was now devoting his full attention to me, not just because we were talking but because he was really interested in knowing me better. There's a difference and you know it when you see it and I was happy to see it.

"Not exactly, as one of the few black kids in school, I felt like I was on the outside. That gets to you after a while and I kind of kept to myself because of it. So I was rarely invited to anything, that's probably why this struck me as being weird. My hope was that things would be different here, that I would have a vibrant social life, and it looks like I just might."

He turned and looked out the window for a few seconds and then down at his book bag, "you know, we did something this week that a lot of people don't do in years, find a place to belong." He made two fists, "I don't want to mess that up... I'm scared. I don't do well with other kids."

"Look at me man, you doing just fine. All of us *Mysfits*, maybe not Gene, don't do well with other kids. You're in the right place." I tried to assure him. I knew then that I needed to be at that hangout time no matter what, not for myself like I thought, but for Wales. I guess that's the definition of friendship. He nodded as though he at least accepted some of what I said and returned to looking out the window.

"Enjoy the party tonight!" I said as he got up for his stop.

"Oh, I will... I'll tell you all about it on Monday."

As I watched him get off the bus, I thought of him and the other *Mysfits*. I felt something that made my heart warm – gratefulness. It was of this, and the thing on the upper field, that I wrote in my journal that night.

Monday morning came quicker than I would have liked. I had to drag myself out of bed that morning and trek to the bus stop in the low sixty-degree weather like a weary traveler sadistically condemned to walk the earth without reprieve. I didn't really wake up until my eyes fell upon Saundra, who was dressed as though she were about to walk the catwalk in Milan.

"Twelve-year-old girls shouldn't look like this." I thought to myself, but somehow, I didn't mind.

To my shame she noticed the extra helping I took in looking at her.

"Good morning." she said with a rather satisfied smirk on her face.

Once again I did the only thing I knew how to do with her. I lowered my voice to a husky whisper, so as to feign trying to keep the other kids from hearing, and said, "Saundra, it's too early to be hitting on me. I'm flattered but I've got a lot on my mind. I'm so sorry to turn you down again." With that I turned to face the street as though I needed to break off the conversation. I quickly glanced back with a playful grin to make sure she knew I was still kidding. The fact that she was laughing to herself, almost with tears, made me feel good. "I'll win her over soon." I thought to myself.

I didn't stop thinking about Saundra until about the time Wales was on his way down the aisle. He plopped down next to me and shook his head.

"Did you see..." he started.

"Yeah... yeah... just leave it alone." I cautioned. I knew he was going to ask if I'd seen Saundra.

He shook his head again and changed the topic.

"So how was your weekend?" he asked.

"Restful, probably not like yours. Spill it!"

Wales chuckled and said, "So we get there Friday night and there are some artsy people from around town, musicians and the like. Then, out of the blue, in walks Mayor Schaefer!"

"Holy crap!"

"Yeah, apparently people knew people and there you go. I spent the whole time networking and I loved it! My mom also let me sip some wine by the way." he said that last part with a sly grin like he'd proven his manhood.

I shook my head and just accepted it all, "Wow, man, I don't even know what to say."

"Me neither, I mean I was speechless. It took me like a whole minute to introduce myself." he reminisced.

This would have been a big thing in any year but in 1984 it was all the more special. Earlier that year, Baltimore's football team, left the city for Indianapolis. The year before, Baltimore won the World Series. The city had been through a lot and it seemed that Mayor Schaefer's leadership was keeping it on track. He went on to tell me more about that night including a rather comical story about the clogged toilet that became the talk of the night much to the embarrassment of the host.

The next few weeks were remarkably uneventful given the events of the first week of school. As I suspected, the *Mysfits* adopted the name and used it proudly. Wales organized the exchange of phone numbers and based on those of us who had three-way calling, he devised a call list that could put all of us on the phone at once. This was extremely helpful later on when that first round of exams hit. The night before the first math exam, Leigh held court on the phone. Our math was elementary to her and she saw to it that each of us understood the material.

THAT FIRST BIRTHDAY OUTING:

Wales's birthday fell on a Friday. It was really cold that day so all of us on the bus understandably wore thick coats. This kid strolls onto the bus sporting a black trench coat under which was a black and white shirt and vest ensemble tied together with a monochrome paisley tie that was just perfect for the outfit. A gray tweed fedora with black trim rounded out his "presentation".

"I've had this outfit in mind for a while now." he boasted.

"Happy Birthday!"

"Thank you, thank you very much!" he responded, trying to imitate Elvis.

For the remainder of the ride to school, we talked about the plans for the following day. This would be the first time the *Mysfits* hung out as a group outside of lunch or on the phone. It was fun thinking of all the ways we could fill that Saturday afternoon.

The next day, my mother drove me to Golden Ring Mall to hang out with my friends at noon. We got there a bit early as planned so she could meet Wales' mother. They hit it off almost immediately. At some point Ms. Wales took me into her arms and held me tightly.

"You just don't know." she whispered.

"Thank you for chaperoning today." was all I could think to say.

"Hey Wales, where's your brother?" I asked.

"With my uncle for the afternoon. Don't worry, he's having fun at the Science Center."

My mother pulled off after confirming that she was to pick me up at six. Ms. Wales waited with us as the Mysfits arrived one by one with a parent in tow. She greeted each parent, which I am sure put them at ease. By noon all of us were assembled at the fountain near the main entrance to the mall.

"So, what now?" asked Wes.

"We eat!" Wales chirped with a grin on his face.

We found an area with a few tables and chairs. Wales' mother brought in two *Baltimorioni* pizzas and assorted sodas. We broke out into the very worst rendition of *Happy Birthday to You* imaginable. Shoppers were laughing at us as we laughed at each other. The six of us pigged out on pizza, soda, and this incredible chocolate cake his mother made. We barely uttered a word as we ate. Actually "grazed" may be a better word as we seemed more like a pack of animals than middle schoolers. "Pack" is the right word for as we ate we all knew we belonged. Wales's mother knew it too; I could see her on a bench a ways off just smiling. I got the sense this was as important to her as it was for Wales.

After we ate, it was my turn. "Wales and I were thinking and thought we should go around and formally introduce ourselves. Seeing as how we haven't really done that, it sounded like a good idea. So, please tell us your full name, best hope, and worst fear... I'll start. You guys call me Joe but that's not my name, it's actually Philip Joseph Mack but please keep calling me "Joe". My best hope is, I guess, that we remain friends..."

"Hear! Hear!" Bruce interjected.

"My worst fear is not knowing what I want to do for like, a job and stuff."

Everyone nodded for a moment as they thought about it and then looked at Leigh sitting next to me.

"OK." Leigh said as she pushed her hair back and set it with a clip. "My name is Leigh Winter Adams."

"Pretty!" Wales emoted.

Somewhat shocked at this outburst we all looked at Wales. Red-faced, he stammered, "Wha... What? It's a pretty name is all."

"Why thank you, Wales." Leigh said with slight embarrassment showing on her face while her eyes lingered on him a bit longer than perhaps she was intending.

"My biggest hope is to be valedictorian and my worst fear is to be stuck in a dead-end career." she added.

"My name is Gene Christopher Tucker. My biggest hope is to have a family and be comfortable. My worst fear is being alone."

"OK. My name is Thomas Deveraux Wales. My biggest hope is to be remembered. My biggest fear is losing my mom and my brother. Another thing, I'm scared of messing things up, I mean, I have a hard time with people my age – I just want things to be different at this school."

We took that in for a moment and kept going.

"I'm Bruce Arnold Edwards. My best hope is be a doctor and my worst fear is going through high school with no girlfriend."

"I'm Wes, um... Wesley Warren Moon. My best hope is to date a high school girl. My worst fear would be something happening to my family."

After that, Wales piped up, "OK, now what's everybody's most embarrassing moment?"

For what had to be an hour we laughed about things from going into the wrong public bathrooms to other things happening in public that twelve-year-olds tend to find funny. Wales took it to another level when he mentioned losing his father at seven years old because of a heart problem. With that, a sense of seriousness came over us like a cloud hiding the sun.

"I uh... had a brother, Michael." Gene said with his head down and continued, "He died when I was in the fourth grade and it messed up everything. My dad left and uh… yeah… it messed up everything. So that's why I said what I did… because I'm alone now." We all encouraged him in some way and if everyone was like me, we began to see why this was important for all of us. That was the watershed moment. After that we all talked openly about people we'd lost or were scared we may lose. Hang-out time went from laughter to therapy – at least whatever therapy twelve-year-olds can offer each other.

When our time was coming to an end, we all agreed that this was probably the single best afternoon we'd had with friends. We all agreed to do it as often as we could and even made plans to see a movie the following month. No one seemed more satisfied than Wales and I was happy for him.

CHAPTER 6:
ANOMALISTIC

The following Monday, Wales and I used the bus ride to talk about the time we all had together at the mall. Both of us felt things went really well and that we all gelled nicely. Then Wales paused and stared out the window for what I felt was an uncomfortably long time.

"Was I *that* obvious?" he asked.

"I, um... don't know what you're talking about." I responded.

"I... I just don't want to mess things up!" he stated.

"Wales, we talked about this. Things are fine... you're fine." I assured him.

"You don't... never mind..." he yielded.

"Come on man, open up." I insisted.

"OK, but just you for now, OK?"

"OK, just me, what's going on?"

"Was... Was I too obvious with Leigh?"

Then it dawned on me. "You like her, huh?" I asked with as much empathy as I could muster.

"What's there *not* to like?" he said, "She's smart, beautiful, ambitious... I mean what more could I want?"

"Yeah, she's all those things but do you think she likes you too? I mean, what's your strategy?" I asked, hoping to bring this wild-eyed dreamer back down to earth.

"I think I'll take it slow, real slow." he said, his eyes staring into space.

"You think that's smart? What if some other guy moves in first?" I asked.

"She's way to busy for that! If I move in slow and give her space, she won't see me coming. Before she knows it, having me around will be normal." he said with a scheming look on his face.

"That sounds like a plan, Wales. But what if that other guy is... well... me? She's everything you said and then some and I just can't let her go!" I blurted, hoping to get the reaction I got.

"What!" he shouted incredulously.

At that everyone on the bus looked at us. Even Ms. Lucy glared at us in the visor mirror she used for observing the riders.

"Wales... I don't know what to..." I burst into laughter, "I'm sorry, I just had to do it. Your reaction was priceless!"

He sighed in relief. "Jerk!" he jokingly said. "Will you help me?"

"You know I will." I assured him.

During the weeks that followed, the *Mysfits* fell into a kind of groove with each other. We were comfortable in our collective skin and it felt right. "Right" is the only way to describe the way we thought and worked together. We ate together at school, studied together, and encouraged each other. It was really something else. Little did we know that normal was something we would soon leave behind and we would have to rely on each other a little more than we thought.

STICKS AND STONES?

The word made me stop in my tracks. The blood in my veins turned to ice-water as the word sunk in – a word that I'd known but never heard directed at me. He said it again. This time, though I'd known the word it was still almost alien. The stench of hate lingered in the air as though the air had been stained by the "N-word" as it pushed its way toward it's intended target - me.

"That's right <n-word>, I got my eye on you!" he said with an almost surreal contempt in his voice.

I was about to leave the boy's room when this "conversation" began. I spun around to face Jake Thompkins, the boy from the first day who'd apparently gotten his confidence back and then some. There was more to it, something worse, I could feel it.

"You don't have your boy with you now, so what are you gonna do?" he asked with a contorted smile like a demented clown.

My first instinct was to kill him but then I settled down a bit. I looked him straight in the eyes. As I looked, he took a few steps toward me such that our faces were a foot apart. There was nothing in his eyes, just a mindless stare, but behind his eyes was malevolence. I imagined it was the same malevolence that turned dogs and fire hoses on the *Freedom Riders* twenty-some odd years before. This was tangible hatred, something I had not known. This was alive somehow and *in* him or *on* him or something.

Just then Mr. Osbourne came in to use the bathroom. Jake pressed past me and left. I took a moment to gather myself.

"Is everything alright?" Mr. Osbourne asked.

"Um... yeah... I guess." I responded in the midst of my shock. It was probably for the best that I didn't say anything then. I figured I needed to think through it some more.

I left the bathroom and bumped right into Meghan O'Neil. Meghan, the attractive girl with blonde hair, stood a little shorter than me. She had this pretty "girl-next-door" quality about her. Meghan always seemed to have this aloof stare on her face, eyes that seemed to stare into nothingness, but she did have this one enduring thing.

"Oh! I'm sorry! I didn't see you there, my mind is just... never mind." I apologized, hoping to be on my way.

"It's OK." she said, staring through me with that stare. Her gaze lasted for a second and then she shook her head and there it was, her rather enduring quality. As it turned out, Meghan too had one of the prettiest smiles anyone could ever hope to see; it was like her super power, and she knew it.

Her eyes lingered on me for a second or two as she walked away. Though I didn't have time to think about this weird exchange, I couldn't help but think about how both she and Saundra had this strange aloof thing going on. "It makes sense that they hang out together." I thought to myself.

Throughout the next period, Algebra, I reflected on what I'd experienced and how I was sure it was an important moment for me personally. All in all, I thought I handled myself well given that I'd never been tested like that. But more than that, what did I see in Jake? What was it that I felt when I looked in his eyes? Maybe I was just imagining all of that seeing as how I was in shock at his choice of words. I just didn't know.

Lunch was next and it just so happened that as we approached our table, Murph and company were just getting up. Murph nodded to Wales as they passed each other and we sat down. Though this was getting ridiculous, I kinda liked it. I sat there with a blank stare on my face while I mindlessly ate my sandwich.

"What's up with you?" Wes asked.

I looked at him for a moment and leaned forward as though I were trying to keep a secret. The others moved closer too.

"I ran into Jake in the bathroom earlier..." I said. I went on to relay to them the whole story of what Jake said and what I felt. As I finished, my eyes fell on Leigh's face. She was visibly upset, moving her glasses to dab tears with a napkin.

"Leigh... are you alright?" I questioned.

"<Expletive>!" she said emphatically as she erupted from her chair.

We were all startled because we had not seen this side of her. I took it in for a moment and realized that in some way this was maternal. I realized this this was one of the ways she fit with us. She was going to protect her own. I guess being the only female *Mysfit* would work out in one of two ways; she was either going to be nurturing or she was going to keep to herself – thank God she chose the former. She fixed her gaze on Jake at the *Country Boys'* table as she huffed and puffed. Jake and his friends looked over at her and chuckled among themselves.

"Hey... hey..." Gene said in calming tones as he slowly rose from his seat next to her and put his hands on her shoulders. He helped her back into her seat, hoping to defuse the situation. Wide-eyed, Wales wisely let Gene talk her down.

"Not like this... Not like this." Gene said disarmingly, "I want to kick his <expletive> too, and I just might before the day is done but not now and not here."

Gene looked at her and gave his signature "nod of finality".

She nodded as she pushed back a few more tears.

"I'm just so embarrassed!" she managed to push out.

"Yeah, you blurted that out kinda loud." Bruce mentioned.

Leigh responded, "Not about that... I'm embarrassed that this happened at all. I guess I was naive in thinking that this kind of stupidity was behind us. I mean I remember what Jake said on the first day but... I guess I was just lost in hope."

It was pretty apparent that lunch ended twenty-minutes early so we walked back to the junior high building. Mr. Philmore was just leaving his room.

"Do you mind if we sit in there for a few?" Wes asked.

Mr. Philmore looked at each of us for a minute and saw that Leigh looked distressed.

"Sure, but remember, you break it you buy it!" he said with a hint of trust in his voice.

We thanked him as we walked into his empty classroom and took seats. They all indicated their support for me and some a desire to hurt Jake. I was still weirded out by it all but one thing I knew for sure was that what I saw and felt was in no way normal. I told them exactly that.

"Of course it wasn't normal, it's not supposed to be." Wes insisted.

"That's not what I meant." I said.

"It doesn't matter what it felt like; it was a jerk being a jerk and we either tell somebody about it or we don't." Wales added, trying to be the voice of reason.

"Tell somebody? I say we just roll up on him and handle some business!" Gene let his thoughts be known though we already knew what he was thinking, "He just best be glad it wasn't me, that's all!"

"He wouldn't have said those things to you, Gene, he picked me for a reason. I'm telling you guys, this was not right. I've been insulted plenty of times, maybe not like this, but I never felt like... like something else was happening" I said.

"Look, whatever man, but what are we gonna do?" Bruce asked.

"Yeah, what *are* we going to do?" Leigh added.

"I don't think we should do anything or tell anyone. We should probably wait until we know more before we make plans. Don't you think?" I thought this was a good course of action.

"No." Gene said emphatically, "But this happened to you so you decide, but I think we should do something – hopefully *to* him and not *about* him."

We sat there for a while in silence, well at least we didn't say anything but we said more with our expressions than we could have with words. Without saying anything we all communicated concern for what the future might hold.

Breaking the silence was easy for Wales and in this case at least I for one appreciated that fact.

"You know what we need?" he asked as he met blank stares from the group, "Another outing!"

Wheels were turning. You could see some people warming up to the idea. I thought about the last time we were together off-campus and began to think it was a good idea.

"We could see a movie this time." Wales said with a kind of luring tone in his voice.

"I haven't seen a movie since *The Search for Spock*." Leigh said unexpectedly.

"You're a Trekkie?" Wes asked with a sense of skepticism.

"Yeah, I've seen everything... I love it." she answered.

You could tell from Wales' face that he was making some kind of mental note.

"OK, it's settled then, we'll get together Saturday and see that new killer robot from the future movie!"

"That movie is rated R, man, how are we gonna get in?" Bruce questioned.

"Leave that to me." Wales answered before asking, "Are we all good with this?"

We all agreed to let Wales do his thing. By this time a commotion began to build in the hallway. It was time to go to next period. I thanked everyone for their support and ideas before leaving the room feeling better than I had all morning.

The remainder of that week seemed to go by slowly. Every time I saw Jake in a class or in the hallways he'd give me the stink-eye. At first it was a bit disconcerting but I got used to this new normal and went on about my business. As the week wore on, the prospect of hanging with friends on Saturday grew evermore appealing.

MALL RATS:

I woke up early that Saturday, knowing I had to get through my chores before I could go meet up with my friends. It's funny what a little motivation can inspire. I had what usually took me all day done by 10:30. So impressed were my parents they kept asking if I'd done something wrong in a way that almost insisted I was hiding something. I was more amused than irritated.

By 1:00, the agreed upon meeting time, my mom and I were pulling up to the main entrance of the Golden Ring Mall. Once again Wales' mother greeted her and she pulled off after confirming she was to be back by six. Ms. Wales and I shared a few words, I joked about Wales' wardrobe before joining the few that had already gathered at the door. We all went in after Bruce and Wes arrived.

Gene pulled me aside for a moment and told me to, "Check Leigh out." It didn't take but a second to note that she was wearing makeup. Leigh never wore makeup. To be fair it wasn't much but it was noticeable and she looked good. It should be noted that this particular day was unseasonably warm, like twenty degrees above average, it had gotten into the eighties or something. Presumably that was why Leigh was dressed in a black tee-shirt and blue-jean shorts. The reason for all this became clear as the day unfolded. It was obvious that Wales had taken notice as well; he was unusually quiet and kept stealing looks whenever he could.

Ms. Wales told us she had some work to do and asked, "So what are you guys going to do with your afternoon?"

"We thought we'd go to the arcade, get something to eat, and maybe take in a movie." Wales promptly answered.

"Oh, OK, have fun!" she said as she found a table and chair near the fountain.

"So, what do we wanna do?" Wales asked as he adjusted his fedora.

"We should probably eat now." Leigh suggested.

"Good idea!" Wes responded.

Likely due to the good weather, the mall was rather crowded that day. The six of us worked our way over to the pizza place near the arcade. After ordering wings and a large pizza, we sat in a corner booth.

"So, *Terminator* huh?" Bruce asked with unashamed skepticism.

"Leave that to me..." Wales answered with an assuring grin and nod.

Just then Bruce went for the hat. We all knew somehow that you don't touch the hat. This was some kind of unspoken rule that sort of emanated from Wales. Wales wasn't much of a fighter but we all knew that he would fight over the hat. Somehow sensing Bruce's attack on the hat, Wales put up his fists and recoiled into the person sitting next to him – which happened to be Leigh. She let out this odd high-pitched shriek and, after a moment of silence, we all burst into laughter, including Leigh.

Our food was ready soon after "the shriek". An onlooker would have thought we'd spent the last week away from civilization because of the way we consumed our precious fattening bounty. Even Leigh, who was known for the civilized manner in which she approached her food at lunch, gave no refuge to wing or slice. In what seemed like minutes, the trough was empty and six satiated kids were pulling their last dregs of soda through the straws of their cups.

"The movie doesn't start for an hour and a half, arcade?" Wales offered as he carefully scrubbed tomato sauce from his t-shirt with a napkin.

"Arcade!" I said, looking at Gene with a sense of competitiveness. Earlier that month, Gene and I got all worked up over this new arcade game, *Karate Champ*. We agreed that should we have the opportunity, we would find out which one of us was the better player. Now, Gene could beat me in everything that had to do with sports or something physical. So, there was no way I was going to cede the digital world to him as well.

"Hey Joe." Bruce said with a quizzical sound in his voice, "How are you doing with all of that Jake crap?"

"It still bothers me, you know, but I'll be alright." I answered, trying to match my body-language with my words.

"You'll let us know if he does anything else, right?" Leigh said with a stern voice.

"You know it." I replied looking her in the eyes. I didn't want her to get upset again.

"You'd better." Gene said matter-of-factly as he glared at me to underscore how serious he was.

The arcade was in sight of the pizza place. We were talking and laughing as we left the restaurant, not watching where we were going as kids often do, and I bumped right into Saundra.

"Oh, sorr..., Saundra! Um, I'm sorry... are you OK?" I asked, embarrassed and stammering comically.

"I'm alright, don't worry about it." she said with a hint of laughter in her voice, "Hi Gene."

"What's up, Saundra?" Gene replied.

So caught up with Saundra were we that we did not see the people she was with.

"You guys hang out outside of school too, huh?" Meghan asked as she looked at each of us with that spaced-out look of hers.

"Uh, yeah." I said.

I don't know if it was because Saundra was there or not but there was this feeling that something was just "off". I can't explain it, I just knew it.

"Aren't you going to introduce me to your friends?" said a wispy yet articulate voice. This voice came from a tall slender woman with blond hair slicked back and set in a bun. She had model-like features and was well-dressed from her expensive-looking shoes and black pant-suit to her white blouse. The deep maroon lip-stick only added to her already striking appearance.

"Certainly, mother." Meghan responded, "Everyone, this is my mother. Mother, this is everyone."

"It is nice to meet you, everyone." Ms. O'Neil said.

We all kind of muttered, "Nice to meet you." to her displeasure. I could tell she was the type that preferred children not mutter, especially when addressing adults. I suppose she endured it because we were not hers.

"Well, everyone, have a nice day." Ms. O'Neil said as she began to walk with both Saundra and Meghan on either side.

We watched as they walked away. When they were out of earshot, the opinions flowed. Gene broke the silence with, "I told you all that Saundra was weird."

"Who calls their mom, 'mother', anyway?" I added, "Meghan weirds me out."

"Me too, I ran into Olympia and Destiny a couple of weeks ago at the store with my dad and they're the same way." Bruce mentioned.

"I'm telling you guys, the whole group of them is weird!" Wales stated.

We hit the arcade and it seemed as though any thoughts of the weirdness we'd encountered melted away as we played games and cheered each other on. Then *Karate Champ* became available and it was time for the showdown between Gene and me. We decided to play a series of seven games, like the *World Series*. I wish I could say that I humiliated him with wide-margin victories. He bested me five games out of seven.

Gene had a way of gloating a bit longer than what some would say is normal. I had to endure it until it died down on the way to the theater.

We climbed the steps and read the marquis. We were disappointed to find that *The Terminator* wasn't listed. This was common because they added other theaters on the opposite side of the mall. You would frequently see people walking fast if not running to the other end of the mall because they guessed which theater they needed and were wrong. We were no different. The six of us nearly ran, dodging people as we went, to the other end of the mall.

We found the right theater and Wales motioned for us to stop. We saw some older kids, about high-school age, try to buy tickets for the movie and fail. A guy was there making sure kids didn't get in. He was a large man sitting on a stool who somehow managed to be physically fit. Though he wore the same uniform as the other workers there, he was decidedly not friendly. The most prominent thing he wore, however, was the scowl on his face.

"You're up hotshot." Wes said with vindication in his voice.

What happened next went down in the annals of history as one of the greatest of Wales' stories.

"Wait here for a minute." Wales said.

He adjusted his hat, took a deep breath and began to walk. We all thought he was going to the box office but instead, he walked right up to the guy who was more like a security guard. We couldn't hear their conversation but after a minute or so the guard erupted with laughter and motioned for us to come forward.

"Go get your tickets and don't tell anyone." the guard said with sternness in his voice.

The man nodded to the teenager in the box office and all six of us bought tickets to the R-rated movie. In stunned silence the six of us filed into the dark theater and found a bunch of seats together toward the back of the theater. We all sat there for a second unsure of what just happened. Wales just sat there with a grin. Wes spoke first.

"How in the world, Wales?"

"I think I'll keep this one to myself." Wales said

"Are you kidding me?" Gene expressed with incredulity.

Wales just glanced at him with a triumphant look on his face and then got comfortable in his seat.

Because the theater was crowded, we had to sit together with no buffer spaces. Buffer spaces seemed to be an unwritten rule among guys, two guys can't sit together in a movie theater, there must be an open seat between them. The exception to this rule being that the seat can be occupied by a girl. Gene and I sat together with Leigh sitting in between me and Wales while Wes and Bruce sat on the end.

Leigh nudged me during the trailers before the movie. "Hey Joe..." she said, keeping her voice down.

"What's up?" I whispered.

"Watch this." As she said those words, she stretched out her arms and interlaced her fingers as if to crack them. She then slowly moved her right arm and positioned it over Wales' head. She'd done this in such a way that he knew exactly what she was doing. She lowered her hand onto the hat and removed it from his head and slowly put it on hers. Then she pulled the brim down in front and sat back in her seat while smirking at me. To my utter shock, Wales didn't say a word nor did he move a muscle. This was when I knew Leigh could read people pretty well. She apparently knew he liked her and this was her way of letting him know it. I supposed the way she dressed that day had something to do with Wales too. I looked at the others only to find blank stares of puzzlement being shared among us.

Afterwards, the movie had our geek senses heightened and we couldn't stop talking about it, that is to say all but Wales. He seemed to be in somewhat of a trance state, his head bare, with unkempt black hair going this way and that. Leigh, fully engaged in our conversation about time-travel, still wore Wales signature possession triumphantly upon her head as though it were a kind of trophy. She looked good in it too. I pulled Wales aside so that we trailed the group as we walked.

"You alright?" I asked him as gently as I could without laughing.

"I uh... guess so?" he replied, "Do you think she knows?"

"I think so, but this is a good thing." I assured him.

"How?" he asked seeming defeated, "I froze, I didn't know what to do."

"She's not making fun of you. I think she wanted you, all of us actually, to know that she felt comfortable enough to do what we couldn't do." I said, trying to cheer him up.

"You think so?" he asked, his face seeming to brighten.

"Actually Wales, I think she likes you." I stated as I continued to walk while Wales stopped dead in his tracks.

Leigh wore that hat until we met up with Wales' mother who almost didn't recognize him in public without it. She slowly removed the hat from her head and placed it on Wales'. He adjusted it and didn't say a single word about it. His mother just sat there, wide-eyed.

That night I wrote about all of these things in my journal. It felt as though my mind was given a reprieve from Jake Thompkins. It's funny, if I were to guess, I'd bet Jake wasn't even thinking about it near as much as I was. I suppose that's the nature of hateful things.

CHAPTER 7:
ALLANTIDE

On the way to the bus stop that Monday, I couldn't help but think about how it was turning out to be another above-average day in terms of weather. It was as if Spring had come early for a few days. I was early so I took a slow walk through the neighborhood looking at all the Halloween decorations on the surrounding houses. I knew that come Wednesday night there would be any number of kids running around in costumes with bags collecting the candy they believed was their due. I thought for a minute about how all of that was behind me now.

I saw Saundra at the bus stop and was somehow put in an even better mood despite the weirdness I felt Saturday. This, however, was not true for Saundra. For some reason she was not acknowledging me as she normally did. I thought I would start the week off right by getting a smile out of her but it was as if she didn't want anything to do with me. I tried to chalk this up to the "weirdness of girls" but this seemed different, almost intentional in a way. I couldn't help but feel a little hurt.

No sooner than I could start to wallow in my disappointment, the bus came lumbering around the corner. I began to think of Wales and how he was doing in light of recent events. A few stops later, he stepped up into the bus. Gone was the annoyingly talkative kid who seemed to exude a confidence beyond his years. Now I beheld a sheepish kid who, though dressed nicely, slowly made his way down the aisle and slid in beside me on the deep-green bench seat. I opened cautiously.

"Uh... hey Wales... how ya doing?"

"Fine... um... terrible... I don't know!" he said, frustration dripping from every word.

"Lemme guess, Leigh?" I responded, daring to "go there".

He returned fire with, "Yes, Leigh, what else could it be!"

"OK, let's take a minute here... What's going on?" I asked in my best diplomatic tone.

"I dunno, I just... I just want her to like me!" he answered.

"Um, I thought we kinda covered all that. Remember Saturday? It looks like she does. How did things go when you talked to her yesterday?"

"Well, uh..." he stammered.

"Wales, you *did* call her yesterday, right?" I asked, bracing myself for the answer I knew was coming.

"Well, no."

I stared at him with wide incredulous eyes until he spoke.

"I know, I know! I just didn't know what to say and I was... am so scared of her thinking I'm crazy or something. What if we got it wrong and she was just clowning around."

"Listen to me." I said, "Cause I'm only gonna say this once. She knew what she was doing. Bruce tried it earlier that day and you almost got into a fight. She even asked me to, 'Watch this', before she took it. She knew and she wants you to talk about it."

"Really?" he said, the word coming out like a sprout growing out of the underbrush toward the sunlight.

"Really." I said resolutely. "Look, one of the reasons the six of us fit so well together is that we're all like adults stuffed into kids' bodies. We should be mature enough to talk about this kind of stuff. True, Leigh is more adult than all of us, but don't let that stop you. Promise me you'll talk to her before the end of the day, OK?"

He replied, "I don't know, you know I'm better with adults than kids my age."

"I know, but man, I don't think you can find a more adult kid your age than Leigh. You got this." I said with my best convincing tone.

"But what if...."

"You got this." I interrupted.

"OK, I get it, I got this." he said. "I got this." he said again, almost to himself in an assuring tone.

"Good." I stated, hoping to have put this issue to bed.

Classes that day were unremarkable and lunch was rather awkward. We all knew something was going on with Leigh and Wales but we kinda danced around it. No matter what we talked about, the elephant in the lunchroom was sitting at the end of our table. I could only hope that Wales would step up so things could get back to normal.

After lunch I noticed Wales had a funny look on his face. Just as I dismissed it as him being too scared to say something to her, he pulled Leigh aside in the lobby of the CAB. Being nosy, I walked slowly out of the CAB with the others, headed to class. I caught a glance from Wales at one point but couldn't tell how things were going. I didn't know what he said to her and I would have to wait until after classes to find out.

I caught up with Wales after a rather boring remainder of the day. Mondays were not my favorite and I suppose it showed in my lack of interest in classes as the day went on. I was, however, interested in the drama surrounding Leigh and Wales. I found Wales on the lawn in front of the school near where the buses pull in. On some days, like today, the buses were already in the lane waiting for students. There he stood, facing our bus, with a blank stare on his face. He didn't even acknowledge my presence until I spoke.

"So, uh... what's up Wales?" I opened.

"Bus. Now." he said in a most caveman-like way.

The thoughts running through my head ranged from bad to worse. My mind was spinning with what I would say to calm him down and try to smooth this whole thing over. I was just hoping that Leigh let him down easy and that we could all still be friends after this.

We stepped up into the bus, greeted Ms. Lucy and made our way down the aisle through the empty bus to a seat three-quarters of the way down. Wales just sat there for a solid minute looking out the window before I felt I had to say something.

"Look, Wales, I..."

Without looking at me, he interrupted me with, "You couldn't have been more..." The pregnant pause was killing me. "Right!" he said. It took me a moment to realize what he said and gather my thoughts.

"I... I knew it? I guess." is all I could push out of my mouth.

"I pulled her aside after lunch and she said she was waiting for me to say something." he said.

"Good... that's good, right?" I asked.

"Yeah, it's good." he said. "She said she wants to figure out what she's feeling but she doesn't have time for immature games, which is why she was worried when I didn't call or step up sooner than I did."

"Good... that's good, right?" I asked again, somewhat stunned.

"Yeah, it's good." he said. "I then said what I think must be the smoothest thing I've ever said in my life. I said I would give her whatever space she needed and whatever time she needed until she understood her feelings like I understand mine."

"Holy crap! I need to write that down!" I exclaimed with a huge smile on my face.

"Yes, you do and you're welcome!" he said, giving me a quick wink.

"So, what does it feel like to have a girlfriend?" I asked, like a hungry reporter trying to impress his boss.

"We talked about that, labels. We agreed that we're in a relationship and that we shouldn't use those labels right now."

"This is all too big for twelve-year-olds!" I thought to myself. Then I reminded myself that none of us were like little kids and that we were kind of mature for our age.

"What are you gonna tell your mom?" I asked.

"I'm going to tell her the truth; that we're trying to figure things out. I think she'll be thrilled." he said matter-of-factly.

We agreed that none of this should affect our group of friends in any way and spent the rest of our time on the bus talking about Leigh. We discussed how we all thought highly of her, how they were going to spend time together, and what attracted her to him. He didn't know what she saw in him.

Except for lunch, the next day was even more unremarkable than the day before. Leigh sat next to Wales, which was not out of the ordinary, but she acted as though nothing happened. She was not like other girls our age, overly enamored with whatever crush they had at the moment. She was, as we'd discussed, mature. This was good because it forced Wales to step up his game. What a thing to watch.

I woke up Wednesday morning like I had the day before, counting off days until the weekend. Though the stuff with Wales and Leigh kept things interesting, that was a tough week for me. I just didn't want to sit in classes all day. I don't know what it was but I just wanted to sleep in and stay home that day. Though I was convinced this was the best course of action, my mother was not. I dragged myself through my normal morning ritual that resulted in my reflective walk to the bus stop. Along the way, I noted that the weather was again unusually warm.

At the bus stop I noticed Saundra had a pair of headphones on as if she were blocking out the world. I somehow took this personally and simply decided not to try anymore. I mean it was a pipe-dream anyway, right? Someone like her would never be interested in a guy like me who had *maybe* a few extra pounds to shed and wasn't the *most* athletic person in the world.

The bus turned the corner, providing a reprieve from the pity-party that was just getting started in my head. As I boarded the bus, I greeted Ms. Lucy who had her portable radio tucked behind her seat and tuned to the local news. I found my usual bench seat and watched the world pass by as we journeyed from stop to stop. I didn't even notice Wales getting on the bus until he plopped himself down next to me. He'd called Leigh the night before and was filling me in on the details. As I expected, there were no details to tell. They talked about school and she helped him with a math assignment. She would throw him a bone every now and then, cracks in her otherwise stern resolve. "She must really like him." I thought.

The bus went down the steep hill and up the other side before turning right to get to the school. As we made that right, a gasp could be heard from a number of people at the front of the bus. Both Wales and I craned our necks to the left to see what was going on. There had to be dozen or so police cars, with lights going, on and around the school's parking lot. There was an officer directing buses to the back of the lot where we disembarked.

As we got off the bus, we noticed various teachers were stationed around the property conducting kids to their respective buildings. Mrs. Wilson, a high school teacher, instructed us to go straight to our homerooms.

"What's going on?" I asked, somehow believing I would get an answer.

"Just go to your homeroom class, everything is under control." she said, trying to be calm and collected. I could tell she was rattled.

"I wonder if this is like the last time." I said.

"Maybe, but worse from the looks of it." Wales replied.

In our homeroom, Mr. Philmore's history class, everyone was chattering at a feverish pace. Rumors from a burglary to murder and everything in between began to fly. The chatter, like a frenetic hum of white noise, ended abruptly when Mr. Philmore entered the room.

The teacher walked to the front of the room with a terseness in his walk. At the front of the room, he leaned against the clean blackboard and folded his arms, his head down as he stared at the floor for a moment that seemed like ten minutes. He was angry and was finding his way back to his normal calm. He finally collected himself and addressed the class.

"You know class, I'm a straight shooter. If I'm going to say something or have to tell you something, I'll give it to you as I see it – no sugar. That being said, I must yield to the will of the Principal and the Dean, my bosses. So here goes..." he said all of this with a hint of defiance in his voice.

"Obviously, you all know that something happened on campus. We were the unfortunate victims of vandalism no doubt connected to Halloween. This sort of thing happens at schools from time to time but it appears that one of our Janitors, Jim MacPhearson, confronted the vandals and was assaulted. They had to take him to the hospital for treatment and observation but he'll be fine. This is why so many police officers are here. They should be here for a few more hours. Because of all this, Chapel is canceled and will resume next Wednesday. I'm sure rumors will spread so the school will send a letter home with you today containing all the facts. Everything is under control and this poses no danger to students. Now, let's get on with our day, shall we?"

I didn't like it and from the looks of it neither did Gene. I looked back at him and he was just shaking his head. We both looked at Wales and gave him a nod. He nodded back, knowing that we were asking him to do what he'd already planned to do – talk to Murph and get the whole story.

There was a strange feeling in the air that morning. It was as though everybody felt like their own homes had been violated. People were quieter in the hallways and there were more huddled discussions, even among the teachers. I'd just gotten out of Earth Science, my second period class, and was headed to my math class when I came across Leigh in the hall. She pulled me aside.

"Hey Joe, crazy morning huh?"

"Yeah, it is. Wales is gonna see if he can find some more information. If anybody can get something out of the staff, he can." I said confidently.

"Yeah, he's good at that. I know Wales tells you everything and that you know that he and I are in a relationship." she said kind of sheepishly.

"I'm all for it!" I assured her.

"I know. I am too, so um..."

"Is everything OK?" I asked.

"Yeah, it's just that... Wales thinks the world of you and Gene, you in particular. He listens to you. He really likes me and I don't want any of this to mess with the group. I guess what I'm asking is that you keep an eye out. You know what I mean?" she was uncharacteristically all over the place.

"I do." I lied, "...and I will" I had to put her out of her misery and end this conversation. Leigh was the most mature of us all so she was over my head on this one. I just figured it would all work out and I would understand over time. I think I was more or less right.

Just then Meghan O'Neil floated up to us with Olympia Dupree, a beautiful thin girl with glasses and long straight brunette hair, in tow. I say "floated" because she was obviously in her "weird" mode. Her eyes had that spaced-out stare in them as they scanned back and forth from me to Leigh. Meghan abruptly burst into that beautiful smile that could calm a rabid dog.

"Hey guys!" she said in her best chipper voice, "Weird day huh?"

"By the minute..." Leigh said under her breath.

"It sure is!" I said loudly, speaking over Leigh.

"Well, you guys have a nice day!" Meghan offered.

Leigh and I both mumbled something to the effect of, "You too." and they left.

"That girl is just spooky!" Leigh asserted.

"I couldn't agree more." I responded.

"I gotta go to class. Thank you for looking out for Wales." she said as she walked off.

"Sure, of course!" I replied with confidence as she walked away, acting as though I knew what her earlier request meant.

"What would Wales find out?" was all I could think about during third period math. As the teacher, Ms. Ethridge, droned on and on about some equation, my mind was spinning about what really happened the night before. I figured it must have happened in the gym or else why would they cancel Chapel? I wondered if it was the same group of people who set up that stuff on the upper field in September. I wondered if Mr. Philmore had a...

"Mr. Mack." Ms Ethridge said in her monotone voice as she held out a piece of chalk. Apparently, she'd called upon me to come up to the board and complete some equation. I looked at the board to see, if by some chance, I recognized what she was doing. No luck there apparently. She really had been teaching while my mind was elsewhere.

"Uh..." I stammered while my mind searched for a way out of this without being embarrassed. Again with the, "Uh..", and then the sweet light of epiphany shown full in my mind. "I'm sorry Ms. Ethridge. I guess my mind is scattered today with all the... you know...." I said with a tone that begged for pity.

"It's alright." she said, "I think we're all scatter-brained today." she sympathized.

Was it wrong to take advantage of the unpleasant events of the day, yes, but a kid had to do what a kid had to do.

After the grueling remainder of the class during which I was sure to pay close attention, lunch had finally arrived. We got to the CAB to find Wales sitting alone at the table. The Janitors, who normally held the table for us, were nowhere to be found. Wales had somehow gotten out of class early and met with the Janitors in the lunch room. As we approached the table, we noticed a look on his face that could only be described as ominous.

"OK, everyone, lean in. This has to stay between us." Wales insisted.

We all learned in from our chairs and Wales began to share what he'd been told.

"They found him this morning apparently drugged and tied to what they called an altar. He was putting in overtime yesterday and they must have grabbed him."

"Wait a minute, that would mean these people were there all night." Leigh stated.

"Murph told me they had to be in the gym for a long time to set up all that stuff." Wales replied.

"All what stuff?" Gene asked.

"The altar, a bunch of candles, the hundreds of flowers in circles around all of it, and... um... a dead pig." Wales answered.

"A dead pig!" Bruce exclaimed, trying to keep his voice down.

"Yeah, Murph said he heard one of the detectives say something about ritual sacrifice. He also said there was a bunch of stuff painted on the walls in there too."

"What the heck do we do with this?" Wes questioned.

We were at a loss, all of us wanted to get to the bottom of this but didn't know how to do it or even if we could. This was bigger than us and we felt as though we were just along for the ride like we were being washed down a raging river. We all sat back in our seats and stared at each other. We eventually got back to normal, spending the rest of lunch lamenting over how eventful our two months at this school had been. I think we all knew without saying that "strange" was the new normal. Somehow, we were comfortably uncomfortable with that.

Days that change your world start off in the same unassuming manner as any other day. Like riding a roller-coaster in the dark, you are completely oblivious to the unexpected twist that changes your point of reference. I can truly say, looking back on it, that this particular Wednesday, Halloween 1984, was one of those days.

CHAPTER 8:
CLOSE ENCOUNTERS

The next few weeks came and went. The school found its way back to normal soon enough and before we knew it, Thanksgiving was upon us. This was a needed break, essentially a four-day weekend during which I could reconnect with my brother, Preston, whom I'd not seen since we moved him into his dorm in late August. I looked forward to sharing with him all the weird things that happened in the past few months and compare notes to see if he'd had the same problems during his time there and kept it to himself for some reason.

It was the day before Thanksgiving and I pondered these things as I made my way to the bathroom through the busy lunchroom filled with the incessant chattering and whooping laughter of pubescence. I found the bathroom empty. I learned otherwise for as I washed my hands, I heard a word from one of the stalls. It was a word with which I had become all too familiar.

"N-Word!" The word ricocheted off the walls in such a way that I was almost inclined to duck. The stall door burst open as Jake stepped out. The stench of what he'd obviously been doing rivaled that of the word he'd chosen to use to address me. Once again, he didn't look right. His face was pale and twisted with hatred, his dead eyes latched onto mine as I resolved to look him straight in the face and not show any sign of backing down. I knew this was a situation in which I was not going to be able to use slick words to escape. I knew that if I was to get back to the throng of hungry kids on the other side of the cinder-block wall I would have to go through him. The time for diplomacy had apparently come to an end, at least this is what the dead-panned face of the hate-fueled *Country Boy* in front of me said. Even with all this, my mind was racing for options. The ugliness of his vocabulary hung in the air as did the sense of an impending fight. I still couldn't shake the fact... I don't know... that it felt like there was someone watching us – perhaps from another stall or something. But now wasn't the time for spooky feelings, now was the time to fight. I assumed a defensive stance, drawing on every bit of the eight Jiu-Jitsu classes I'd taken the Summer before. My opponent put up his fists in the way every American moviegoer is taught. We stood there for a moment – long enough for him to rattle off several other racial epithets. The coiled viper in me was about to strike when the bathroom door opened.

"Whoa... Whoa... What's going on here!" said a familiar voice. Gene stepped around Jake to stand beside me. His physique and the intimidating look on his face had a cooling effect on Jake such that he stood back and put his hands down.

"Are we gonna have a problem here? Cause you best believe I been wanting a reason to beat your <expletive> for a while now!" Gene said as he took a step toward Jake. The door opened again and a few others came in along with a teacher.

"Boys." Mr. Langford said as he chose a urinal. Jake took this chance to quickly exit the bathroom. We followed, not to find Jake, but to get back to the table.

"You were taking too long and I saw that Jake wasn't with his friends so I thought I'd take a look." Gene explained.

"Thank you!" I said with heartfelt appreciation, "I was about to get into it with him and I'm not sure how it would have turned out."

"Either way it wouldn't have worked out for him in the long run." he assured.

I knew then something I think I'd known for a while, that Gene would have my back whenever he could. He wasn't the type of kid who would say something like that, no, he didn't value words all that much – he valued actions and that was the way he communicated.

Back at the table I related all that transpired in the bathroom, including the spooky feeling I had that someone was watching us. Again, I could see the fire in Leigh's eyes and Wales could too, so he worked at calming her down which apparently worked. Though they were all ticked about the confrontation, they didn't know what to make of the spooky part.

Thanksgiving was everything I wanted it to be, a brief respite from whatever was going on at school as well as a time to reconnect with Preston. These few months were the longest time I'd spent apart from him in my life and it was apparently long enough for me to forget how easy it was to think out loud with him. I told him the whole story from day one forward.

"So that's what's been going on." I said.

"Wow little bro, it's like I don't even know that school at all. I never saw anything like what you're going through." he replied, staring at the ceiling while lying on the sofa in the family room.

"I don't know what to say about all that vandalism stuff but I am concerned about the racism. I don't want you to get beat up or anything." he added.

"Me neither..."

"What did Mom and Dad say?" he asked.

"I didn't tell them yet." I replied.

"That's alright for now but you have to tell them. They need to know. I understand why you haven't yet, Mom will fly off the handle, but you can't let this go for too long. Who did you tell at the school?"

"I didn't tell anybody at the school." I answered.

"When you get back to school, I want you to tell Mr. Philmore everything you told me about Jake. Mr. Philmore and no one else; He's good with problems. He'll tell you if someone else needs to know." he advised.

"Why Philmore?" I asked.

"I got a chance to know him a bit. He's the assistant coach of the basketball team, you know. I think he's your best bet." he said convincingly, "About this vandalism stuff, I'd keep that to myself. You're not supposed to know as much as you do anyway. Besides, you don't want to give up your source."

"OK." I said, "Thanks, I think I have an idea of what to do now."

Preston went on to tell me that he was sorry I had to put up with all of this and how surprised he was that the school had changed so much over one Summer. He then went on to tell me about college life in Delaware.

GUIDANCE COUNSELING:

I got a chance to talk with Mr. Philmore when I returned to school the following Monday. He was kind enough to spare some time during lunch for me. I told him that Preston asked me to share with him my situation with Jake. As I expected, he took offense to what Jake said and done but what I didn't expect was his reaction to the spooky feelings I had when I was with Jake. He kept pressing me about what I'd felt and asked if Jake mentioned anything about feeling watched. In truth, I began to feel a little weird about that conversation. But then he laid this on me.

"Look Joe, I could be honest with your brother and I hope I can with you too. I'm gonna go out on a limb here and say some things I probably shouldn't say. This isn't the first time I've heard someone say that they felt they were being watched. However, all of the times I've heard this have been in the last two months, here at this school. Now, you can take that to mean whatever you want. I choose to believe it's not a coincidence and that something is going on."

I was taken aback and he knew it.

He continued, "I've said too much as it is, I can tell. If this keeps happening to you and you want to talk about it, my door is open. Now, about Jake, if we call him into the office, he'll just deny he said any of those things and nothing will happen - your word against his. But rest assured, if he goes off like that with people around, there will be consequences, there's no place for that stuff at this school."

"But what about the first day of school?" I asked, holding out some hope that the school could somehow help.

"Unfortunately, that was months ago. Maybe if you'd said something then, but I'm afraid now is a little late." he said with empathy in his voice.

In that moment I knew I had to weather the storm as best I could until the school got a chance to do something about it. However, I felt good because he did something I wasn't sure other faculty and staff would do – believe me. I was sure the other *Mysfits* believed me when I said that I felt as though someone was watching but I got the feeling they didn't take it seriously. I thanked him for his time and advice and headed to the CAB to take advantage of the lunch time I had left.

THE ADAMS FAMILY:

The next few weeks went by quickly. The anticipation of Christmas and the two weeks of vacation that went with it lingered in the air and was heavy on the minds of students. It was a wonder that anything got done that week before the holiday.

Leigh invited all of us to her house the Saturday before Christmas for a get-together. She lived in the Historic Northwood section of Baltimore City, a posh neighborhood lined with old-growth oak trees and well-manicured lawns dotted with just enough leaves to make you think they were placed just so. Mom dropped me off a half-hour late due to family obligations.

The house was situated in such a way that you had to go down a few steps to a walkway that wound its way to the house. Though the surrounding trees were now bare, I could only imagine how well-shaded the house would be in the summer months. It was beautiful, with just enough ivy creeping up the walls to give it that old-world collegiate look that seemed fitting when thinking of Leigh. I stepped up to the door and rang the bell. The door opened after a few moments and there stood Wales, wearing a maroon and black smoker's jacket with the letters "KA" monogrammed on the left side. He welcomed me into the house and I stared at him like he was crazy as he greeted me and took my coat. I caught Mrs. Adams out of the corner of my eye, she was shaking her head with an incredulous smile on her face. I could tell he'd already won her over.

The house was immaculate and everything was in perfect order. The staircase banister was wrapped with gleaming white Christmas lights. The other decorations were meticulously placed and the tree looked as though it'd been ripped from a greeting card. This living room was trimmed with mahogany and the white rug completed the picture perfectly. Everything was in such order that I imagined that the inside of Leigh's brain must look like this.

I greeted Leigh's mother as her father came up the steps from the basement where everyone was gathered. Mr. Adams gave me a firm handshake as he welcomed me. He took one look at Wales and shook his head. Not many kids could pull off wearing their girlfriend's father's clothes and get away with it but somehow Wales pulled it off. I was about to go to meet the others when *she* came downstairs.

"Who was at the door, Mom?" she said.

"Another of Leigh's friends, honey." Mrs. Adams replied.

"Oh hi, I'm Laurel, Leigh's sister." Laurel said as she shook my hand.

Leigh spoke of her sister often; she admired her actually. Laurel was ten years older than Leigh, a brilliant woman like whom Leigh aspired to be. What Leigh failed to mention was that Laurel was absolutely stunning. I was probably too young to know what a perfect ten looked like but if I had to guess, Laurel would qualify.

"Uh... hi Laurel, I'm Joe." I managed.

Just then, Wales put his arm around me and led me to the basement stairs.

"You can stop drooling now." he whispered.

We had the best time that night. We ate, played games, and talked. It turned out to be one of those nights we would never forget, not because of anything in particular but because we simply spent time with the people we loved. Leigh, by the way, also could not believe the audacity Wales displayed in wearing her father's jacket. But, like everyone else, she thought it was somehow charming that he could feel so comfortable being so bold.

Christmas and the vacation weeks that followed were just what the doctor ordered for all of us. We all needed that break to get ready for the rest of our seventh-grade year. During that time, I got to enjoy my family and get a pep talk or two from Preston. He was always in my corner. We didn't have the sibling rivalry that was so common among my peers, the six years between us may have had something to do with that. He encouraged me to follow Mr. Philmore's advice concerning Jake and to keep him updated whenever I could.

Gene's mother, a senior nurse, transferred to the hospital where my mother worked in the clinical labs. They became fast friends and I began to see a lot more of Gene outside of school. This period of time was when Gene and I really clicked. We still got on each other's nerves from time to time and occasionally argued but that was a good thing because we wound up understanding each other better. He became the brother I was missing since Preston went off to college and I kind of became the brother he was missing.

Spring couldn't have come soon enough. Though I was thankful for snow days during the winter, I was not a fan of the season. I never liked being cold. Spring was here now and I could put being cold out of my mind. With spring came spring fever and what I'd come to believe was myth came true – boys get girl-crazy. I know this because it happened to me. I had Saundra on my mind a lot and the only thing that kept me sane was her apparently not wanting anything to do with me. One day I might have gotten on her nerves a little too much trying to get her to smile and got this for my trouble...

"Look, could you please not talk to me? I'm not interested in you and we're not friends." she said with emphasis on the word "not" both times. Rough huh? Yeah, that's what I thought.

It was April now and the year was winding down. With a month to go before the end of the school year, there was a sense of excitement in the air that would increase until its inevitable crescendo at the end of May. On one Friday evening, my mother dropped me off at Gene's house so she and Ms. Tucker could have a girl's night or whatever. Gene and his mother lived in a white single-family house a few miles from me, near Memorial Stadium. In the basement of his house was an area with a couch and an over-sized television. The basement was painted a dusty rose color and was equipped with a ceiling fan and an arching gold metal floor lamp that seemed to hit me in the head whenever it could. We would come to spend so much time there that we called it "Headquarters" or "HQ" for short. "New Coke" came out on the Tuesday of that week and, being fans of Coke, we decided to share the experience of the next evolution of soft-drinks. It was... terrible.

It turned out that Gene had been hung up on one of the Sidity Committee girls, Imani K, but he was too shy to talk to her. I was surprised because under all the bravado and muscles, he was just like any other kid – a slave to his emotions. We drowned our sorrows that night in terrible New Coke and a fantastic *Baltimorioni* pizza. We played games on his Commodore 64 well into the night and I wound up sleeping over.

On the bus on Monday, Wales asked about my weekend and I told him about the time at Gene's. I had to ask, "So, Wales, how was your weekend? Did you do anything? I know you do something every Friday night so... what's up?" I asked this question whenever I remembered because I secretly hoped, for once, that his life would be normal and mundane... like mine. Wales must have caught on to my routine because he smiled that wincing smile you give someone when you want to apologize for something.

"Um... private party on the *The Pride of Baltimore*." he stated sheepishly.

"OK... I see." I said, taking it well. "Did you take Leigh?"

"Uh... yeah, and her family. Laurel even came up." he said, his voice beginning to betray the fact that he was excited. "It was... AWESOME!"

"I probably know the answer, but how did you manage to get invited to a private party on that boat?" I asked, knowing what was coming.

"My mom knows a guy from work whose stepson's father knows some of the crew. I talked to the guy a few months ago and I got three invitations in the mail. Each of them had a plus one so that meant six people. It gave my mom and her parents some time together and of course Leigh and I got to hang out."

"Wow, I'm glad things are so good with you guys." I meant it but I still wished I had a similar story to tell.

"Oh yeah, the Mayor was there!" he added.

"Oh wow! That's the second time seeing the Mayor at a party, huh?" I said, with no more surprise left in me.

"That's right, and uh..." he muttered.

"Yeah?" I prodded.

"Uh... she kissed me." he said, as though to keep a secret.

"You mean on the cheek like before?" I asked. This innocent cheek thing started in the Spring.

"No, it was quick and all but it was on the lips. I couldn't talk for the rest of the night." he recounted.

"Well now..." I said with fresh energy and then joked, "Now Wales, do we need to have 'The Talk'?"

"Fun-ny." he said as he play-punched me in the shoulder.

EVER-PRESENT HELP:

I'd been raised in the Church all of my life. At that time, my faith was based more on knowledge than relationship. I knew God was there and I could call on Him when I needed Him. Sometimes He throws you a curve-ball to get your attention. That Tuesday something happened that changed my world. Out of all of the weird things that happened that year, this was by far the strangest. It was not strange in a bad way, in fact, it was the most important thing that happened to me.

Gym was held out on the upper field and afterwards I was collecting loose equipment as I was asked to do. We'd played flag football so strips of material were strewn about as well as a few footballs. I was alone on the field by this time and didn't think anything of it. Then it happened, an overwhelming sense that I should duck. It was so strong that I did so without pondering for a second. Just then, a football came zooming through the air where my head had been. I stared at the football that was now skipping along the ground some ten feet away from me.

"Hey N-Word!" Jake yelled, the word snapping me back to reality like a slap in the face. I spun on my heels to find three of the *Country Boys*, Jake Thompkins, Terry Elsmore, and Milton Edwards charging at me.

"We're gonna finish what I started!" Jake yelled, now ten feet from me and running. I might have had a chance with any one of these guys but three was a problem... a big problem. I hate to admit it but in that moment

I froze. I was out of options and began to brace for a beating. Then it happened again.

"Spin to the left!" These weren't words, it was that compelling feeling again. I spun to the left just as Jake tried to dive into me with his arms open. He landed on the ground and the others tripped over him. They wasted no time in shouting obscenities and epithets as they got up and launched their attack.

"Lean right!" - Dodged a punch.

"Jump!" - Tom tried to sweep my legs and missed.

"Crouch!" - Milton came flying over me, grabbing nothing but air and crashing into Tom. Both on the ground now.

"Leapfrog!" - I leaped over Jake as he lunged at me and went to the dirt.

"Run!" I was easily fifty feet away before they got up and realized I'd gone.

I got back to the CAB and went into the empty lunchroom. I. FREAKED. OUT. Well, for a minute or two. Trying to get my composure I wondered if I was crazy; did any of that happen at all? I mean, it couldn't have been better choreographed if it were a Kung-Fu film. I settled on the fact that I wasn't crazy and that it simply had to be, because there was no other explanation, God. It just had to be God.

I went back to the now empty field, collected the equipment and returned to the CAB. The locker room was empty except for a Janitor and three angry-looking *Country Boys* who, if looks could kill, did me in several times. No words were exchanged and I didn't take my eyes off them while I changed clothes. "No shower today." I thought. All the while I was thinking about how I would explain my lateness to my next teacher and that I needed to see Mr. Philmore.

I only had a few minutes after school to meet with Mr. Philmore before I had to get to the bus. Buzzing with urgency like a little kid waiting in line to get to the bathroom I waited outside his classroom. His class had obviously gone late that day. As the door opened, I fought through the tide of upperclassmen that streamed from the room like a salmon trying to make it upriver. Finally, I stood before his desk with him seated, reading over some kind of homework assignment.

"Mr. Philmore, can we talk for a minute? I've only got about ten minutes before the bus." I asked hurriedly.

"Sure, what's wrong?" he asked having heard the urgency in my voice.

I went on to detail what took place on the field leaving nothing out. When I was finished, he sat back in his chair and stared at me intently. I wasn't sure if he thought I was crazy, lying, or what. He pulled a tissue from the box on his desk and slowly took off his glasses. He looked down at his glasses as he cleaned the lenses with the tissue.

"You remember King David and how he fought in all those battles?" he asked.

"Uh... yeah..." I responded as I wondered where he was going with that.

"Ever wonder how he could possibly live through all of that?" he continued.

"I guess I never really thought about it." I answered.

"I figured that God must have been keeping him safe somehow but I never knew how until you told me what happened to you today. It took a lot of guts for you to tell me this and I hope this means that you trust me. I've been praying for you and I'm always encouraged when I get to see Him answer those prayers. Thank you!"

"You're welcome." I said. I could tell he had more on his mind but was being careful with what he shared.

He continued, "I wish there was something I could do about Jake but again, there is nothing concrete to go with here. Besides, it seems God has the situation well in hand, don't you think? Look, you need to get to your bus but please don't hesitate to see me if something else happens, OK?"

"Thanks, I will!" I said as I began to head toward the door.

I didn't tell anyone else about my encounter with Jake until I got some time with Gene that Friday night. Gene and his mother had dinner with my family that night. After dinner, in my room, while we played a game on my computer, I calmly mentioned that Jake and a couple of *Country Boys* tried to jump me on the field after gym. As I expected, his response to my calm matter-of-fact statement was not so calm. He spun me around in my desk chair and growled, "What! Why didn't you tell anybody!"

"I... I told Mr. Philmore." I said calmly, trying to cool him down with my tone.

"Great! What the heck is he gonna do about it? Huh?" he asked, staring at me as though I was supposed give a convincing answer.

"Uh... I..."

"Of course you don't know!" he interrupted. "Did they hit you!?"

"No, that's just it..." I began to offer with a bit of excitement in my voice.

"Oh what? You all made friends and sang Kumbaya together?" he interrupted again.

"No, listen!" I insisted as I went into the story in complete detail. When I was done, he sat back in the chair and said, "Are you <expletive> me?"

"Um... no." I never really knew how to respond to Gene when he chose to speak with such... diplomacy.

He made me go over the story again paying special attention to God's intervention. He wanted me to describe the compelling feeling and the timing of each attack in great detail. Apparently, the mechanics of all this was of particular interest to him.

After a while we got back to the game and spoke of other things, mainly Leigh and Wales. I could tell, however, that his mind couldn't let the incident go. That was one of Gene's quirks, he never really let something go, it was always simmering on the back-burner. He would dwell on things, everything really, sometimes for the better and sometimes not.

The school year came to a close uneventfully. Summer finally arrived and with it the sense of freedom that only a few months off could bring. Though I thought Wales would spend his time planning things that he and Leigh would be able to do, he got all of us together a few times. To celebrate me and Gene's birthdays in July we went to see *Back to the Future* and hung out all day. This was really special for Gene because he'd never really had a birthday party. He wasn't the nostalgic type so birthdays and holidays were never his thing. This was somehow different. Maybe the fact that people were genuinely happy to celebrate his being in their lives did something. Whatever it was, he never said.

Another month passed and with it the joy and freedom of being a teenager in the Summer. The dark cloud of another school year loomed on the horizon as precious carefree days, once plentiful, now slipped away like water down a drain. The *Mysfits* had sort of a back-to-school party, a barbecue with our families, at Bruce's house. As fun as that was, it was not enough to make the specter of September disappear. I think the only one of us that wasn't having a hard time was Leigh.

So, with that, the carefree school-less days of Summer 1985 came to a close. Looking back on the Summer and proceeding school year, I had to admit to myself that things turned out much better than I thought they would. I had friends that I knew would be part of my life for a long time, experiences I could never forget, and I grew in ways I couldn't believe. Considering those things, I actually looked forward to whatever was next – I just wished I didn't have to endure a school year to get there.

CHAPTER 9:
RHYTHM AND BLUES

I'd been through a number of Septembers by then but none instilled the feeling of uneasiness I carried with me in September 1985. For days I searched for a way to come to grips with the foreboding feeling that hung over me like the twisted limbs of a gnarled old-growth tree on a dark night. I couldn't keep myself from wondering if the *Country Boys* were going to be lurking around every corner or if the twisted cult or whatever it was that targeted the school the year before had more in store or worse things, things I couldn't even imagine. My mind was besieged with these terrors until that Friday night before school started when I got a chance to talk to Gene about how I was feeling. After using a few choice words meant to imply how weak-minded I'd become, he actually began to make sense.

"Look man, all I'm trying to say is that you run scared like this, they've already won. What do they need to do to you? You're already doing it to yourself!" Gene opined.

We were in his living room when we had this conversation. There in the papasan chair I sat, staring at the floor as he spoke, confidence returning to my bones like the sun breaking through the clouds after a bad thunderstorm. I was embarrassed but that quickly went away as we agreed his harsh words were for the best. He ended the conversation with his signature single nod and on we went to some other topic as we went downstairs to Headquarters to watch TV.

I always admired how Gene exuded confidence. He was never concerned about what people thought, nor did he worry like I was given to doing at times. I had not seen him shaken, nor did I get a feel for the types of things that could shake him. I came to learn that seeing those sorts of things came with time in relationships.

The following Tuesday, the first day of school (Monday was Labor Day), my alarm clock erupted with its mocking morning cheer like some kind of demented electronic cheerleader who could only manage an annoying beeping noise. I'd almost forgotten this torturous event that set my morning routine into motion. As sadness hung on me like the backpack I would soon wear, I went through the motions that produced a presentable student who, from all outward appearances, seemed ready to take on new challenges and learn new things. All I wanted to do was sleep.

On the bus I saw several new faces and many I'd become accustomed to the year before. Saundra, like an oasis in the desert, was a particularly smashing sight on such a depressing day. I was disappointed to find that she still ignored me. Wales, on the other hand, was as talkative as ever.

Eventually the bus came to a stop at our destination, the doors opened and everyone began to file out. We stepped out onto the ground and started up the same walkway where we met Jake Thompkins the year before. I strode down the hall of the junior-high building with a renewed confidence. It seems Gene's pep-talk the Friday before actually did the trick. This fact crossed my mind as Wales and I walked and talked.

"Look at it this way, at least we're not the lowest class in the school." he said as he slapped me on the back.

"Yeah, but as much as I like being with you guys, I could have used another month or two of Summer."

As we walked, he adjusted his hat and said, "This is a whole new year, full of new opportunities and stuff."

"Whatever!" I said as I began to realize why he was not as bummed about returning to school as I was. I could see it in his eyes as we rounded the corner and approached Leigh's locker. "Must be nice I thought to myself."

"Hi guys! Joe, are you excited about this year?"

I expected this crap from her so I was ready for it. "Um... not yet but I guess I'll get there." I lied but it was better than getting into a conversation about her advanced classes.

"I am! They let me into Precalculus!"

Too late. She droned on and on about her classes. Wales didn't mind at all. I suppose he'd gotten used to it. She went on for a torturous while before I realized just how cute she was in what had to be new school clothes. I noticed that my mind tended to wander more and more in this direction whenever I got bored. They told me this would happen. "I'm a teenager now so I guess it's true what they said." I thought.

A bunch of the other *Mysfits* eventually showed up and we compared class schedules. I was delighted to find that both Wales and Gene were in most of my classes. That thought brought a lot of relief.

The morning wound on with class after class doing the "welcome to the new year" thing. Syllabi to lose, lectures to forget and all that. Mr. Philmore's class was interesting, they always were. He was the kind of teacher I could listen to for hours. It wasn't long before I realized that I'd missed his insight and I began to find myself actually looking forward to what this year had in store. Funny, I know...

As the morning drew to a close, I thought of only one thing, lunch – when and what to eat. Being the first day and all, we assembled by the door nearest the eight-grade lockers in the junior high building to go over to lunch in the CAB. Some things just felt right and walking with them like that was one of them. I tend to be a creature of habit and fall into ruts sometimes but this one made me feel at home. It's funny, we called our-selves *Mysfits* but right then, I felt anything but.

We got to the lunchroom just as Murph and the other janitors were just getting up from our usual table. This was the case all last year so it was not strange, actually it was nice that they continued to do this for us. The only difference today was that Murph pulled us into a tight huddle and said, "You know, people ask why we do this for you guys. We say this or that and after a while they get used to it. You got used to it too but I want you guys to know that we pray for the students and it's different when we pray for you. When we pray for you guys it's like you got something to do. I don't know what it is but you guys got a purpose. So, we try to help out when we can. Never forget that you guys got a purpose. It's good to see you guys, have a nice lunch."

Of all the welcome speeches we'd heard that day and even at chapel the next day, this one was the one that struck us the most. We felt both good and weird at the same time. It's hard to explain because at that time we were thirteen; we didn't have the tools to really understand how profound and precious that was but because we tended to be a bit more mature, I think we received it well. Then Bruce made a fart joke.

As we ate, I noticed that the lunchroom was divided into the same groups as last year with a smattering of new faces here and there. "Yup, we're the upperclassmen of the middle school." I thought to myself as I scanned the room. Gene was sitting across from me and over his shoulder I could see the table where the *Country Boys* were sitting and the prominently extended middle finger of Jake's left hand. I kept that to myself because I knew Gene was always looking for a reason...

"So, you know what's coming up this year, right?" Bruce asked the group.

There was some murmuring with the word "no" popping up a few times.

"The 'Middle-School Gala' and the 'Eighth-Grade Overnight." he stated with a smile. We all just looked at him with blank stares expecting more. Gene helped him out.

"And what are those things?"

"Oh... the 'Middle-School Gala', last year it was called the 'Sock Hop', is an eighth-grade dance in October and the overnight is when the eighth-graders spend the night in the CAB in the spring." he said as though we were supposed to know.

"I'm going to volunteer for the planning committees."

"You do that..." Gene said with an almost concerned look on his face.

It didn't take long before my imagination caught up with me and reminded me that the "Middle-School Gala" was a dance and that meant needing a date which I would likely not have. The pressure was starting to mount and this thing was still a month and a half away.

The rest of eighth-grade day one was rather uneventful except for running into Meghan O'Neil. I was about to go into the last class of the day when I felt someone tap me on the shoulder. I turned to find Meghan with that distant look on her face and then that smile. I'd forgotten that weird, intoxicating smile. I wished I had a picture. She was cute... my mind went there again. I didn't get all the words and somehow, I knew that she knew why. She said something about starting out on the right foot and this year being better than last. I don't know, I just knew that talking to her was always spooky.

After school I met up with Wales who'd just walked Leigh to her mother's car. We made our way through the throng of kids to our bus and sat down. I mentioned the encounter I'd had with Meghan and before he could say anything, something weird happened. Saundra walked by and as she did, she said, "Hi." and shot us a smile. The fact that she was so stunning kept me from thinking. All I could think was that maybe she would talk to me now, never-mind the fact that she stopped talking to me and asked me to leave her alone. Hormones make you stupid.

I went home and per my usual routine, I recorded the major events of the day in my journal. I was amazed that I'd become so disciplined as to keep a journal in the first place. Nevertheless, I recorded, with great detail, the things Murph said, my encounter with Meghan and, of course, Saundra's apparent thawing toward me.

That night was rather normal. I spoke to my parents about the day and what I thought of the year ahead. I left out the more *interesting* things. I knew if I were to ever take my brother's advice and let them in on that stuff, they would either worry or try to get involved – how embarrassing (yeah, I was at that age). I did homework, ate dinner, and watched television. *Who's the Boss* was on at eight. I liked that show mostly because the girl, Alyssa Milano, was my age and it didn't hurt that I thought she was cute. This was home life with two professional parents and a brother away at college, no frills.

The next morning brought with it about as much fun as the one before, none. I woke up with the usual groggy weight on my shoulders while my alarm clock cursed at me with the most annoying sound in the world that only it could produce. Somehow, without much thought, I made it through my morning routine and I don't think I was really conscious until I was on the bus stop. I'd hoped to strike up a conversation with Saundra but she seemed a little cold.

"Hey Saundra, good morning!" I opened.

"Hey." she said staring down at her Walkman as she inserted a tape.

"You, uh... excited about this year?" I questioned.

"No." she told me as she slipped the earphones over her ears.

I got the message and felt awkward. I wasn't sure what to do with myself when, thank God, the bus came around the corner.

As we got off the bus, I paused for a moment and took in my surroundings. I'm not sure why but I just paused and looked at the throng of students making their way to their respective buildings.

"What's going on? Why'd you stop?" Wales asked.

"I dunno... I guess I'm just people-watching"

The sun was rising behind us and shining on the buildings. As people walked up the slight incline, their shadows cast long in front of them. It was a warm morning that eventually would lead to a rather hot day.

As it was the first Wednesday of the school year, that meant the first chapel. Starting this year, the new-year rally was moved to the first Friday. I didn't mind the shortened class periods throughout the day but I did mind chapel if it was boring. You never knew what you were going to get but I do have to say that most of them were fine. Just not this one.

The ten-o'clock sun streamed through the high thin vertical windows in the gym at the bottom of the CAB. The floor was recently polished and a few gray metal chairs were set in a line in front of the mobile altar which was set at mid-court like normal. The bleachers had been pulled out and kids filled them as they filed into the gym from different directions.

As usual, and the *Mysfits* were no exception, kids sat in cliques clumped together on the bleachers. Leigh, who somehow managed to always get to chapel first, held a few spots for us. Chapel was at least one of those things that disrupted the veil of monotony that at times seemed to settle over the school. It was sort of like lunch; you could be with your friends outside of class for an hour.

We had a new Vice Principal, Patrick Finnegan. This Chapel was to be his formal introduction to the student body and sort of an installation service. He was a somewhat portly man with fire-red hair. For a while some of the kids jokingly called him a clown but this ended quickly as we learned to fear him. He was very strict and very fair in that he did not treat anyone any differently than anyone else. His character was in stark contrast to Adam Valentine, his predecessor. The Wisconsin Congress, the governing body for the denomination to which the school belongs, reassigned Mr. Valentine to be the principal of a school in Virginia. Mr. Valentine and even Principal McIntyre are laid back and fun to be around, not true with this guy.

Lunch was somewhat slow. We all seemed to be rather quiet that day. That's when, whom else, Wales had to break the ice that seemed to be forming each second we were there.

"We need an outing, something to look forward to!" he said with more excitement than the combined lot of us. "Bruce, when is the dance?"

"The 'Middle-School Gala' is on October 19th, a Saturday." Bruce answered.

"We should do this thing right. What do you say we all go shopping and dress up... wear cool clothes to the dance?"

Of course we agreed because that's what we always did whenever Wales opened his mouth about an outing. All this did was add some more stress for the dance. I could dress anyway I wanted but that wouldn't change the fact that I wouldn't have a date. I had already come to grips with the fact that I would probably chicken out and not ask anyone.

"OK, what about Saturday the 5th?" Wales asked.

The date seemed to work for everybody so I just went along with it.

After lunch, Gene pulled me aside and so began the first of what would be several "talks" about dating and such. I was about to say something because I could tell by the look on his face that he had something challenging to say but I was too late.

"So, who you gonna ask?" Gene asked the question with a quick nod of his head backwards like a basketball player about to shoot a free-throw. I hesitated. This was not the best thing to do because it led him to say...

"Come on man, I know you too well! Right now, you wish we'd all stop talking about this thing because you think you'll be too scared to ask someone."

"Well, if you knew that already, Gene, why ask at all." I retorted with a look on my face as if to indicate that this was an obvious waste of time.

"Because you need me to help you with stuff like this. You're confident when you think you have to be but you're chicken anytime else. You know I HATE that. You need to man up!"

"Excuse me..." I began to argue like a litigator, "Excuse me, you want me to man up? You, who could probably go out with any girl on the *Sidity Committee* you wanted including Imani K. but you're too scared to talk to her; you want *me* to man up?"

"Alright, hold up... that was a while ago. I plan to ask her to go. You can check me out this week and see what she said but what about you? You gonna step to Saundra or not?"

I hesitated.

"Just what I thought. You're my boy and all, you know I got nothing but love for you, that's why I want you to man up! We'll talk."

Great, not only can't I get away from this dance, Gene is committed to getting me to ask somebody and when he's committed, you can pretty much count on him following through.

Days went by, days filled with mounting stress over this dance – a dance that was supposed to be fun and somehow I turned it into something to dread. I did check back with Gene and he actually did ask Imani K. to the dance and she actually said yes. It bugged me sometimes when he was right.

THE GREATEST SHOW ON CAMPUS:

That Friday the student body filed into the bleachers on the main field. The field was divided into three large rings. Before long, the band started to play from... somewhere. Turned out they'd encircled the gathering and came from all directions, pretty neat. What took the cake were the animals that were then led onto the field while the band played. Two horses, and a llama were each led into one of the circles. Their handlers had them perform various tricks with balls. I came to find out that the school contracted a local circus troop. As if that weren't enough, Lyle Tidewater, the music instructor and band leader walked onto the field in a tuxedo complete with tails and a top hat. He was accompanied by his rising-star band majorette, Stephanie Anders. She was dressed as a magician's assistant and as they directed the band's performance they performed tricks, badly, which was the point. This comedy routine had us rolling in laughter! I would have paid real money to see that ridiculous spectacle. It was hard to go back to class after all that.

A SURE FOUNDATION:

A couple Saturdays later, I had my first Confirmation class at my church. In our denomination, the same one the school was in, we confirm someone's baptism and faith in Jesus Christ. This is done through a series of classes with the Pastor once a month for the length of a school year ending with a public profession of faith in Jesus. I was looking forward to this about as much as I would if I were taking a history class on Saturday. It turned out to be much more than I'd bargained for.

That Saturday, I got up and got my chores done early. I knew that if I waited until class was over, I would have no time to myself. It was a nice clear day, the kind of day you didn't want to waste in some lecture. Anyway, my mother dropped me off at the church where I met up with some of my church friends who were also in the Confirmation class.

Paster Summerstone was a rather tall, bearded, white man with salt and pepper hair. His face had somewhat severe features in that he had an angular jawline and a rather intense gaze. He took us to the youth rec-room on the second floor of the Church's administration building. The room had a few tables. There were some books on shelves interspersed with a few board games. I hadn't been in this room but a few times so I was kind of curious. We pulled a few metal chairs across the multicolored checkerboard tile floor. I got comfortable but not too comfortable because I knew that sleep was a distinct possibility.

The Pastor started by asking us what Confirmation was and if we thought it was necessary. The more he talked, the more I got engaged in the class, we all did. From his sermons on Sundays, we'd never have guessed that he could be this interesting. He laid down some foundational history about our denomination, some I'd learned in religion class, and some I'd never heard of before.

He intended this class to be introductory so he ended early to give us some time to mingle before we were picked up. I thought I would tell him how much I enjoyed the class.

"Pastor Summerstone?" I said as he collected his belongings.

"Yes, Joe..." he responded.

"I just wanted to let you know that I really enjoyed the class. In a way it's a lot like my religion class in school."

"You go to Towson Christian, right?"

"I do."

"Eighth grade, so you still have Max O'Leary, right?"

"That's right, you know him?"

"You know that school was founded by a group of churches including this one, right?"

"Yeah, we went over that last year."

"That was in the sixties, before my time here. Did you know that the planning committee met in this very room back then and that members from the founding churches are on the school's board along with concerned parents?"

"No, I did not." a weird feeling of nostalgia washed over me slowly as the thought took hold in my mind that I was in the birthplace of my school. It felt like connections were taking place in my head.

"Uh... Joe?"

"Yeah!" I said with a start.

"Lost you there for a moment."

"Yeah, I was letting what you said sink in. There is something fitting about that"

"Oh?"

"Long story..."

"I've got time. How are things at the school? From your perspective I mean."

I knew to be very guarded with what I knew so I told him about the racial stuff because I had to give him something. He looked at me as though he knew I was holding back but he didn't press it.

"That's terrible. I'm going to bring this up to the board but I'll be discrete. Hopefully we can work something out. No one should have to go through that."

I thanked him for his time and was off to the lobby to meet my mother who was sure to be there in a few minutes. As I walked away, I heard...

"Why don't we talk more often, I think it would be good for both of us."

OK, getting a little weird. As I walked, I turned so I could see him.

"OK, sure..."

I seem to say that too easily but what could I say? I didn't think it would be right to refuse him.

CHAPTER 10:
"THE POLITICS OF DANCING"
- RE-FLEX

I awoke to the sound of my alarm clock singing its song of annoyance. Only today was not a school day. It was Saturday, the Saturday I was to meet the *Mysfits* at White Marsh Mall to go clothes shopping for the dance. I was of mixed emotions; I didn't want to go shopping but I did want to hang out with my friends. However, I didn't have mixed emotions about pulling out the three-hundred or so dollars I'd managed to save over the past year and a half to buy clothes for a dateless dance. The thought of spending my saved allowance, birthday, and Christmas money just burned me. There were some things I wanted for my computer that would now take forever to get. Nevertheless, I had to get my chores done so I could meet them at twelve.

My father and I got to the mall a little before twelve. We were to meet at the food court where we would eat first. It was a fairly nice day weather-wise and the mall was rather busy. My Dad had to get something from Sears before he left so we parted ways there and I had a bit of ground to cover before we were to meet. As I cut my way through the throng of people, I kept trying to convince myself that this would be a good thing and that even if I didn't have a date, it could still be fun. Who was I kidding?

I knew that Gene would constantly remind me of my fears as he had over the past few weeks. I also knew that sitting around watching my friends dance with dates was *not* my idea of fun. Why was I so scared? Or was it insecurity? Or are they the same thing in this case? This was too much for my teenaged mind. Run-ins with the *Country Boys* I could understand. The secret art of talking to girls might as well have been something I would have to study under a master in a foreign land like Kung-fu. I started playing with the thought of what that art would be called, "Date-Fu", "Girl-Fu", ah it didn't matter what it would be called, I still didn't have a date.

As I walked, I started paying attention to my surroundings. All sorts of people were there, some were sitting on benches whiling the day away under the sunlit skylights. The mall opened just a few years before and still had a sense of novelty that brought shoppers in droves. The walkways were lined with shiny new stores offering just about anything you could possibly want. I especially liked the computer software store and the video store which had these amazing new LaserDisc video players. No time for that now though, I had to "go shopping" ... joy.

White Marsh's food court felt more like a carnival than anything else. Along with the usual cacophony of diners and the dizzying blend of colorful lights from restaurant signs, there was a clown making balloon animals and even a carousel in the center complete with a line of little kids and parents. As usual it seemed every table was taken and vultures, people with trays of food in their hands, were circling, prepared to swoop down on any table whose occupants appeared to be leaving.

I picked a spot out of the way of the stampeding herd so as not to be trampled and began to scan the crowd for my people. It wasn't long before a tweed fedora caught my eye and sure enough, I found Wales underneath it. He was standing on the opposite side of the court with everybody but Bruce. I managed through the crowd and greeted them...

"What's up?"

"I don't know, what's up with you? Buying new clothes, huh? Sure would be ashamed to be all dressed up and nobody to share it with." Gene had a way of cutting right to the quick. The jerk. I loved him for it though because I knew where it came from.

"Well then..." Wales said in a failed attempt to break the tension.

"Uh... why don't we get going? We can eat later..." Leigh had his back.

We started to move and forgot about Bruce who was just then walking up to us.

"Hey Leigh, you think you can handle going shopping with a bunch of guys?" Bruce asked, not even realizing that we were about to leave him.

"I already have clothes for the dance. The question is whether or not I can be the responsible adult." Leigh retorted.

Wales smiled a little and patted her on the shoulder and we were off to the stores. Like a calamity in slow motion the group of us was set free in the mall. Yippee.

Amazingly, I could not have been more wrong. This was becoming a pattern. I should not have been surprised but to my astonishment, Wales was an incredible fashion consultant. I knew he dressed well for school but I guess the gloves came off when it came to special occasions. Attendants in the stores couldn't get enough of him. His worst suggestions were better than most of our best ones.

Not only was I stunned at Wales' fashion sense, I was equally stunned when I realized I'd spent $186 on an outfit... for me, an eighth-grader who hadn't even stopped growing! I must have lost my mind. All this talk of asking out girls and what not must have warped my brain. I made the mistake of expressing that thought to Gene...

"But you'll look nice though... Look, I did the same thing." he said with confidence as he perused a shirt rack.

It was easy for him to say, he was going with one of the hottest girls in the school. Imani K. was the type of girl who turned heads wherever she went. Too bad she knew it and her personality followed. All of those *Sidity Committee* girls had that kind of air about them. He continued...

"Sure *would* be a waste if I were going alone though." his eyes got big as though he were embarrassed to say something he shouldn't and then they slowly moved and settled on me – a sarcastic grin on his face.

"Ha ha... fun-ny." the dryness in my expression was not lost on him.

"All joking aside though. You know why I keep getting at you about this, right?"

"Because you want me to grow or something like that?"

"That's part of it. Look man, I just don't want you to be the guy who never speaks to girls. You'll be asking 'what if' for the rest of your life and I just can't let you do that."

Stunned again, I nodded my agreement and walked away. I needed a moment. How could such... such wisdom come from a kid his age? I had a lot to think about but was too hungry to do it now.

Back in the food court we managed to find a table. I was glad it was over, but apparently not yet, Wales needed something from *Chess King*, a vest he said would "make the outfit". He was probably right but I was *Chess King'd* out. The only thing I wanted to consider at the moment was the mall Chinese food that sat on my plate.

We talked and joked for what must have been an hour. Wes had to mention that he couldn't get a certain *Cosby Show* episode that seemed relevant out of his mind the whole time we were shopping. He did have to admit though, that he would have never pulled off the look he had without Wales. I know I couldn't have. Just then Bruce brought up what I thought was a really good point.

"I just have to ask, we're all gonna look this good and have our moms and dads drive us around that night? I mean, Liz and I will already be there because we're volunteering and all." Bruce had asked Elizabeth Walker, a friend of his that he'd known from elementary school. I didn't think there were any feelings between them but at least they wouldn't be alone.

Leigh cracked a smile, put her arm around Wales and looked at him with what I thought was the cutest look of admiration.

"Well, I didn't want to say anything too early but I have a plan for that night that I think you will all like... a lot. The only thing is I won't know if I have the biggest part of it until a few days before the dance, so hold on."

We'd all learned to trust Wales so no one questioned him further. That's not to say that we weren't curious about what he was working on.

That next week, in addition to school and all of this dance stuff, I had reading assignments for Confirmation class on Saturday. My mind was pulled in several directions, one of them happened to be whether or not Pastor Summerstone was going to ask any probing questions about my experiences at school. I grew up in that church and he'd been the pastor there my whole life. I was seriously contemplating his admission into my tight circle of trust.

On Friday, dance fever was clearly on the rise. Rumors were going around about who got asked and who got rejected. Girls were snickering in the hallways. I must have looked like Scrooge as I worked my way through the sea of hormones with my best humbug face. I was on my way to history when I ran into a smiling Leigh. It was not unusual to see her smiling while coming from or going to a class; it usually meant she did well on some assignment or aced an exam, but this was different somehow.

"Hey Joe, how are you?"

"Good... I'm doing just fine." I lied.

"Are you really?"

"Truth be told, no! Maybe I'm just not ready for all this boy – girl social stuff!"

"I know Gene is riding you pretty hard about this but look, you don't have to have feelings for someone to go to a school dance. You just need to work up the courage to ask. You might have to move quickly, word got around that we're going all out and now it looks like everybody else is too - like a competition." she said that in hush tones and with the best intentions in the world. That's why I didn't get annoyed.

"Thank you..." I said that with my best "thank you for thinking of me" voice.

"OK, then... off to class..." she said as though she were on an adventure.

For the rest of the day, I was useless. My body was at school but my mind was nowhere near school. My thoughts were nothing but a mixture of worries and trying to focus on any one of them was like trying to pull just one of those plastic monkeys out of that barrel. I did notice more and more that my confusion was turning into frustration and anger.

Confirmation class the next day was amazing. Pastor Summerstone decided we should work through the book of Acts. I was learning so much because I began to ask questions I didn't feel I could ask anywhere else. Questions about spiritual gifts. All the kids in the class found it as intriguing as I did.

After class, Pastor Summerstone and I had our planned chat in his office. He'd discussed with my mother that we would need an additional thirty minutes after each class to give him what he called a "fresh perspective" on the school. His office was finished with wood paneling. Everywhere it seemed possible, the wood was carved in the shape of a flower or some other design. The place felt like an old English library.

"I decided to go through the book of Acts with the class. I think we'll find it... relevant." Pastor Summerstone said leaning back in his chair.

"Yes, and I really enjoyed class today. I thought the discussion about the Holy Spirit was great." I really did enjoy that class.

He leaned forward, put his elbows on his desk and paused. He fixed his eyes on me as though he was weighing what he would say next. He broke the silence with a question that made me a bit uncomfortable.

"Joe, you know I stand by the beliefs of our denomination, right? I mean, I wouldn't pastor this church if I didn't, right?" he chuckled a bit.

It almost sounded as though he was trying to convince himself of what he thought the answer should be.

"Yes... I suppose so." best I could do.

He paused again before saying, "There are times. Times when it seems some of the things our denomination believes just don't square with the Bible."

"Could you give me an example? I must admit, I am a bit confused."

"OK, I've been trying to figure out how to say this for a few days now but I think the best thing to do is to say it and hope you feel you can ask if you don't understand. You see, ever since you told me what you were going through at the school, I've been praying for you and I felt this week the Lord lead me into some truths. Are you with me so far?"

"Believe it or not, I am." I mean, come on, with the things that Murph said and what God did on the upper-field. Yeah, I was with him.

"Listen, I need you to be brutally honest with me. I need confirmation of the things I think the Lord was saying. Can you please do that for me?"

"Yes, I think I can"

"OK, this is what I think I heard. Yes, you are having a problem with racially motivated bullying."

"Yes..."

"But there is more to it... much more. You are in the midst of a spiritual battle. You have seen the working of God in your life and will continue to do so. You keep these things mostly to yourself, and do well to do so, but you are not to diminish them in any way and are to recognize them for the miracles they are in the midst of the battle you're in. You are not in this alone for God has raised up people with whom you will walk and when it is darkest you will strengthen and encourage each other in the Lord."

We stared at each other for what seemed like an uncomfortably long time before he asked, "Does that sound right?"

Leaning forward, I answered, "That is exactly right, the part at the end hasn't happened yet but you are exactly right."

He stammered a bit, "I mean, I've heard about this happening but... just wow!"

I went on to tell him everything that happened since day one. He was, for lack of a better word, amazed. He left it up to me concerning who I would tell, considering what he'd heard. He then went on to say...

"Our denomination has no framework for what we discussed today. The official position is that things of this nature ended with the Apostles. I know that is not true." He paused, turned to the credenza behind him and turned back with a book. I bought this for you this week. I read it, I think it's good. It goes over some very good confidence-building scriptures to help you remember them, even committing some to poetry. I want you to have this.

"Thank you!" I was excited that God gave me another ally.

"You know, I was intending to go through the book of John with the class but it seems Acts is more appropriate. We need to raise a generation who understands the spiritual reality of the world around them."

I agreed wholeheartedly and thanked him for his time. We both agreed that we looked forward to the next class and talk. Regarding the time I hurried to meet my mother who by then was waiting in the lobby.

"Did you and Pastor Summerstone have a good talk?"

"Yes, we did, Mom. I'm getting a lot out of this class!"

"Great! That's what I was hoping for."

I started reading the book that night and found it as good as advertised. That Monday was Columbus Day that year, a day off, and by that afternoon I'd finished the short book and had begun to read it again. It *was* a confidence builder. I would need all I could get because the dance was

Saturday and, according to Gene, "The Tock is Clicking!" He thought that was clever. I didn't.

Somehow, I made it through Tuesday without being reminded that I would be alone at the dance. It was half-way through Wednesday, at lunch, when it started. Lunch turned out to be an intervention, a concept with which I would become quite familiar but more on that later. The *Mysfits* truly did care for each other and it was my turn to feel the love. Leigh started, probably because it would go down easier if a girl started off.

"Joey, you know we love you and would do anything for you, right?"

The awkward pause that followed her statement and question forced me to answer.

"Yes, I do..."

She continued with concerned looks on the faces of the others, "We know this is really just a school dance, but it's much more than that because it's through things like this that we stretch ourselves to be more than we are. If you don't grow, you'll have this problem for the rest of your life."

This was right out of Gene's playbook. I glanced over at him and his eyes ran from mine as I caught his gaze.

She went on to say, "We really want you to pick somebody and ask them, it's for the best."

As annoyed as I was, I knew they weren't playing or teasing in any way. The looks on their faces were real and I needed to really listen to what they had to say. Hard pill to swallow but it did go down... eventually. It all ended with a hug from Leigh and pats on the back. I hated that kind of attention.

In the bathroom after lunch, I ran into Jake. Even he was taken with this whole dance mania. We looked at each other for a moment, then went on about our business. Washing our hands at the sinks, he just *had* to say something.

"Who you taking to the dance? Slim pickin's for you huh? Aren't that many black chicks around."

"I'll be fine, thank you!" I said with a hint of bitterness.

"No problems with me, I know who I'm going with."

"How nice for you."

Not being able to take this conversation anymore I just left and went to class. On my way my mind was swimming with things the others said and images of me in expensive clothes sitting by myself at the dance. As I wallowed in my misery, Mr. Tidewater walked up beside me.

"Hi how ya doing?" he asked in his winsome way. He really did exude both confidence and fun. I was never into music but seeing him made me want to take a class with him.

"OK, I guess." I wasn't feeling it right then.

"You're Joe, right?" he asked.

"Yeah… I'm Joe." I felt like a deflated balloon.

"Wow… not having a good day huh?" he deduced.

"No. Everybody's all into this dance thing but me. I don't have a date and don't have anyone to ask." I knew the conversation would get there eventually so I just jumped to the end.

"Oh… I get it. Listen Joe, when I was your age, I was awkward and a band geek. I couldn't talk to anybody, let alone girls. It took me years to learn this so I'm gonna tell you so you don't have to wait so long. Just be yourself. If it comes it comes, if not… that's fine too. At the end of the day, it's an eighth-grade dance. Believe me, there will be many more things in life to worry about."

"Oh, OK… thanks!" I was actually starting to feel better.

"Sure thing. Look, I need to get going but find me if you ever want to talk again, OK?" he offered.

I couldn't help but think that he was a really cool guy. His advice did make me feel better... for all of ten seconds! No pep-talk could get my money back or keep me from being alone at that dance.

The rest of the day was unfolding uneventfully. There was so much buzz about the dance that the sounds of giggling girls and the ever-present rumor mill was getting on my nerves. I was full-on Scrooge on my way to my last class. It was in the Senior-high building so I decided to go the long way rather than chance running into a *Mysfit*. I would have to deal with Wales on the bus so I needed all the alone time I could get. I pushed open the double doors and stepped out onto the platform about to go down the steps when who should I run into but spooky Meghan. It was a warm day and the sun was beaming. Though she was wearing sunglasses I could tell she was looking at me. Then she smiled that smile of hers. In that moment I thought to myself no matter how weird or spooky she might be, and she was, she was one of the prettiest girls in that school. She pulled off her sunglasses and shook her hair out of her eyes.

"Hey Joe, how are you?"

"Honestly, I've been better."

"Sorry to hear that, I'm sure things will get better."

"Thank you." I said believing she meant it.

"So, the dance is coming up, that's a good thing, right?"

"Right..." I wanted this to end.

"Are you going?"

"Yes."

"Who are you taking?" she asked.

"No one." I officially just wanted to go to class now... please!

"Take me!" she blurted with a bit of nervous laughter, "I'm not going with anybody either."

Her words hung in the air as if dangling from some magical sky-hook. Understandably I was taken aback as I looked into the face of this weird girl who always made me feel strange. At that moment, with that smile on her face I heard, "OK, I guess, sure." Now, I was looking at her the whole time but I never saw her lips move. It didn't take long to figure out that I was the one who spoke.

"Great!" she exclaimed, "See, now neither one of us has to feel weird about being there. You should pick me up about 4:00, we should probably get something to eat first. I've got to get to class but here's my address and phone number."

She scribbled on a piece of paper and handed it to me.

"See you later!" she said, smiling.

All through the next class and half-way into the bus ride, I didn't say a word. Wales was so preoccupied that he didn't notice. He was going on about some limo deal or something when I blurted out, "I'm taking Meghan!" Life stopped. Everything seemed to pause, even Wales. This was one of the precious few times when Tommy Wales truly had nothing to say. "Say something!" I exclaimed.

"Do... wow... do you like her?" he asked.

"No, man, she weirds me out, you know that."

"Then why..."

"I don't know why! I guess I just didn't want to go alone." I interrupted.

"So, you thought of her and asked her out?"

"She kind of asked me..." I said. The look on his face begged for the story, so I gave it.

Stunned, he managed to say, "Well she *is* hot and it's just one night, right?"

I managed to agree and we spent the rest of the ride with strange looks on our faces.

That night, as it turned out, Gene's mother needed to drop something off for mine. I answered the door and found Gene on the porch with his mom. I shook my head thinking that Wales filled him in over the phone.

"What?" he asked.

I paused, let them in, and took him to my room. There I didn't say a word but waited for him to ask about Meghan. He didn't.

"Look, man, I'm sorry about lunch... it's just that we're all concerned and..."

I interrupted, "You really don't know, do you?"

"Know what?"

"I'm taking Meghan O'Neil."

He plopped down on a chair.

"But you always said she was spooky."

"She is."

"So, you asked her anyway?"

"She asked me."

The look on his face begged for the story just like Wales' and so I gave it to him too.

"So, how do you feel about it?"

"I dunno..."

"No, think about it. Do you feel good?" The volume and sincerity in his voice was mounting, uh oh, a speech was in my future."

"Not really, I don't know what to think and I'm a little intimidated. If I was going to go with someone, I didn't think she'd be white – let alone somebody who weirds me out."

"You bothered by the white thing?" He was looking at me like he was both surprised and puzzled.

"Well... yeah? Kind of? I mean it's just something I haven't thought of, especially the way elementary school went, you know?" Even I was surprised with how open I was being with him.

"Look man, I get it. I think about stuff like this a lot and I think I got it down now. I think we can't let that matter no more. I mean this stuff gotta change sometime, right? So why not with us. Besides she is fine... right? I know you checked her out before! C'mon man, don't lie!"

I was trying not so smile and failed so I gave in, "Yeah man, she's incredible!"

"I'm like, I don't care what color you are – there's something wrong with you if you don't notice Meghan! Look man, I know it's all new and all but it's just one night right, I mean y'all aint dating or nothin!"

When he was right, he was right. "You're right, it's just one night, nothing to worry about, just have fun, right?"

I don't know what I said that fueled his fire but I knew I was in for it when he stared at me like he wanted to knock some sense into me. Then he started...

"You know what I think?" He was using the most argumentative tone he could muster. This meant he was about to go all broken English and curse words on me. (Gene objects to that assessment – he made me write this objection).

"No, what do you think?"

"I think you don't know who you are!"

"What?"

"You think you this shy boy when really you a warrior! You think God was doing His thing out on that field so you can go shrink back? No! You a <expletive> warrior! You need to get yo swagger back. So what she white! You need to own that night! Take her out and have a good time! You need to act like you in charge. You need to be da top dog ROO! ROO! Boy! Take yo place!"

As crass as his tirade may have been, I felt something I hadn't felt in a long time... confidence. I began to wear it like a well-worn robe that knew just how to make me feel comfortable. He could see it too.

"That's right boy! Rise the <explctive> up!"

Just then we heard his mother's voice, "You boys alright? Gene, it's time to go..."

"Alright Ma..."

He opened the door to my room and pointed at me while he stepped backwards into the hallway.

Later that night the phone rang and I answered.

"Hello?"

"ROO! ROO! Boy! Yeeaahh! <Click>

CHAPTER 11:
ONE NIGHT IN BALTIMORE

The next morning, I woke up before the alarm clock and assaulted it before it could assault me. I felt confident and was laughing to myself as I realized that I had what only could be described as my "swagger" back. This was bound to be an interesting day.

On the bus my head could not stop shaking as Wales unfolded the plan for Saturday that he tried to tell me the day before. He'd done it again and I understood why Leigh gave him that look of admiration at the mall that day. This is where I would usually ask how he'd managed to pull it off so I contemplated whether I really wanted to know. I did, so I asked... more head shaking.

"The bottom line is that you need to tell Meghan that you'll pick her up at three o'clock."

"Got it..."

I caught Meghan at her locker. She was with Saundra, Destiny, Ivanah and Olympia. This was funny because it was the first time I'd actually went looking for her.

"Hey Meghan!"

"Oh, hi." I caught looks from the others.

"I need to pick you up at three on Saturday and here's my phone number." I scribbled down the secondary line used for the computer so I could control who answers the phone if she were to call. Handing her the paper I added, "See you then, and uh... wear something nice." My swagger-filled attitude made me walk away without even waiting for her reply. *I didn't even recognize me at this point.* I just figured I had to ride it out. The part of me that most wanted to be a gentleman forced me to at least look back which I did for just a second. There she was, standing in the middle of her clique with the cutest grin and brightest eyes as she returned my gaze. I went to class.

Don't ask what class was about, heck, I'm not even sure I was in the right room. I just sat there taking inventory of what transpired since she and I talked the day before. I felt that I owed it all to God for structuring things this way though I had a looming sense of dread because of what the Pastor said about the darkest time coming. I also realized I needed to thank Gene for his pep talk. Whenever I needed it most it seemed God put Gene right there to help even if it was in his own way. Think about it, Gene just showed up at my house without even knowing I was going with Meghan. I just couldn't get the look on her face from a few minutes before out of my head. There it was again... hormones.

Lunch was decidedly different from the day before. The *Mysfits* were shocked but got over it. Wes and Bruce even congratulated me. We spent the time going over the game plan for Saturday night. Questions were asked and answered, every detail was scrutinized to make sure no one would miss out.

Wales was in the zone, holding court like a king addressing his subjects. I took a moment and reflected on how much he'd grown from when I first met him. We all had. Each one of us had benefited from being friends with each other. I couldn't help but remember what Pastor Summerstone said, "God has raised up people with whom you will walk and when it is darkest you will strengthen and encourage each other in the Lord."

Normally I would have shared this with them but honestly, I didn't know how. I guess I figured I would when the time was right.

That night I managed to finally get this stuff off my mind. It seems easier to put things out of mind when they're going well. I decided to rest and take in the *Cosby Show* with my Parents, a weekly tradition. Turns out, it was an episode that seemed oddly relevant to my current circumstances. I also thought about how I'd forgotten that the girl I really liked, Saundra, was probably going and I didn't know who she was going with. So much for clearing my mind.

Why did we even have school on Friday? None of the kids had their heads in class... well, maybe Leigh. I found her at her locker brushing up on something or other in the few minutes we had between periods.

"You know, Joe, it's like having the old you back."

"I think I know just what you mean. I feel really good."

"I'm so glad. It would've been bad if you decided not to go or went by yourself. Here's something you might be interested in... I heard that Meghan is getting her hair done tonight."

"That's cool." I said, hoping Leigh wouldn't notice I was giddy.

"Well, gotta run, looking forward to tomorrow!"

"Me too! I think it'll be really great!"

Rounding the corner in the hallway I almost ran into Meghan on her way to class. The first thing I noticed was that she was wearing a hint of makeup and dusty rose-colored lipstick. She did not need these at all, she was already very attractive. She broke into her signature smile.

"Hey... good morning!" I said, trying to act as though I didn't notice her makeup.

"Good morning!" she said with a little nervous flutter in her voice.

There was an awkward pause during which I just gave in and let "Joe Swagger" take over. I could feel the confidence rise as I leaned towards her and said, "I am really looking forward to tomorrow, I think we'll have a lot of fun."

"You know, something's different about you. Is everything alright?"

"Is it a bad thing?"

"No... it isn't." she said reassuringly as she looked me dead in the eyes.

"I need to let you go to class..." I said, realizing I was in control of the situation.

"OK, class... right..."

"Can I call you tonight?"

"Yes... of course." she said with a look that indicated that I needn't ask.

"OK, talk then..."

"Yeah..."

We both continued on and I was amazed at myself. I wondered if this is what Gene felt like all the time. I was actually looking forward to the the thing that had been the source of dread for me just days before.

Lunchtime came and as expected the topic was the dance and once again Wales was holding court. He'd told us to bring another $40 for what he called "special corsages". He said he'd gotten some kind of deal and, as was our custom, we blindly agreed. Confidence or no confidence, this was hitting my wallet pretty hard. This night of Wales' was already costing $80. Now we were up to $120 not to mention the $180 or so I spent on clothes. I figured I might have to get some cushion money from the parents for this one.

"You know, we all thought your finest hour was getting us into that *Terminator* movie, but you pull this off and we'll be legends for as long as we're here." Bruce said staring off into space. We all nodded our agreement and went over the plan once more. Wales had the forethought to get his mother on board and have her call our parents to put away any fears of having a bunch of young teenagers with dates running around without a chaperon.

I pulled Gene aside after lunch. I was standing tall just like he was and he knew it.

"Feel's good, doesn't it?" he asked.

"What do you mean?"

"The confidence and looking forward to going out on a date."

"I wouldn't call it a date. We're just going so we don't have to be alone."

"There you go again! Look man, don't downplay nothin!"

"Here we go..." I thought.

"Did you see that girl today? She looks unbelievable! She's wearing makeup, man. I saw that in class and just knew she's looking forward to this thing. She made herself up for you! How can you not see that!"

"We'll see about that but I just wanted to thank you for the talk the other night."

"Look, I've got your back and you've got mine; I know that. One day I might need you to be the one doing the talking."

Sometimes I felt like I was the most immature *Mysfit*. I was just glad to have people like this in my life. I nodded in agreement and we went on with the day.

That night, I gave Meghan a call around 6:30. This was no small thing for me. Even in full "Joe Swagger" mode I had to work up to it.

"Hello?" she answered.

"Hi Meghan, I just wanted to confirm that we'll be picking you up sometime around three. Is that still good?"

"Yes... Um Joe?"

"Yeah?"

"Did you um... never mind, we'll get to that later. Listen, I've got to get to the hairdresser at seven so..."

"Oh, OK... Uh... by the way..."

"Yeah?"

"You looked *great* today!"

There was an awkward pause. She broke it with, "I'm sorry... I'm blushing... Thank you."

"I'll see you tomorrow around three?"

"Yes."

"Goodnight..."

"Bye."

ZERO HOUR:

The day was here. I forced myself to get as much sleep as possible figuring I might need it. I did my chores that morning and got a chance to talk to my parents. I put them at ease about the night which was easy to do because they trusted Ms. Wales and thought highly enough of Leigh (I was surprised they brought her up). They knew that Leigh wouldn't put up with any foolishness. They were right.

About 1:00 I began to get ready. My heart was starting to race a bit in anticipation but "Joe Swagger" stepped in when I replayed Gene's pep talk in my mind, "You a warrior! Roo! Roo!" I could see the confidence return to my face in the mirror. The only thing to do now was dress the part. Wales made sure of that.

I took a long shower after which I added just a hint of cologne. I pulled the new clothes out of my closet and began to dress. When I was done, I stared at myself in the hallway's long mirror. The black dress shoes, the sporty black dress pants, the white shirt with thin black stripes, the very thin black leather tie, and the sports jacket that looked as if it were made to be "fly" all combined to make me look the part. Actually, not quite... I needed to add Wales' "splash of color". I reached for the hat that would become a signature of mine over the ensuing years. Wales picked this hat and he was right. I ceremoniously placed the maroon flat *Kangol* on my head with the kangaroo logo to the front. What can I say, it was the eighties.

After getting the nod of approval and some cushion money from my parents, I stepped out of the house, walked the sidewalk, turned right and proceeded to the boulevard. I got there at two fifteen as I was told and as if on cue, there it was, the stretch limousine that was the first part of Wales' plan. The boy had a gift. He had a cousin who ran a limo service. He was also our driver and chaperon. He worked it out so we needed to pay forty dollars per person which was eighty dollars for each guy so the girl didn't have to pay.

I got in and examined him. His gray tweed blazer over dark pants, white shirt and deep purple tie said it all. No need to mention that he was wearing his hat, of course. He and I were the first to be picked up because of the location of our houses. After I got situated, we were off to get Gene and Wes.

"So..." he said, looking for approval of the limo.

"I guess it'll work for tonight. It could be better though."

He sat there with a smirk on his face because he knew I was joking.

Then I gave in, "Are you kidding me? This is amazing!" The lights outlining the ceiling, the dark tinted windows, the mini-fridge stocked with cokes, all of it was crazy.

"Thank you." he said with a smile and a nod.

"This is gonna be one crazy night!"

"Yeah it is!"

We talked about fashion and the flat box he had on the seat beside him. They were his special "corsages". He never let us in on those and even now he kept them to himself.

As Gene got into the limo, I could tell by the look on his face that he was impressed. I don't mean "well-done on a test" impressed, I mean "bench pressing twice as much as me" impressed.

"Wales, I don't even know what to say, man. I'm just blown away!"

"Well, you look good at least." I said. He did, he was wearing a rather stylish dark pin-striped suit with a black shirt and navy-blue tie with a silver tie-pin.

"When prom comes around, we're gonna have to get a helicopter!" Gene was right, if we put it all on the table now, what in the world would we do then?

"Funny you should say that..." Wales said with a serious look on his face before admitting he was "Just kidding!"

We were off to get Wes and then the ladies.

Just like Gene, Wes was gob-smacked by the level of luxury Wales managed to acquire for us. He wore a dark blue suit with light pinstripes, a black shirt, and a deep gold tie. I must say, fashion by Wales was on point today. We all commented, of course, on the limo then we were off to pick up the ladies. We were sad in a way that Bruce and Elizabeth, since they volunteered for the dance and had to be there so early, would miss out on all of this.

The protocol for picking up the ladies was that as we arrived, the respective guy would get out, go to the house, greet the lady and parents then escort her to the limousine. Leigh was up first because of how close her house was to Wes'. Wales stepped out, ordering us not to look in the "corsage" box, and proceeded with the protocol. A few minutes passed. I later learned that her parents wanted pictures. As they approached the limo, we could see that Leigh looked amazing! She coordinated her color pallet with Wales and the two of them looked like a well thought out system of fashion. Her makeup and hair were expertly done and she carried herself well. That was impressive. She lavished comments on us and we felt like knights of the round table.

Wes was up next. He went through the protocol and returned to the limo with Carolyn, a girl from his church. She too looked good but I am sure she felt a little under-dressed in Leigh's presence. I felt a slap on the back from Gene as it was my turn. My palms started to sweat as we rode through the neighborhoods of Roland Park. The limo stopped at a house with a very well-manicured lawn. The house was clad in gray stone and brick. The driveway was a semi-circle through the front yard with a parked car that kept the limo on the street. I took a breath and made my exit. As I walked up the driveway, it felt as though it got longer the more I walked like the driveway was itself teasing me – taking pleasure in my nervous agony.

By the time I got up the steps and to the front door, I was noticeably nervous. I looked back at the limo beyond the longest walk I'd ever taken and turned to the door. It was then that something clicked in my mind and my new friend "Joe Swagger" stepped to the plate. I pressed the button and could hear the melodic doorbell through the door. I waited and was about to press the button again when I heard the sounds of the door being unlocked. Ms. O'Neil opened the door and invited me in.

I knew her to be a rather terse if not harsh woman from our chance encounter in the mall a year ago. However, nothing could have been further from the truth. She asked about school, family, the dance, even my interests. I was so off-put by this that I hardly realized how weird I felt. I didn't feel weird because of the situation but because of her. I just supposed it ran in the family somehow. Then it happened. Meghan came down the stairs. If my mind had thought to faint, it would have. It was as if I looked at "Joe Swagger" and he said, "You're on your own, man!" There I stood, transfixed on this... this beautiful girl who could tell what I was thinking. She stopped on the stairs, blushing and stared back at me.

"You kids are just too funny! Just have fun tonight." her mom said as she left the foyer.

"Um... Joe?" she said, trying to rouse me from my shock with a coy smile on her face that usually goes with the notion of having someone wrapped around their finger. "Joe Swagger" returned in force as I replied.

"You are going to outshine every girl there tonight. You look absolutely gorgeous!" my face was blank but my confidence was off the chart.

She *was* beautiful! Her black dress seemed to know where every curve was supposed to be if she were all grown up. She had a thin gold-colored belt around her waist with a small matching clutch bag in her hand. Her heels were perfectly coordinated as were her stockings. Her hair made the outfit. It appeared wet but was only styled that way. It was pulled back with some in the front hanging a bit over one eye.

"Thank you!" she replied as she finished her trip down the stairs. "You look very handsome yourself!"

I thanked her and we left after she grabbed a sweater in case it got chilly. She locked the door and before she turned she asked, "So is your mom dri..." At that point all of the expense on Wales' plan was absolutely justified. She was stunned when she turned and saw the limo while she was speaking. She slowly turned her head to me with a blank stare. It was a perfect setup for a joke to break the tension.

"I uh... really like you, Meghan, and I guess I wanted tonight to be perfect." I paused for about three seconds of watching her not know what to say and then I followed it up with, "Just kidding... Now you see how I felt when you asked me to take you tonight... let's go have some fun!"

As we got into the limo, I noticed the group of blank stares she received, even from Leigh and Carolyn. She blushed the whole time but I could tell she was enjoying herself. I introduced Meghan to Carolyn and we were off to collect Imani K. Imani lived in Towson, which was fitting because the restaurant where we were to have dinner was there.

Gene returned to the limo with the very model-like Imani K. She too was stunning. Like the other girls of the *Sidity Committee*, Imani K. was beautiful and she knew it. With her use of makeup and the way her maroon and beige dress complimented her mocha skin; she could easily pass for an older girl. She was stunning and somehow, she and Gene just looked right together. However, like the others, even she reacted to seeing Meghan. I don't even know how to describe my state of mind at that point. We were all laughing and joking. Every now and then Meghan would look at me with that coy smile which seemed to indicate that she was just happy to be with me and I would shoot it right back at her in an attempt to express the same.

The limo came to a stop in a parking lot. "Time for dinner" Wales said, "But first..." Wales leaned forward with the "corsage" box in a way that everyone could see. The limousine was configured with sort of a semi-circular seating pattern so it was easy for everyone to lean in and see.

"OK, I thought we could use these instead of traditional corsages." Wales opened the box and there before us were ten classic *Ray-Ban* sunglasses, the quintessential sunglasses of the nineteen-eighties. These things went for around eighty dollars a pair and this joker worked out some crazy deal for twenty bucks a piece. He encouraged all of us to take a pair and wear them, which we gladly did. So what if I looked like "The Black Panthers Meet Prep School", we all looked so good! I had no idea Meghan's outfit could be improved upon until she slipped on those *Ray-Bans*.

So, there we were, eight teenagers in *Ray-Bans* streaming into *Beefsteak Charlies* on the upper lot of what was then the small *Towson Town Center Mall*. The driver, Wales' cousin Robert walked in and sat with us to make everything look right with the management. I mean, you can't just have a bunch of kids walk into a sit-down restaurant like that.

We dined on steak, rice pilaf, and joking conversation all dinner long. Everyone looked as though they were having the time of their lives. I wasn't paying attention to the fact that I still felt annoyingly weird around Meghan since this was pushed way down every time I looked at her. I needed to get my mind right.

We ended dinner at 5:30, plenty of time to get to the dance. Back in the limo, Wales briefed us on how things were to go. This was something he'd worked out with Bruce and chose not to tell us. I guess he figured it would be fun to have a surprise up his sleeve. By now we didn't care, Gene was chatting up Imani K., this was the most I'd seen her laugh... ever. Wes was relaying the *Terminator* story to Carolyn and I was puzzled over something Meghan said just then. Whispering, she'd leaned over and asked if we had time to talk after the dance. Knowing Wales' intention for the evening, I told her we would. But what did she want to talk about?

The limo had been circling an area of Towson for a while so we would get to the school at precisely 6:00. When we got to the school, all went according to Wales' plan. The limo pulled into the driveway behind the Junior high. When we opened the door, Meghan and I stepped out first. Even though it was mostly dark by then, as directed, Ray Bans were worn. Before I could even suggest a pose, her right hand was on my left shoulder and we were standing sideways to the camera. The yearbook photographer's flash went off. Gene and Imani K. stepped out and she took the opportunity to get a few additional personal pictures. The others stepped out and went through the same routine with Wales and Leigh being last. Bruce and Elizabeth met the limo when we arrived. Wales handed them their sunglasses and they too went through the routine. We all took a group picture and proceeded to the CAB for the dance.

As we were walking, we noticed other students arriving and taking note of our photo routine and the way we were dressed. Some of the kids came dressed up too, as rumored, but none of them like us. What was just a dance where kids were pretty much expected to wear their school clothes, we treated like a middle-school prom. Again, we followed Wales' protocol for walking to the CAB, arm in arm with our dates, somehow, I didn't mind. Walking with sunglasses in the dark was interesting but I guess fashion prevailed. Always the joker, Bruce started singing "Sunglasses at Night" by Corey Hart. He stopped after the first few words when he realized we were not amused, even though we really were.

When we got to the gym, which had been decorated well for this occasion, "Everybody Wants to Rule the World" by Tears for Fears was playing. An area in the middle was designated for dancing. Some kids were already dancing but those who weren't were checking us out. We all complemented Bruce and Elizabeth for their work on the event.

Every now and again Meghan and I would dance if a song we liked was played. Most of the time the group of us had fun goofing on each other and trying to sing badly to make everyone laugh. George Michael's "Careless Whisper" played and we all had fun screeching out the chorus. It was like this the whole time and we just had fun with it. We felt as though we were celebrities who owned the night. Speaking of owning the night, Meghan turned so many heads I was getting a bit offended. "Joe Swagger" rose to the occasion and the next thing I knew, whenever I felt that way, I just took her to the dance floor. Problem solved. During one dance, I happen to catch Jake Thompkins staring at us. His face was beet red like he had a rash or something. I saw Saundra too; she was with a guy I knew to be an upperclassman whose name I didn't know.

Getting close to eight o'clock, Foreigner's "I Want to Know What Love Is" was played. Apparently, Meghan liked this song because she pulled me to the floor. Staring into my eyes she put her arms around me and her head on my chest. We didn't say a word... I surely wasn't going to. In my mind, the hottest girl at that dance was slow-dancing with me. I was doing all right. The photographer caught a picture of it. To this day, that yearbook picture of me and Meghan O'Neil slow-dancing with her head on my chest haunts me.

When we got back to the others, I noticed I was holding her hand. I let it go as politely as I could.

"We need to be somewhere by 8:30." Wales reminded us. All the women except Leigh of course, questioned what he meant as they thought we were going to end the night at the dance. "Joe Swagger" tapped me on my mental shoulder and said, "I'll take this one..."

"We've got the limo all night, the weather's right, and Baltimore's a big city. Trust us..."

The ladies looked at their respective escorts who all nodded in agreement. So with Ray Bans on, the now ten of us headed for the limousine. Bruce and Elizabeth worked it out beforehand so their responsibilities ended at eight. Elizabeth thought it was because he wanted to dance but given that the other ladies went along with it, she did too.

As the limo pulled away, I handed Gene a coke from the fridge which he gladly took. As usual, we pulled the tabs at the same time and toasted before taking the first sip. The limo found its way through Towson to the Beltway and then onto 83 south. Knowing what was coming I projected complete confidence to Meghan who surprisingly just leaned back on me. I didn't mind.

We all seemed to sit in a kind of reflective silence as each successive street light provided momentary illumination through the windows. As I looked around, I could tell we were all feeling the same thing, the wish that this night would never end. I glanced down at this head full of styled blond hair leaning upon my chest. I knew something was happening between us but I didn't know what nor did I dare to guess. I caught Gene's eye and for a moment I thought he would do something like give me a thumbs up or smile but he did neither. He just settled into the reflective haze we all seemed to enjoy. This was a rare moment, a special moment I knew should not be disturbed by words.

Familiar things sped by the window the Pepsi sign on the Jones Falls Expressway, the off-ramp to Northern Parkway. These landmarks I'd seen all my life made me feel at home but, for some reason, nothing felt more comfortable than sharing the ride with the best friends I'd ever had. I was nervous about the new feelings I seemed to let myself have for Meghan as well as the constant weirdness she made me feel.

Off the JFX now, the limo navigated its way through the streets of downtown Baltimore. The constant light from the streetlights broke the mesmeric trance in which we basked. Elizabeth interrupted the silence.

"Where are we going? I don't come to the city often but when we do, this is the way we go to the harbor."

"Don't worry about it." Bruce said, "just relax and enjoy the ride."

In the twenty-first century, these words would be cause for concern but among eighth-graders in 1985, relaxation and anticipation.

By this time, we were all alert and looking around at Baltimore on a Saturday night. We turned left onto Pratt Street and in a short while the limo parked with its hazard lights on in front of Baltimore's World Trade Center. The weather had been rather warm all day and that night was near perfect. We got out of the limo and the trunk popped. Wales and I pulled three bottles of sparkling cider from a cooler along with plastic toasting glasses. When the trunk closed, the limo continued down Pratt Street.

We walked over to the entrance where a guard was walking patrol around the now-closed building.

"Can I help you kids?" the Guard asked.

"Could you please let Albert know that Tommy Wales is here?" Wales replied.

"Fifteen to base, fifteen to base." the Guard spoke into his radio.

"Go ahead fifteen." the man's voice said on the other end.

"Hey Al, I got a Tommy Wales and friends here at WTC."

"He's on the green list, open the door for them."

"Seriously?"

"Open the door for them fifteen, he and his friends are green-listed, we're good."

"OK everybody, follow me, I guess." he said with a resigned sigh.

As the guard led us through the entrance, Meghan looked at me with a quizzical expression.

"Just accept it, it's like this all the time." I whispered.

The Guard got us into the lobby and said, "Well here you go." and left. We got onto the elevator and rode it to the twenty-seventh floor, the Observation Deck. The Observation Deck was empty and dark, illuminated only by the city lights below. Much like the ride on the highway, this set a peaceful mood. We set up on a nearby table. Everyone took a glass and Wales offered a toast to our "very fine" ladies and a wonderful night.

The city lights were beautiful from here. We could see the city from every window on that floor. Meghan and I, glasses in hand, chose a far corner overlooking the Harborplace Light and Pratt Street Pavilions. As I stared out the window, reflecting on the night, I could see her reflection, she too seemed to be reflecting so I just enjoyed the moment. For some reason, my eyes kept finding their way to her reflection. Every now and again, her head would turn toward me as if she wanted to say something. She finally broke the silence.

"What are you thinking about, Phil?"

"I was just thinking that... wait whoa... nobody but family, and only a few of them, calls me that!"

"I'm sorry but hear me out. We have this great energy together; you must have felt that tonight. I mean I knew it all along, that's why I thought it might be nice to go to the dance with you but I had no idea we would blend this well. We just do. The problem is that we hardly know each other and I thought maybe if we had something between us that was just for us, maybe it would be a start."

"Um... OK... So, what are you thinking?"

"You let me call you Phil when we're alone and I'll let you call me by my *special* name."

"What is it? Is it 'Meg'?"

"No! Never call me that, I don't like that..."

"OK, I won't."

"You have to agree first?"

"Yeah, sure..."

"This is important to me, Joe. You have to promise me that you will not share my name with *anyone... ever*! Will you do that?"

I looked her in the eyes for a moment and was met with the softest, most lovely pleading look I thought I'd ever seen. "Yeah, Meghan, I can do that... I promise." I said softly.

There was a long pause during which I noticed the others had the same idea, the couples were all off by themselves talking the night away.

"You said that we would use these names when we were alone. When are we..."

"I don't want this to be the only time we spend together." she interrupted.

"You don't?"

"What do you want, Phil?"

I took a moment to gather my thoughts, "Joe Swagger" helped a bit.

"I want to get to know the girl who turned everybody's head tonight. But not for that reason."

"Did I turn *your* head?"

"You know you did, that's why I can hardly look at you now."

"Challenge yourself, that's how you get stronger. Look at me now and tell me something you normally wouldn't."

I turned to her and looked her straight in the eyes. She had the softest look in her eyes as the city lights illuminated most of her face. "Joe Swagger" wanted to say something but I knew I had to be myself so I suppressed the "Swagger mask" and answered.

"Meghan, from the moment I saw you yesterday, I wanted to be the guy you dressed up for, not just for some event. It was my privilege to have you on my arm tonight and it would be my honor to consider you my friend."

She beamed her signature smile and glanced around nervously.

"What?" I asked.

"You just... I don't know... I just feel so good." she said blushing.

"I'm glad I have that effect on you"

"By the way, silly, I *was* dressing up for you. The other day when you walked up and changed our meeting time, you were so confident without being arrogant. When you looked back at me, it felt like there was this gentleness about you that you wanted to share with me and Friday, I don't know, I just wanted to catch your eye."

"You did that..."

She closed her eyes for a moment, took a breath and said, "OK... It's my second middle name which I don't share with anyone at all. My closest friends don't even know it. It's Shivawn"

"How do you spell that?"

"S-I-O-B-H-A-N" she said nervously looking at the floor.

"What?"

"It's an Irish thing, go with it." she replied with nervous laughter.

"It *is* a pretty name."

"Thank you, it's *very* special to me so I'm trusting you."

"I appreciate that."

"So where do we go from here?"

"I think we need to do just what you said, spend time together and get to know each other. Maybe I can figure out why you weird me out so much."

She laughed a little and said, "Maybe it's because you've never met someone on your frequency like I am. Let's explore that together."

"By the way, I wasn't thinking when I was holding your hand at the dance, I'm sorry."

"I'm sorry you let it go."

"Why Siobhan, are you flirting with me?"

"Yes, and you're flirting with me too, aren't you?"

"No need to lie. I absolutely am. Now it's your turn."

"What's my turn?"

"Your turn to tell me something you normally wouldn't."

"OK... two things. One, I am a very shy person and the confidence you see right now I am literally drawing from you. Two, and this is definitely too forward for now but we have to start with brutal honesty... I would like it if you would hold me, just this once. I know we need to take it slow and all but just once."

I slipped my arms around her and she did the same. I held her tight and said, "We'll figure this out."

"I know we will."

As I held her I let myself notice how she felt in my arms, the scent of her perfume, and even the scent of her hair gel. I realized I was getting hooked and needed a reason to let go. Found it...

"So, Siobhan?"

"Yes, Phil?" she kept holding me.

"You said that you knew we had great energy all along, what did you mean by that? How long have you been thinking about me?"

She released me and looked at me. "I thought we'd get to that later but do you really want to know tonight?"

"Yeah... I don't think I'll get any sleep tonight if I put it off."

She let out a little nervous laughter and asked, "Do you remember your little sparring match with Jake Thompkins on the first day of School last year?"

"How could I forget?"

"You were in a completely new situation with strangers and yet you were in complete control. I thought that was... impressive. You need to understand that I couldn't have done that. I wanted to get to know you from that moment on. Every time we had a conversation it didn't go the way I wanted but I would get a glimpse... so... yeah."

"You know, this is one of the most honest conversations I've ever had." I didn't know what else to say.

"I'm glad you see it that way. I was hoping we could be honest. So let me take it a step further. This energy I feel, am I wrong or do you feel it too?"

"I don't know what to call it but we do have a strong connection. I feel so comfortable with you. Why didn't I see it before?"

"I weird you out, remember? That's the opposite of comfortable. Who would want to be around that? Do I weird you out now?"

"Honestly, yes. But at the same time, I don't want to be anywhere else."

I gently took her hand and let myself feel it in mine.

"I love that you like to hold my hand." she said staring at our hands.

"Is it too soon?"

"I think we can deal with a little hand-holding."

At just about ten o'clock Wales corralled us and before we knew it we were back in the limousine. Meghan and I kept exchanging awkward glances which Gene noticed of course. I knew he wouldn't let it go and when we got a chance to talk, I would have to fill him in.

We returned the ladies to their homes with each of us walking them to their doors. When my turn came, I walked Meghan to her porch and took her hand. She looked at her hand in mine, smiled, and said, "Good night, Phil. I had the best time!"

"Good night, Siobhan." As I started down the steps I turned and said, "I really like that name!" She smiled at me again.

CHAPTER 12:
"DRINK ME" - ALICE'S ADVENTURES IN WONDERLAND

I awoke Sunday morning to a decidedly different world than the one the day before. I was in a relationship, kinda? I was bristling with nervous excitement and I'd just spent the previous night "on the town", literally. I laid in bed contemplating these things for a while before getting up to get ready for Church. I downplayed the night to my parents because there was no way I could let them in on all of that, heck I didn't fully understand it myself.

After Church I noticed my mother was making a list of errands she had to run which would take her all afternoon. I made a quick call to Gene only to find he'd gotten up an hour or so earlier. We talked a bit and agreed I should come over. My mother added me to the list and I was dropped off at Gene's house.

I made light conversation as if the previous night didn't happen, a game we played until he'd had enough. At that point, we were in HQ and he just sat there, looking at me as though I were his kid and he knew I'd done something for which he wanted me to confess.

"Well?" he asked, the look on his face betraying the fact that he was intensely curious.

"Well, what?" I replied, making him suffer.

"So, do you like her?"

"Yes, I do." I was confident.

"Does she like you?"

"Yes, she does."

"What changed? First, she's weirding you out and now you want to date her."

"I couldn't tell you any one thing. It was all of it put together. It's like she said, we have great energy and we blend."

"Just what the <expletive> does that mean?"

"Whoa!"

"Sorry, I just can't figure girls out!"

"Imani K.?"

"Yeah, now back to you, we'll talk about that later."

"Well, I understand it to mean that we fit together really well."

"OK, Yoda, break that down for me."

"I've done a lot of thinking about this, actually. I think we both noticed that we were building on each other's strengths last night. Slow-dancing is not my thing but it was last night. Confidence is not her thing but she was last night. When she needed me to be open with my feelings, she helped me. When she needed to be bold I helped her. We just... fit."

"Yeah, I could tell she was into you but I didn't know why." he said as he sat back in the chair and stared at the ceiling.

"Thanks!"

"That's not what I meant. What are you gonna do about this?"

"We're gonna hang out and take it slow. Build a solid friendship and see where we go from there."

"Slow? The way you were hugging last night? Did you kiss her?"

"Slow, yes. We were just being honest last night, that's all. Believe me, I'm gonna tone that stuff way down. We were getting ahead of ourselves and we both knew it. Oh and no, I didn't kiss her. Shoot, I can barely handle this!" I paused for a minute to collect my thoughts and said, "So, bottom line is that she is *not* my girlfriend, not yet anyway, she's just someone I want to be friends with."

"But she *is* your girl, right?"

"What do you mean?"

"What if someone else wanted to be her *friend*, would she like that or does she want to work it out with you?"

"No, I think it's just me."

"So, she's *your* girl then, right?" he prodded.

"Well, put it *that* way, yeah, I guess she *is* my girl. Wow, this is so weird."

"You're telling me, you're the one in a relationship and I'm the one by myself?"

"Yeah, now *that's* weird. But you know, you'll be fine, I bet you could go out with any girl you wanted."

"That's the problem, 'any girl' is not the *right* girl. How do you find the *right* girl?" he pondered.

"Man, I don't know. Look at me, I have feelings for a girl that flat weirds me out. Do you really want advice from me?"

"No... no... not really."

He went on to tell me that though his time with Imani K. went well, she just wasn't interested in dating anybody. She did throw in that if he ever needed a date for a night like that, she would be *very* interested. We talked about how we thought this was what *Sidity Committee* girls were like and how he'd bounce back.

I had dinner with Gene and his mom that day. All the while I was wondering what Meghan was doing and if she regretted anything she'd said the night before. I started getting antsy with the thought that maybe I'd read her wrong and that she wasn't as "into me", to use Gene's words, as I thought.

"Joe, are you alright?" Ms. Tucker asked, noticing my uneasiness.

"Yeah, I guess so." I answered.

"Girl issues." Gene added bluntly.

Ms. Tucker gave a wide-eyed flat smile and continued with her food. I glanced at Gene as if to condemn his words. He just smiled at me like a taunting little brother.

Almost an hour later I was home, pacing back an forth in my room wondering if it would be OK to call her. Was it too soon? Seven thirty was a good time, right? Finally, "Joe Swagger" couldn't stand it anymore and reached for the phone on the computer line but it rang before I got there. I just stared at it as it rang through the second ring. This phone *never* rang. We don't give that number out... except when I did just that once last Friday.

"Hello?" I answered.

"Phil? Can you talk now, are you alone?"

I got comfortable and my heart warmed as she spoke.

"Siobhan... It's great to hear from you. I've been out all day. Funny thing though, I was about to call you."

"Sounds like my day... So, um..."

"Let me start." I interrupted.

"OK, shoot."

"We said a lot of things last night, none of them I regret. I just want to know that we're still on the same page and it wasn't the dance, the night, or the sparkling cider that made us say those things."

She laughed a little.

"What?" I asked.

"It's just that I was thinking the same thing. I gave you my name, I don't share that with anybody and I got worried that I might have been too quick with that. You don't know how good it is for me to hear that you don't regret what we talked about."

"If anything, I feel more sure about it. I just need to get to know you better so we can build this friendship we want."

"I am so glad to hear that, Phil. Where do we start?"

"Let's start with questions and see where that goes"

"Great! So, what's your first question?"

I laid down on my bed and got comfortable.

"You said 'Siobhan' was your second middle name, what's the other one?"

"That's true but not the whole story. My name is Meghan Laurel O'Neil. When I turned twelve we had a ceremony at my church in New Jersey..."

"Like confirmation?"

"Exactly! There's this tradition of adding a special name that you don't share with anyone and so mine is 'Siobhan.'"

"I must say that Laurel is a pretty name too." I added.

"Thank you, but I don't want you to miss how special this is. I've never told my mother my name and never will."

I was shocked. The line filled with deafening silence for longer than I knew.

"Phil? Are you still there?"

"I am, I think I just now got how important this is to you and how honored I am."

"Thank you... It really is *that* important to me."

"You said your church in New Jersey, is that where you're from?"

"OK, this is your second and I have yet to ask my first but I'll play along. I was born in Leipzig, Germany. My parents were into international business law back then. We left when I was seven. We were in New Jersey for a while but moved around some. We still go back there for church from time to time."

"OK, this begs the question, and I promise I'll let you ask yours, but is your father still in the picture?"

There was an uneasy silence on the line.

"I'm... I'm... uh... not exactly over that yet." I could tell she teared up a little. She went on to say, "I do want to be open with you so... He... um... he died in a car wreck when I was ten and I've never been the same."

"Meghan I'm so sorry, I wish I hadn't brought it up."

"Thank you, I know you care, but to know me is to know this stuff and there's a lot of it. So, this is good... My turn now."

We went back and forth covering everything from family to schoolwork. We covered so much ground that it felt as though I knew her better than some of the *Mysfits* and that was just one conversation, albeit one that went on for a while.

"So, Siobhan, it's 10:00, I don't want to keep you from sleeping or getting ready for school tomorrow."

"I'm OK if you are."

"I just wanted to be considerate. I'll let you decide when to stop. I feel like I could talk to you all night."

She laughed and told me she felt the same way and then she went here...

"So, um... Phil?

"So um, yeah?" I thought I was funny.

"It's been fun sharing all this stuff but can I ask a hard question?"

Sick upside-down stomach feeling and all I answered with, "Uh... sure?"

"Elephant in the room. I'm white, you're black. Is that a problem?"

So, there it was. She was braver than me for sure. In that moment I felt like I should have gotten there first but truth be told I wanted to avoid it. "I've noticed that too... so weird!" My pathetic attempt at humor to lighten the moment was not lost on her.

"I'm serious, Phil... and I need you to be too. Is this gonna be a problem?"

"Gene and I had this conversation. He thinks that people have to get over this stuff sometime... why not now?"

"I like him. He's right. We do have to get over it."

Right there I just knew she would be all like, "I don't see color" and whatnot. I was wrong. I got this instead...

"I want to know what it's like to be you and maybe you can learn some stuff from me too."

From there we went on to talk about our families. She was saddened by the fact that I could only go back about four generations before hitting the "Slavery Wall" while she could go back much further. Apparently keeping a family tree was important to her family. She said she was taught that knowledge of her ancestors, who they were and what they did was, "A kind of foundation that ties us to our past and points to our future." I couldn't relate.

We talked on the phone until almost two the next morning. I was careful not to share any of the spiritual things I'd experienced, it just didn't feel right for some reason. I was sad that we had to get off the phone. I knew I'd pay for it the next day. I hated being tired like that at school, days like that seemed to never end, and for it to be a Monday too – joy.

Later that morning, the alarm clock sounded as though it were laughing at me, "HA HA HA HA HA" it said in its piercing monotone voice. Its taunts were too strong, I had to get out of bed and shut it up. I wanted so badly to climb back into that bed but I knew I could never get away with it. I slowly accepted my situation and dragged myself through the morning routine. I'd somehow managed to avoid questions of looking tired and before I knew it, I was buffeted by the brisk morning air.

Nothing spectacular about the bus stop, I saw Saundra and amazingly didn't care. I did catch her looking at me in a strange way. I imagined she was curious about me and Meghan. It didn't matter though; my mind was preoccupied with how Meghan may have been doing this morning.

The bus ride was uneventful until Wales sat down next to me. I'd sorta been preparing for this so I braced myself. I thought I could get the jump on the conversation if I injected a little humor.

"Morning Wales, kinda hard to ride the bus after the limo, huh"

"Yes... yes it is." he said with a sly look and coy smile on his face. "Here we go." I thought.

"That was a cool night, Saturday, huh?" I asked.

"Yes... it sure was..."

I let him meet silence.

"Look Joe, I'm not gonna let you off easy but I'll make it as painless as possible. Spill it..."

"Why Wales, whatever do you mean?"

"Come on man, do you like her?"

"Alright, I guess I'm going to have to answer this question a lot today so... Yes, something clicked between us on Saturday and we realized we need to figure it out."

"But she weirds you out, you said so yourself."

"And she does, but there's something between us and whatever it is, I think I want it." I said this without thinking; this was way above my grade-level so to speak.

"OK, wow. I don't know what to say exactly except I'm happy for you. Leigh and I couldn't stop talking about how good the two of you looked together. She's so funny and full of life. That took us by surprise too, we would have never known it."

"Thank you. Wales, can I ask you a question?"

"Of course..."

"When did you know there was something between you and Leigh?"

"That's easy, the *Pride of Baltimore* party. As you know, I liked her before that and asked her to go with me and all but there was something so easy about talking to her that night. I guess it was like you said, I wanted whatever was between us."

"How do you feel about her?" I caught myself after asking the question but it was too late, this likely out-of-bounds question was out there.

"Well... um... you know..."

"Do I?"

"I think I love her. I'm still figuring it out. She just makes it so easy. I love the fact that her brain is faster than mine, that she's thirteen going on thirty, and that she's the hottest nerd in school. That last one isn't a reason but it is nice."

"It does sound like her though." I agreed.

"It does, doesn't it? You know this conversation was supposed to be about you!"

I answered some of his questions and may have tried to dodge a few before exclaiming, "Oh look, we're here already!"

"It's not gonna be that easy, I've got you on the ride home!"

He was right of course, but at least I had the whole day to prepare.

As I was walking to second period, I was jolted from my Meghan-laced fog by a hand spinning me around. Startled, I spun around to find Leigh grabbing my arm. She had this really worried look on her face.

"Um... good morning, Leigh?"

"Joe, you've got a problem!"

"OK, what is it now?"

"I just overheard in the bathroom that Jake asked Meghan to the dance a whole bunch of times and she kept turning him down!"

Right then my mind flew to that time at the dance when Jake was staring at us, red-faced.

"Oh... there's something she could have told me." I stated plainly.

"You think? Listen Joey, watch your back, OK?"

She pulled that big sister to little brother "Joey" thing. She only did this when she was really concerned like, "You're gonna fail that test, Joey", or "Joey, you know we love you and would do anything for you, right?" She hugged me and went off to class.

Great! Another thing to think about. All that period I was wondering about it. Little wonder why my grades suffered during that semester. I even considered the possibility that Jake would just let it go. Not a chance, the way he'd gloated in the bathroom that day about him knowing who he was taking and me having "slim pickins", something was likely going to happen. I couldn't get the question out of my head of why Meghan failed to mention this. She knew Jake and I were at odds, heck she'd even brought it up on the Observation Deck!

After class, watching out for Jake, I ran into Meghan, like literally. I was looking behind me when I turned the corner in the hallway. We both took a moment. I don't know what we were doing but it felt good. She was wearing a green sweater thing with a teal blouse underneath over black pants. I don't know why I remember that but I do. It took me a minute to snap out of it and then to ask her, "Hi Meghan, look I need to ask you something."

"OK...?" she answered with a hint of worry.

"Word on the street is that Jake asked you to the dance a few times, is that true?"

"Yeah... but I said no."

"You um... know that Jake and I, we're not the *best* of buddies, right?"

"I do. But you should know that he doesn't have a say when it comes to who I go out with! You might not have gone if you thought it could stir up something."

"True but..."

"I couldn't risk that. I'm sorry if it caused a problem but I think we both know whatever problem it causes can't be bigger than what we would've missed if we didn't spend that time together, right?"

She had me and she knew it. "You're right..."

"I've got a quiz in this next class; can we talk later?"

"Yeah, of course."

She took my hand for a moment and we both held on for a second before going our separate ways. I thought that maybe this hand-holding thing was too much. Nah...

Lunchtime rolled around and there he was at a table on the other side of the room. Jake caught me looking at him and told me I was "number one" again in the rudest of ways. I resolved to put it out of my mind, I would just deal with that situation when confronted with it. Leigh didn't exactly like that idea and neither did Gene but this wasn't their decision.

As lunch got started, several people came by and congratulated us on the way we handled the dance. Once again, we felt like we were on top of the world. Someone sat down next to me and, thinking it was another fan, I turned to find Meghan. I was as surprised as anyone at that table.

She grabbed my hand and took it under the table where she interlaced her fingers with mine. For a "shy" girl she sure got over it quickly.

"Hi everybody. I just wanted to say that I had the best time Saturday and I really liked hanging out with you all."

"We thought you were fun to be around too." Leigh responded.

"Thank you! Also, as you may have picked up, something happened between me and Joe. We're not sure what it's about but we're working through it together. It's a *good* thing! I know you guys are the most important people to him and he's becoming important to me so I wanted to make sure you guys understood where I am with all of this. I have no intention to hurt him and I didn't share the fact that Jake asked me to the dance because, and I know this might be selfish, because Joe might not have gone. I can't let Jake or anybody else control who I go out with. I know you care for Joe and I hope that maybe someday you can care for me too."

With that she let go of my hand, took her tray, and went to her table but not before I leaned over and whispered, "I am so impressed with you right now, you don't even know!"

"That makes my day, call me tonight." She said this out loud which drew looks from Gene and Wales.

"What can I say... Respect." Leigh said as she watched Meghan go to her table.

"You got that right..." I managed to say as my emotions tied themselves up in knots. This was all too much for my male teenaged brain.

"Now that's a woman!" Gene said, "She came over here and laid it all on the table."

I had the biggest grin and just ate my food.

Later that day, as I pulled my tired self to sixth period, my mindless walk to class was interrupted. The interruption was not by Meghan's pleasant grin, Leigh's concern, or one of Gene's encouraging talks, no, it was an anger-filled wild-eyed Jake Thompkins. In that moment with the number of kids in the hallway starting to lessen as they receded into their class-rooms, since there was no compulsion like on the field, my mind began racing for a solution. I was less than a foot from the locker behind me. I figured his arm reach should have been sufficient so that if he attempted a head shot and I ducked he might hit the locker.

"Alright <N-word> where do you get off taking Meghan to that dance!"

"I didn't know it was illegal and I didn't know you asked her!"

"Well, it should be illegal and now it's time for you to pay the price!"

In that moment I realized his full intention to hit me and lo, Patrick Finnegan, the new Vice Principal stepped into the hallway some twenty feet behind Jake. My mind began to make calculations for getting rid of Jake for three days. It all depended on if he tried to hit me in the chest and if I could sell it just right.

"We had a good time though!" I said, tipping things off.

He went for it, the punch was definitely aimed for my chest, likely center of mass to get me winded so he could rain down more blows with-out retaliation. Locking eyes on Mr. Finnigan, I leaned back toward the lockers so as to "pull" his punch to soften the blow. When his fist hit my chest, his arm was almost fully extended so it didn't hurt at all really. When I hit the lockers behind me, I made sure to throw my arms in the air so my books would go everywhere. I then dropped to the floor like I was hurt. As if on cue, Mr. Finnegan grabbed Jake in a take-down hold and yelled, "My office, now!"

"I didn't hit him that hard!" Those were the words Jake yelled as Mr. Finnegan suspended him for three days after hearing my side of the story. I almost laughed. Heck, I did on the bus when I explained it to Wales.

That night I called Meghan right after dinner. The anticipation was... exquisite.

"Hello?"

"Siobhan, can you talk?"

"Absolutely, Phil, how are you, I saw..."

"Oh, let me speak first, please."

"Sure..."

I let silence sit on the line for dramatic effect.

"How did you know Leigh was the one who told me about Jake asking you out?"

"What...?" she asked, dragging it out like a kid caught with her hand in the cookie jar.

"You're as smart as you are pretty, spill it!"

"Stop it, I'm blushing!"

"Get used to it. spill it!"

"When you talked to me in the hallway about it, I realized she must have been in the bathroom when Ivannah and I walked in. I figured she must have overheard our conversation."

"When did you realize you would need her on your side?"

"Saturday night."

"Really?"

"Yeah, it didn't take long to figure out that her maternal instincts go out to all of you and that she feels like the big sister in the group. So after you and I talked in the hallway I knew I needed her to feel safe with you and me together. If she felt that you were in any danger at all, you would be torn between me and your friends. So I made my appeal at lunch today not to the group, but to Leigh. Did it work?"

"Incredibly well. She seems to have nothing but respect for you right now."

"Phil, you know I wasn't trying to manipulate her, right? I was just trying to fix stuff."

"Yeah... I know. You're so smart though, you said all the right things. Even asking me to call you tonight so they all could hear it. Sort of making sure they knew you were serious."

"You picked up on almost all of it."

"What did I miss?"

"Me."

"What do you mean?"

"I told you that I'm a very shy person."

"Oh, I got that. You overcame it quickly."

"No, silly, I took your hand and drew from your strength. If I didn't I wouldn't have been able to say those things. I need you to understand that we have a synergy, it's like one plus one is three when I'm with you."

"I guess this is something I have yet to understand but you can't deny the fact that you have to be pretty smart to say what you did, the way you did."

"I'm smart? What about that bit of theater you pulled in the hallway with Jake?"

"What...?" I asked, dragging it out like a kid caught with *his* hand in the cookie jar.

"Oh, come on, you controlled that situation. You played Jake and used Mr. Finnegan to get what you wanted. Now Jake is gone for three days and will likely leave you alone for fear that he would get expelled if he tries that again."

"I didn't even think about that last part."

"Did you make him throw that punch?"

"I kinda told him that we had a good time Saturday night."

She laughed.

"Did I lie?"

"Not at all."

There was a pause.

"Siobhan, I've never met anybody who could think through stuff like me." I stated.

"I think we're figuring out what it means for us to be on the same frequency, we think alike. That answers some questions."

"Yes, it does."

It was a sobering conversation after which we both knew that we couldn't do another school day without sleep so we agreed to see each other in the morning.

The next day I walked through the halls as though a weight had been lifted from my shoulders. It was a kind of lightness that came from Jake being suspended for three days. I thought, "At least I can think without having to look over my shoulder for a while." Wrong! At that moment Al Stonebridge, another *Country Boy*, stopped me and whispered in my ear, "You know, <N-Word>, Jake might be gone for a few days but we've got his back!" With that he let me go. Al was tall for our age, maybe 5 foot 10 or so and seemed to have a receding hairline. I just kept walking. It seemed that stuff like this was becoming so normal that days without it were precious few.

Over the next several days I found that Jake's time off only made matters worse. Meghan was right, Jake seemed to steer clear of me, but just as Al Stonebridge said, they had his back. They would say things in passing and sling racial epithets. What bothered me most was that some teachers would see these things, and do nothing – a valuable lesson.

Despite the apparent objections of the *Country Boys*, Meghan and I continued to grow close. Our school days would start and end with hugs that seemed to draw odd looks from some and jealous looks from others – boosting my ego. From time to time, she would even eat lunch with us. One time I ate with her friends, a starkly different experience. Whereas the

Mysfits seemed to emanate a feeling of welcome and inclusion, love if you will, her group was cold. Conversations were surgical. I was left wondering how she could stand it. I mean I knew her and knew full well that she couldn't be comfortable with that. I figured it had to be because I was there that they were like that. With that assumption, I put it out of my mind.

The day before Halloween was a normal day in terms of whatever "normal" had become for me. It was normal, that is, up until the point when I went to Meghan's locker for my goodnight hug. As soon as I saw her I could tell something was off. We embraced and as we did, I asked, "What's wrong"? She didn't say anything. I pulled back and looked her in the eyes to find that she was using every ounce of strength to hold herself together.

"I'm going to call you at seven. Would that be alright?"

She shook her head, yes, very quickly without saying anything. I backed away with a quizzical look on my face and made my way to the bus. Wales and I had a pretty interesting discussion about what could be wrong. Two thirteen-year-old sages riding the bus trying to make sense of the world – epic.

7:00 couldn't have come soon enough but when it did, I was on the phone. It rang almost five times which meant she was trying to get to privacy in her room. A while ago we'd compared phone procedures and were amused that we both had methods of ensuring privacy.

"Hello?" she said. At least she sounded fine.

"Siobhan... are you OK?"

"Um... no... I'm far from OK!" With that she fell apart.

I let her sob, noting my overwhelming sense of helplessness. I wanted to comfort her in some way but couldn't. I didn't even know what the problem was! After a few minutes, literally, of her trying to get herself back together, I began to pry the information from her brokenhearted grip.

"So... Siobhan," I didn't have a term of endearment for her, I wished that I did, "tell me what happened." This is what I got through the sobs...

"I was coming out of sixth period about to go to seventh when I went to the bathroom. You know my sixth period is in the senior high building. I was washing my hands when that tall girl on the basketball team with the braided hair came in."

"Dominique Jeffers?" I asked. There wasn't a guy in that school who didn't know who Dominique was. She was the black, stunningly beautiful, star of the varsity ladies' basketball team. Physically fit... smokin!

"Yeah, that's her... she said... she said..."

"It's OK, you can tell me."

"She said, 'So you're that little white <expletive> that's going with that black guy, huh?' I was shocked so I said, 'what about it?'"

"Wait a minute, you challenged her? That's not a good strategy in that case."

"Well, it wasn't! I'm just glad she didn't hit me or something. I didn't want to have to go down that path! She went on about how we're stealing their men and all. Oh Phil, it was horrible. I've never been ridiculed for being white before."

"No surprise here." I thought to myself. She started sobbing a little.

"It's OK..." I said, trying to comfort.

"No, it's not!"

"You're right, it's not, but you've got to understand that this is something I'm used to. This is my normal... in a way."

"How can you stand it! How do you deal with it?"

"Finish the story and I'll tell you."

"There's not much to tell, she backed me into a corner, literally, as she was yelling at me and then she left. I didn't know how to feel! I was mad and confused at the same time. I sat on the floor, cried some, and pulled myself together. Gosh!!! I wish that people would just evolve already so we can all get on with it!"

"OK, weirdness..." I thought and then said, "I'm sorry this happened to you."

"I know... how *do* you deal with it?"

"It's not smart and you're not gonna like it."

"What is it?"

"I kind of push it down and... let the fire burn higher."

"OK... that's pretty scary." she said with a hint of concern in her voice.

"Yeah, I know, but it motivates me somehow."

"I guess everybody deals with things differently."

"Absolutely!" I agreed.

"You know, I feel better talking about it. It kind of gives me a glimpse into your world."

I replied, "Yeah, well welcome, it isn't a pleasant place at all when it comes to racism. It just makes me feel so... so..."

"Inferior?"

"Yeah, that's right."

"For me I think Dominique made me feel... uh..."

"Worthless?"

"Yeah, that's a good word."

"Jake and his friends' constant attacks sometimes leaves me feeling... like..."

"Empty?"

"Yeah, like I have nothing left inside... just spent"

"When I was sitting in the corner after she left, I just felt..."

"Small?"

There was a pause and then we both laughed. "We're doing it again..." I said.

"Yeah, we're in each other's heads. One of these days it's not gonna be weird to us anymore."

"OK, but today it's still weird."

"Oh, Phil, I just can't help but think that it must be horrible to go through this as much as you do at school."

"It is... but you get thick-skinned, I guess. I wonder sometimes that if these are the people willing to say how they feel, how many more people feel the same way but keep quiet. You know what I mean?" I asked.

"Yeah, that's a scary thought. What do you think people think about us? I mean do you think there are more Dominiques?"

"I think there are a lot of Dominiques out there. Dominique thought we were like together – together. What are we really?"

"What do you think we are?" she questioned.

"I think we're two people who are just trying to figure out if we shouldn't be together."

"Should we? Should we be more than friends?"

"I think that's where we're going, what do you think?"

"I think so too, but we need more of what we're doing now – building something."

"I agree. No need to rush."

We continued to validate each other's experiences with racial issues and explore what they meant to us and what they might mean for us together.

"It's getting late again... Where does the time go with you?"

"I don't know but I do know it's been some kind of day. See you tomorrow morning at my locker?"

"Of course. Tomorrow's Halloween, I hope things don't get weird." I added.

"Yeah, that reminds me. My mother has a fund-raiser tomorrow night so I won't be home until late. I guess you'll get a chance to get to bed early for a change."

"I don't know what that feels like anymore."

The next morning, I woke up before the alarm with Pastor Summerstone's words about the *Mysfits* having to support each other in the future ringing in my head. It took a while to shake that foreboding feeling. On the bus, Wales and I swapped girl stories; things that we do that irritate them and vice versa. Our conversation was just getting good when we pulled into the school's parking lot. We agreed that we needed to get together outside of school sometime. At the mention of this I could see the wheels turning in his head which prompted me to tell him that this didn't have to be fancy, just hanging out. His reaction was such that I thought maybe he'd never had a friend just hang out with him - I mean Leigh, sure, but other than that. I quickly filed it away as we stepped off the bus.

As we talked while walking toward the building, Leigh joined us. Wales put his arm around her and she put her arm around his waist. It was good to see the difference between Wales at that time and a year earlier. Leigh snapped me out of my reminiscent fog.

"So, Joe, stop me if I'm intruding but how are things going with you and Meghan?"

"Leigh!" Wales said as though trying to keep her out of my business.

"Wales, it's not a problem. We've all been through stuff and we still have a lot to go through... My business *is* your business." This drew some weird looks. I would have given myself some weird looks too. I guess I hadn't shaken Pastor Summerstone's words yet. "Um... I don't know what you don't already know but we're good." I stumbled over myself trying to alleviate the weirdness of my former statement.

Leigh stopped and turned to me, "I mean I know you guys are friends, and getting close and all, but do you see it going anywhere or are you good with what you have?"

Wales turned to me with eyebrows raised as if to say, "See? Too much, huh?"

"Funny you should ask; we were talking about that last night. We're good where we are right now. Besides, we're thirteen! Where could it go?"

"That's good, but the way you guys hug and hold hands every now and then..."

"I know, weird, huh? We do have a strange relationship; I mean heck, she still weirds me out, but it's a good friendship."

At that, we entered the building. As we maneuvered through the crowded hallway, I felt a tap on my shoulder. The last time this happened, I was just overjoyed to find Jake behind me. With some hesitation, I turned and found Meghan standing there. Something inside me stirred. Given what she'd been through and our conversation I wanted nothing more than to scoop her up in my arms and hold her as if we were the only two people in the world. At that point I realized my caring for her had changed from just that to something more. I was embarrassed, elated, and scared at the same time. The weirdest thing, however, wasn't the feelings I had but that we were in sync again and I could read from her expression that she felt the same way. We stared at each other for a few seconds and then slowly embraced and told each other that we would be OK. I knew she needed to hear that but I didn't know I needed to hear it too.

The rest of that day was uneventful, thank God. It was one of the good days where I suppose I was below the radar so to speak. I found myself thinking of a question Meghan asked me in one of our phone conversations, "Why do you think Jake bothers you but not Gene?" I told her that it is not in my nature to be threatening, but for Gene, threatening was easy – besides, he had the physique to back it up. I considered becoming more like Gene and then thought that I like being me and that Jake doesn't get to control that.

Halloween night came and went. I remember running out of candy for Trick-or-Treaters and not a few teenagers going door to door with no costumes. The airwaves were full of Halloween episodes for this sit-com or another. One of my favorite shows couldn't resist and had to air a Halloween-themed episode dealing with middle-school relationships.

The next morning however, was anything but routine. When Wales and I got off the bus we couldn't help but notice an inordinate number of teachers on the school's front lawn. They were spaced out, as if guarding something or at least keeping people away from an area of the grass. Wales and I looked at each other and I said, "Now this feels about right." Wales nodded in agreement recalling the strange occurrences of the previous school year.

As we walked, we noticed Principal McIntyre talking to a police offi-cer. Mr. Finnegan stood nearby but his attention was on the students, not the principal. It was as though he made sure to look each student in the eye as they passed by. After he scanned us, I couldn't help but to look at the guarded area of the lawn. It was weird to say the least. There was a cir-cle on the lawn drawn with chalk like from a baseball diamond. It had to be twenty feet in diameter and every few feet around the circle the chalk was interrupted as though something had been moved from those spots. The ground was charred in the center of the circle as if a campfire had been there.

Wales shook his head as we continued to walk and said, "I know the drill, I'll try to get with Murph and the guys and see what's up."

"Yeah, and here I was thinking that we might not have to deal with this kind of thing this year."

"Well, no such luck, I guess..."

The hallway was abuzz with chatter about what was going on outside. I could hear students who were there last year telling new students what happened then. The words "Halloween" and "prank" seemed to be thrown around a lot. We met up with Leigh, Bruce and Wes who were obviously talking about what was going on outside. I didn't see Meghan.

Lunchtime rolled around and I happened to run into Meghan on the way.

"Hey, missed you before school..." I said as we hugged.

"Yeah, Mother and I both slept in. We didn't get back from the fundraiser until almost one-o'clock."

"Who was it for?"

"Small Business Women of America, the local chapter. She's been a member for years and yes, it was as boring as it sounds."

"Oh... OK"

"I heard some stuff happened... stuff like last year."

"Yeah, I don't know much but if I find out anything, I'll let you know."

We entered the lunchroom as we were talking and afterwards joined our separate groups.

Wales came in late, we learned that he'd met with Murph and his crew in private after they held the table for us. He got his food and sat down at one end of the table and leaned in as if to be secretive and then said, "They're calling it a prank but it's more than that."

"More how?" Wes responded.

"There was a chalk line drawing on the lawn and they set a bonfire in the middle. People in the neighborhood called the fire department sometime early in the morning, like 3 or 4 and told police that there were people dancing around the flames."

Blank, incredulous stares.

"A little far for a Halloween prank, don't you think?"

"Wow, this is all kinds of messed up!" Gene declared.

He was right, this was all messed up. We all sat back and thought about the strange scene that played out on the lawn the night before. I remembered the book Pastor Summerstone had me reading about light and darkness and how the darkness longs to overcome the light, but can't.

"Well, I think there are some crazy people out there who don't like Christians."

"I agree with you, Leigh. I think they were obviously mocking our faith on Halloween. I mean who would go that far for a prank?" I wondered.

The official statement was read in seventh period and letters to parents were given out. Both dismissed the "incident", as it was called, as a Halloween prank which included some defacing of property, namely the lawn. No further details were given. I understood not wanting to alarm parents but still, I would have wanted to know more if I'd had a child in that school.

After school, in the few minutes I had before getting on the bus, I visited Meghan at her locker and filled her in on what we learned. As we were talking Leigh interrupted.

"I'm sorry to interrupt but Joe I've got that study guide for the math test you and Wales were talking about. I wrote it based on what I'd put on the test if I were your teacher knowing what you'll need in higher math classes."

"Thank you, Leigh! I appreciate it. The last one you did was right on the money!"

"Oh, and Joey, some of this stuff is really hard but you'll need it so you have to study hard, OK?"

"OK, I will... gosh..."

"You know I just want the best for you guys, right?"

"I do... Thank you, I mean it."

"You're welcome. Good night you two." Leigh smiled at me in a way that said, "Y'all are cute." as she walked away.

"Does she do that a lot?" Meghan asked.

"Only when we have a big test. It's cool having someone who knows what you'll need to know later on. It's a big help."

"I guess so."

"I'll share it with you, don't worry."

"Thanks. Um... another thing..."

"Yeah?"

"Did you tell her to call you that or did she make it up?"

"What?"

"She called you 'Joey'."

"Oh, that... She made it up. That's just something she calls me when something serious is going on."

"You shouldn't let her call you that, Phil."

"Why not?"

"Oh my gosh you've got so much to learn... There's power in naming someone."

"OK... huh?"

"I'll tell you more sometime but for now you've got to get to your bus."

CHAPTER 13:
MORE ANSWERS, MORE QUESTIONS

I opened my eyes. The room was dark but for the amber stripes across the ceiling from the street lights shining through the semi-opened mini-blinds. With angry red glowing numbers, the clock revealed the time to be 3:34 AM. I was still tired but something else was going on. I stumbled my way to my desk and flipped on the lamp. As I pulled the journal from the hiding place, I thought about how I could get some sleep if I could just get these thoughts out on paper.

My mind was racing. I was contemplating my life and there was something I couldn't figure out. I mean, I'm the type of guy who thinks things through, heck, I even prided myself on that - situations, conflicts, plans, and... relationships. Could it be that as a teenager I had been so blinded by emotions and raw hormones that I didn't think through what-ever it was that Meghan and I had between us? I mean, this *is* the girl who's weirded me out for so long and now, now... I don't know what.

I was in uncharted waters. My teenaged brain was scrambling to come to grips with these new feelings. The only thing I knew for sure was that I had a deep need for this to make some kind of sense. It went on like this for about an hour before I got back to bed. At least it was Saturday.

That morning, I got up, did my usual chores after breakfast and was off to Confirmation class.

I went through the motions in Confirmation class, my mind was clearly not present. This did not go unnoticed by Pastor Summerstone who promptly called me aside afterwards. I can't say I was surprised given how well he was able to read me… no matter, I wanted to talk to him anyway.

"So… how are you doing?" he asked, knowing full well that I was distracted.

"I'm getting along, I guess. You can probably tell I've got a lot on my mind." I responded.

"I know that look. I suppose it has something to do with a girl?" he said half-asking, half-knowing.

"Well, yeah. The truth is, I like her very much. I mean Meghan and I fit in a lot of ways but from time to time… I don't know, I guess on some level I'm still weirded out by her or maybe just by how fast these feelings came around. I don't know."

"You're certainly not the first and won't be the last young person to deal with this. She's probably just as confused as you are. Don't put up a front, acting like you've got it all together. You don't have to be strong for her. Both of you are young and have a lot of time to sort all of this out. Talk to her about it, it'll be easier if you do even though it might not seem like it now." he said as if speaking from experience. Imagine that, some adults might actually get it.

"That makes sense. We'll see, I'll let you know. By the way, did you hear about the Halloween prank someone pulled at the school?"

"Yeah, I heard about it. Looks like some kids pulling a prank. What about it?" he asked.

"Yeah, OK… that's the official line. I heard the whole story, and it wasn't a prank. I don't think drawing stuff on the lawn and a group of people dancing around a bonfire is a simple prank." I stated, staring him in the eyes.

"So… OK… that's not what I was told. I was told it was just some defacing of property." the expression on his face was deadly serious.

"Property was defaced by scorching the lawn with the bonfire they built." my expression matched his now. "We think someone was doing this because of our faith."

"I don't think you're wrong there, and I think the school administration thinks so too or they would have told the whole story. They don't want to alarm anyone." He was looking up at the ceiling now as if deep in thought. "This isn't the only time something like this has happened at a Christian school."

"It isn't?" my eyes begged for more information.

"Tell you what, let me make some calls and we'll talk about this some more." he was still looking elsewhere with a look of concern on his face. "For now, though, let's just keep this between us, OK?"

"OK… who'd have thought going to school could be so… interesting?" I joked.

That following week seemed to go by faster than expected, same number of hours but somehow it felt as though there were less hours in those five days. The impact of my preoccupation was noticed by more than a few that week. I fended off questions of illness and the ever reliably ambiguous, "Is something wrong? You can talk to me…" from well-meaning *Mysfits*. Either way something *was* wrong or at least if felt that way; I just couldn't figure it out.

That Saturday Wales, Gene, and I arranged to hang out at the Golden Ring Mall. Just us men as it were. We did all the obligatory things before taking in a movie – arcade, walk a lap of the mall taking in the sights, people-watching, talking about the week. About half an hour before the movie, Wales turned to us and told us to wait by the water fountain while he got the tickets. We gave him the money and he melted into the crowd. Gene and I sat on the fountain's ledge. As this was about 2:00, the sunlight was beaming through the skylight in just the right way for it to shimmer not only on the water but on the minor treasure trove of loose change which lined the bottom of the fountain. A little kid on the far side, trying to entertain himself while his mother talked with a friend, was dipping his hand into the water to claim a bit of the treasure. To his displeasure, which was more than evident on his face, his arms were too short. He whined a bit when his mother shut down his little expedition.

"You ever wonder why there's a water fountain in every mall?" I asked.

"No." Gene replied, giving me the inquisitive side-eye.

"Think about it, every mall has one and it seems the newer the mall the bigger the fountain." Whether this was true or not, I didn't know but I was trying to rest in the distraction of the thought.

"I guess so, White Marsh, Hunt Valley, heck, even Towson. I don't know, maybe for malls it's like having a living room in a house. Every house has to have one, even if you don't use it."

I pondered his idea for a moment and was interrupted.

Gene cut in, "Look man, I've sat back for a whole week and didn't get on you for whatever it is that's got you... I don't know... 'not right'. I think I've been real patient but that ends today. After this movie, when we eat, you're gonna spill. OK?"

"I sorta guess that's why I wanted to hang out with you guys today." I said, hoping it would make him stop.

Just then, as if on cue, Wales came back with the tickets. We were going to see *A Nightmare on Elm Street 2: Freddy's Revenge*". To this day I still don't know how thirteen-year-old Wales could come up with R-rated tickets whenever we needed them. We'd ask and he would say something about sausage being made and play it off. A few of us reasoned that he had a family member at Golden Ring or something but we realized that it didn't matter what theater we chose, he always came through. Every time it was almost surreal, unescorted children handing in tickets for R-rated movies only to have the attendant accept them and direct us to the right theater.

After the movie, a sequel that, wait for it… surprise, didn't live up to the first movie, we made our way to the pizza place.

Not ten seconds after we sat down my gaze was met with a determined stare from Gene and one word, "SPILL!"

Wales figured it out pretty quick and fell in line with Gene, "Uh… yeah, Spill!" he said.

I opened the tennis match with, "So… I suppose you guessed it… Meghan."

"Obviously." Wales blurted in an "oh come on" voice.

"Whatever it is, it's got you down so what is it?" Gene said with actual concern in his voice.

"When we talk, well, it's just so easy. We can talk for hours without thinking about it."

"So… that's a *good* thing, right?" Wales asked quizzically.

"Yes, that's a good thing. But that's just it, everything is good but I feel like something is holding me back… Keeping me from getting any more attached than I already am. I just can't put my finger on it."

"So, like a feeling on the inside – something weird you think you know but can't possibly know?" asked Gene, concerned voice and all.

"Yeah, that's probably the best way to put it."

"You know this has happened to you before."

"When, Gene, when has this happened before? When have I been in this kind of friendship with a girl?"

"Not a girl thing but isn't this kind of like the time on the field with the *Country Boys*"?

"I never thought of it that way. But that was WAY stronger than this."

"How strong or weak does it have to be to be true? I've been thinking a lot about that experience of yours, I don't know why so don't ask, but I think... well, maybe not."

"Say it, I may need to hear it."

"God was, for lack of a better word, 'loud' on the field. I think maybe because that was urgent. This isn't urgent, yet, so maybe He's not as loud."

Silence.

"Pardon me, but just what the heck are you guys talking about?" Wales interjected incredulously.

Over the next few minutes I shared the "upper-field" story with Wales. I thought he'd be hurt somehow that I didn't tell him until now but he seemed to get why I hadn't. He was rather speechless but for the infrequent syllables he managed to press through his lips.

"Yeah, it's like that." I said alluding to the fact that such experiences were not exactly the norm. I continued, "One day when we're all together, I'll share this stuff with everyone but for now, I'd appreciate it if you would keep it under your hat."

"Sure, buddy, you got it." Wales responded, obviously still processing.

"So you see, what Gene was saying was that maybe this is like that and God is telling me something... something like, 'you shouldn't be here.'"

"I get it, I really do and your problem is that you really want that friendship."

"Yeah, Wales, that's the honest truth." I admitted.

"Maybe you should give it some more time. Have you talked about this with Meghan?" Gene asked in a tone suggesting action more than anything.

"That's part of the problem, I just don't know how to bring it up with her."

Wales offered, "Well… maybe that's the problem. I mean, you've got this big part of you that you don't think you can share, of course you feel funny about it. Maybe you should try."

The three of us sat in silence for a minute while we considered this simple and rather obvious suggestion. I broke the silence.

"I just don't know. Out of all the ways we work well together, I don't know where she stands spiritually. From some of the things she'd said, I can't be too sure."

"I'm with Wales. This is the biggest part of you, your faith – I mean, you're getting confirmed in the Spring. How can you *not* talk about it. This yo problem right here man. You need to stop being a <expletive> and step to the plate. If you care about her, you will."

"Gene's right." Wales said. "You owe it to her to be honest about your feelings."

I knew they were right but for some reason that didn't make it any easier. I wound up agreeing with them that I would bring it up at the next best opportunity and, I guessed, see what would happen.

We rounded out our time together in the arcade before being picked up.

I had a problem you see, I wanted to find a way to slyly get Meghan to open up about her relationship with God but I knew that she was too smart for that. She would just come right out and ask me why I was trying to manipulate her. I knew the only thing to do was what Gene told me to do, man up. The next time we really got a chance to have a real conversation was the following Wednesday night. She and her mother had been away for the weekend, taking advantage of the fact that we were off for Veteran's Day.

"Phil, I've been looking forward to talking to you since we got back."

"I've been looking forward to talking to you too." I lied. "How were things in Jersey?"

"Pretty boring. It was basically a trip for Mother. She caught up with old friends and stuff. We got a chance to go to our Church though so seeing people there is always good."

"Yeah, so, about that. We've never really talked about faith and all."

"No… I suppose we haven't."

She was waiting for something, I could tell.

"What denomination are you and what kind of church do you go to up there?"

"OK…" she chuckled, "I wouldn't be going to a Christian school if I didn't believe. Mother wouldn't have sent me there if she didn't. We do believe some things that aren't taught at school or in its denomination. You know, kind like the way Pentecostals are different."

"OK…" I took a moment to consider this and remembered that even Pastor Summerstone thought the denomination's beliefs were a bit limiting. I took another moment, wondering if I felt better. Not sure, I decided to give it some time. "Cool." I said.

We went on to discuss the weekend, the time I spent with the guys and all. I couldn't shake the feeling that we would revisit the subject at some point.

I would later learn as an adult that if you don't pay attention, time has a way of sneaking past you. As a teenager I knew no such thing. Before I knew it, it was the day before Thanksgiving. That's what happens when you fall into routine and fail to appreciate each day for its own uniqueness – a lesson I learned much later. Anyway, It was just before last period and the halls at school were abuzz with the anticipation of being off for the next couple of days. The common goodwill was palpable and then it wasn't. The *Country Boys* were clustered near Jake's locker. One of them caught me looking over there and alerted the other three. The other heads turned and Jake mouthed something I'd rather not mention here, but I'm sure you get the picture. All of this would be bearable except for the fact that just then

Megahn rounded the corner, looking fine as ever I might add, and beamed when she saw me. The only problem was that the *Country Boys* saw it too and just could not help themselves. By this time Jake knew that he had to stay behind the scenes for this stuff or he would get into real trouble so he had one of them run up to Meghan and whisper something in her ear. He lingered there behind her with a demonic grin. She had to be twenty feet from me when this happened and I couldn't hear what was said but her face said it all. Her face went from her signature megawatt smile to that look she had after her encounter with Dominique to some kind of angry determination as her fists curled. She dropped her books, wheeled around and decked Terry Elsmore so hard it sounded like a slap. Life in the hallway stopped. He went down and scrambled to get back up. Just then Gene flew from behind me (I didn't even know he was around) and jumped in front of Meghan who was now wringing her right hand in pain. I just stood there like the proverbial deer and watched all of this unfold.

"What's up now!" Gene yelled as he spread his arms as if he'd been the one who'd hit Terry.

The *Country Boys*, as stunned as I was, started towards them. I noticed my feet were moving too. Just then, Mr. Finnegan came around the corner and sensed the tense situation. Looking at Terry and Gene who were in a standoff he said, "What's going on here?"

"Nothing Mr. Finnegan." they both said in unison and the situation began to slowly unwind. Life began to creep back to normal like when a thunderclap silences a bustling forest and the animals fall silent only to meekly begin to make noise again after a few seconds.

When I got to Meghan, she put her arms around me and said nothing.

"That was an impressive punch." Gene said to the back of her head.

"Yeah, that was something." I added.

She let me go and looked at Gene, "Thank you for jumping in."

"We protect our own..." he said as he walked away.

I could tell Meghan was touched by this. She just stood there watching him leave with a blank stare.

"I'm sorry I didn't jump in like Gene did, I was shocked."

"That's OK, trust me, I know violence isn't your first thought. I like that."

"How's your hand?"

"Nothing a little ice won't cure when I get home, my punch landed wrong. I've got to get to class, hey call me tonight, I wanna ask you something."

"Sure..."

I was stunned a bit that she could go back to normal so quickly after something like that.

That night, as promised, I called Meghan on my good ol' safe computer line. I was still beating myself up for not being the one to throw myself into harm's way to protect her. I was sure Gene and I would discuss that in the near future, oh boy!

"Hi Phil, sorry to run off like that but I had to get to last period."

"No problem, look, I want to apologize for..."

"No, you don't have to apologize for anything." she interrupted. "It's like I said, I know its not your thing and that's fine."

"But..."

"Drop it. We're good!"

"Are you sure?"

"Couldn't be more."

"OK, then. What did Terry say to you anyway?"

"He referred to you in a way that disgusted me and implied how I felt about you. Listen Phil, Dominique Jeffers got away with that because she caught me by surprise and I didn't know how to deal with it, but that was then. I won't give anyone the power to make me feel that way again."

"Good..." I commented.

Just then the house line rang.

"Do you need to get that?" she asked.

"No... Someone else will get it."

"Listen, I wanted to ask..." she started.

Her voice was sounding a lot less confident as she continued so I knew this was going to be a doozy.

"I wanted to ask if Mother and I could come over tomorrow for dinner. We have no where to go tomorrow and I thought..."

"Of course." My turn to interrupt.

"Don't you have to ask?"

"I'm sure it will be fine. Come over about four."

"OK. Great! I have to do something with Mother now but I look forward to seeing you then!"

"So do I."

So, I uh... didn't fully understand the gravity of what I'd just done. I looked up at my bedroom ceiling and asked God to make it OK. I called Gene and told him what happened. He laughed and laughed before telling me...

"Yo! My mom just got off the phone with yours... Guess who's coming to dinner too!"

"Oh... My..."

"Yup son! I'll be your chaperon for the evening." he said between chuckles. "We need to talk about you stepping up, or not, anyway."

"Are you serious?" I asked, knowing it was going to happen.

"Yeah man. Look, you had a date for the dance, big step forward there by the way, now we have something else to work on."

"Great..." I said flatly.

"Dinners at five so lemme guess, you told Meghan to be there at four. That means I'll try to get mom to get us there by 3:30; you know, so we have some time to prepare."

"Shut up, Sherlock!"

THAT ONE THANKSGIVING:

All my life Thanksgiving mornings were a time of lounging and anticipation of what was usually the year's best meal. A day of computer games, television, and reconnecting with my brother, Preston. However, because I was expecting company and my family was "so excited to meet Meghan", I had nothing but anxiety. I got up early and was fidgety. I stumbled through a few games on my computer at 5:30 that morning only to find no relief. I tried sleep... no joy there either. Giving up, I simply resigned myself to what I believed would be a day I looked forward to looking back on.

The clock wound its way to 3:30 as slowly as possible so as to milk my anxiety for all it was worth as if it were nourishing itself and savoring every drop. The doorbell rang. I heard mom open the door and exchange pleasantries with Gene's mother. I soon heard feet beating their way up the steps and my door flung open.

"Honey, I'm home!" you know who said in a terrible Ricky Ricardo accent.

"Shut. Up." I said, annoyed.

Gene sat on the corner of my bed while I sat at my computer trying, and failing, to distract myself from being anxious. I put down the controller and shut the system down. I spun around in the chair to find Gene with that contemplative pre-lecture look on his face.

"Look man, we don't have that much time before they get here. I just wanted to say that I didn't mean to make you look weak or anything by standing up for your girl. When stuff like that happens, I run on instinct.

"I didn't think that. Don't worry about it."

"You *do* need to stand up for her in times like that though. I mean, what would've happened if I wasn't there and Finnegan didn't show up?"

"I… I don't know." I said, taking his logic seriously now. He had a point and I couldn't deny it. "I guess I would've jumped in. I was going to when I saw you and Terry square off."

"Yeah, but that would've been too late. Terry might have done something by then." he replied, arms crossed.

"When you're right, you're right. What can I say? One thing, though. Please don't bring this up tonight. She said she's good with what happened and that it was over."

"OK, I won't bring it up if she doesn't, fair enough?"

"I guess that'll have to do."

We talked some more about random stuff. I was just trying to pass the time as easily as possible and then came the doorbell.

Gene clapped his hands together and said, "Let the fun begin!"

I took a deep breath. "Just give me a minute, OK?" I took a minute, like a real minute then headed for downstairs.

Gene and I came downstairs to find all the parents sitting in the living room getting to know each other. Preston had already begun to ~~interro-gate~~ "get to know" Meghan while interested adults in the room did a poor job covering the fact that they were eavesdropping. I came along side of Meghan, who was surprised to see Gene, and asked the group if the three of us could be excused.

"Actually, is there anything I can do to help set up for dinner?" Meghan asked, making me look bad.

The next hour or so was full of place settings, trivets, napkins, and all the fun stuff I came to love about large dinners – not. The three of us made the most fun of it that we could. Meghan was kind enough to volunteer us for cleanup duty afterwards, to my brother's delight, during which we had a really good time making fun of each other.

After the whole affair, which I must say included one of the best meals I'd ever had, the three of us retired to the basement. With all the people and that oven running all day, the basement was a much more comfortable place to be. It was good that Gene was there because the three of us going down there was likely more palatable to some adults than just Meghan and myself. We could hear the laughter of a bunch of adults that seemed to hit it off mysteriously well. Meghan's mother was once again in social, not creepy, mode and that in and of itself creeped me out. I was glad nonetheless.

The basement had a couch, a couple of lazy-boy chairs, and a television not to mention a ping-pong table. The previous owners built an L-shaped bar in the basement with an orange top and a massive mirror on the wall behind it. I always thought it was so cool. For some reason, my father's exercise mat was still on the floor, a thick blue awkward pad.

"Thanks for having us, it was a lot of fun. Mother and I couldn't have hoped to have had a better time today."

"Don't mention it, you actually made my day. I was sure they were going to ask all kinds of awkward questions and those they did ask you handled like a pro." I never really filled everybody in on what happened the night of the dance and they were trying to get details out of the three of us.

"My mom's been trying to do the same thing. I try to blow it off the best I can." Gene added.

"You guys are too funny, I told Mother everything." she said, then she looked me in the eyes, "just about everything, anyway."

"So, we all held back, and we should have. It's not like we did anything wrong and they might not have even believed the whole downtown thing." Gene reasoned, defending his choice to be tight-lipped.

"Say, Gene, thanks again for yesterday. What you said meant a lot to me." she stated.

"Oh, the thing about protecting our own? Sure… It's true though." he said.

"I'm just glad he didn't do anything stupid - like hit you." I interjected.

"Yeah…" she said with a distant look, "If not for Gene and Finnegan he might have tried, and I would've destroyed him." She gave a quick shrug of the shoulders and began to look around the room.

"'Destroyed? Yeah." I said with a bit of a chuckle and glanced at Gene who had a kind of "yeah, right" polite smile on his face.

"What?" she asked, looking back and forth between us.

"It's just that… you know… 'destroyed'? Is that how it would've gone?" I sheepishly asked so as not to offend.

"Well, pretty sure. My dad, well, before he…" she caught my eyes, "When I was younger, he had me in Krav Maga training. They had a kid's program."

"Krav Ma-what?" I asked

"You have got to be <expletive> me!" Gene exclaimed, staring at her?

With the most robotic movement and dead-panned face but for a few blinks she looked at Gene and said, "Oh… I <expletive> you not."

"OK, what is it?" I asked.

The show-off, Gene, answered for her, "Krav Maga is the martial art used by Israeli Special Forces. I know because I read all those martial arts magazines." Gene was into that stuff, almost obsessively so.

"Yup, that's It. I still work out when I get the chance. Close your mouth Ph-, Joe" she said with confidence.

I shot her that "you almost messed up and you know it look" she retorted with the "you got me there look".

"OK." she said taking off her shoes and stepping onto the exercise mat that seemed to have been there just for this occasion. "Throw a punch, Joe."

"I uh… I can't do that."

"If I thought I was in any danger, I wouldn't ask."

"Still, um… no."

"I will." Gene said coming forward like he was stepping up to the plate.

"Sorry Gene, I'm pretty sure I can win Joe's forgiveness faster than yours if I hurt somebody."

"Um... no." all I could say.

She walked over and led me to the mat by the hand and said, "It's OK… It's all part of getting to know me."

I stepped onto the mat and took a deep breath.

"Like you mean it!" she said, forcefully.

I drew back my fist and, doing what was probably not wise but bowing to the pressure of being wrapped around a girl's little finger, fired with all my might, right for her nose. What happened next happened so fast I can only remember it in flashes. I felt my arm get hit. I felt several fast strikes to my torso. I felt a strong tug in my armpit. I felt something hit the entire back side of my body and then I saw the ceiling… from the floor.

"What happened!" I exclaimed. Amid the laughter I heard from Meghan I looked over at Gene who had both fists covering his mouth and a most incredulous face as if to say, "Yikes".

"Everything OK down there?" somebody called, I don't even know who.

"Yes" we said in sing-songy unison.

"I should probably teach you some stuff… it'd be a bonding experience."

Getting up I just nodded my head in the affirmative.

"You alright?" she asked, rubbing it in with a smile when she knew I was. She continued, "I don't fight but I will if I have to... and I will win."

"<expletive>" from Gene

"Yes, ma'am!" I responded.

Gene was just shaking his head.

We went back upstairs and mingled with everybody because we'd been away for a while. When it was time for them to go, I walked Gene and his mother along with Meghan and hers to the porch. At one point while everyone was walking to their respective cars, Meghan and I were out of their earshot.

"You are without a doubt one of the most interesting people I've ever met. Goodnight Siobhan, my mysterious girl."

"Oh... is that what I am? Your *girl*?" she said coyly

"I... I um..." I stuttered.

"It's alright, if I'm not your girl, I don't know what I am. Goodnight. Call me tomorrow." she said dismissively as she walked away with a grin.

Why is it that women get to drop bombs like that as they walk away? If a guy were to do that the girl would be all, "What do you mean?" and, "We need to talk."

Later that night I got to express all of these things to my journal. My journal just looked back at me as if to shake its head and say, "I can't believe any of this. You live in a world where your girl and your best friend can protect you better than you can." My ego *was* bruised, I must admit, but probably in the best of ways. My ego was bruised while being impressed by Meghan. All in all, I thought it was pretty cool. Yeah, it was pretty exciting and then I started to really think about it. Why is it that I can't shake the feeling that there's a lot more that I don't know than I do? "This is true of just about anybody at the beginning of a relationship." I said to myself, "So she can fight, a lot of people can..." No. it was something else, something I picked up that I can't put into words. Something was there, lurking in the shadows and I only had my sense of foreboding to prove it. "Sooner or later..." I said, "Sooner or later I'll find out why I get so weirded out."

When Monday morning found me, I was lost in dreamland. This is the dream that still creeps me out when I think of it. All of us *Mysfits* were together in a park or somewhere. The sun was shining and we were all laughing, probably at each other. I looked around and saw everyone there but for some reason I knew someone was missing. For some reason, I was really worried about this – like my life depended on it. I tried to get everyone, anyone to tell me who was missing. Everyone just kept laughing. Just then the sound of the alarm came piercing through what I thought was reality with all of the force of the sound effect in that Hitchcock shower scene. Startled, I sat bolt upright wide-eyed and breathing heavily.

THAT ONE DECEMBER:

Even though it was the first week of December now, the gray days of Winter had already begun to be the norm. Walking through the halls with Wales that Monday morning we found the atmosphere to be saturated with winter-break fever. There was just a prevailing wind of nonchalance – sort of an adolescent scent that wafted through the halls like the funk of the boys locker room after a shower. Even though I told Wales on the phone over the weekend about all that happened Thanksgiving he had me retell the story on the bus. He took particular interest (and humor) in how Meghan kicked my behind. That was our mindset as we passed through the crowd of kids that were most obviously faking their interest in doing the school thing that day. Well, all but Leigh whose locker we were approaching. She was apparently in a good mood seeing as how she took the fedora off Wales' head and positioned it on her head in that cock to one side way that only women can do well.

"You best be glad I like you." Wales said with a warning finger that only made Leigh smile.

"Morning Joe!" she said with a giggle. For as long as I'd known her, she'd gotten a kick out of the whole "Morning Joe" / coffee play on words. She'd run that into the ground long ago. I was only amused that she was still amused.

"Morning Leigh." I said flatly.

"Did Tommy tell you about New Year's?" she asked with a smile. Leigh was the only person to refer to Wales as "Tommy". Other than a few select teachers, everybody called him "Wales" or "Mr. Wales".

"No..." Wales cut in, "I didn't get a chance. We were all about Thanksgiving on the bus."

"No, *you* were all about that on the bus." I clarified.

"Well, that *is* an interesting story, Joe. Can't wait 'til lunch." she added.

"So sure..." I said.

"Anyways… I was thinking we need to have a New Year's Eve party. You know, just us *Mysfits* and 'friends." Wales added with Groucho Marx expressive eyebrow raising.

Having already been down this path and learning that you can't fight this crowd on such things I agreed, "Sure… let's."

Right then I felt a hand pull on my shoulder turning me around. When I turned, I saw a fist headed for my face. I was truly startled for all of a half-second before I realized the fist belonged to Meghan.

"Oh, you're funny." I said with all the humor of a flat tire. Wales and Leigh thought differently, they laughed before greeting her. I felt really good about the way they both accepted her. There was something about the way she smiled and looked back at me that made me feel great.

"Did I scare you?" she said in her most condescending voice.

"Of course not." I lied as I took her into my arms.

"Am I still your girl?" she sheepishly whispered in my ear, teasing me while hugging.

"Of course." I whispered back.

"I'm so glad." she said as we parted for our respective classes.

Wales laid out the party plan at lunchtime like a general conspiring with his commanders before a battle. We all crowded Wales' end of the table with our chairs while we tried to eat. This odd configuration drew looks from around the cafeteria but we didn't care. I shot Meghan a smile at one point when she gave me furled eyebrow look from across the room that asked, "What's going on?" By the end of lunch, we'd locked everything down except for the venue.

The end of the day came with all the slowness of watching a clock do its thing. When the day finally ended, I got a chance to brief Meghan who promptly told me to give her a call that night because she had an idea, whatever that meant. When I told Wales about this, he was as curious as I was and of course, sages that we were, decided to try to figure out whatever it was she could have been thinking. The two of us on that bus ride home philosophizing as the sun was going down like we did so many days before. It's funny looking back on it all, how much we thought we could figure everything out - solve the world's problems, so to speak, in the space of a bus ride. It doesn't matter if that's naiveté or wisdom, it was the confidence of youth in full bloom.

As I climbed the steps to my room, I was excited to have another event to enjoy with my friends. Before I knew it, I was in my journal contemplating how different my middle school experience had been from my expectations because of my friends. I thought about the fact that this is exactly why we were friends. We somehow realized that we needed each other's support. If it had not been for them, I guess I would be some kind of loner and, knowing me, telling myself that I loved it. I was genuinely excited for the future and the fact that we had something truly special wasn't lost on me.

That night my curiosity was sated with a two-hour phone call. We talked about a lot of things, the highlights of which went something like this.

"So, what idea did you have about the party?"

"I had to check with Mother first and she thinks it's a great idea. We'll have the party here at my house."

"Really? That's great!" I responded. Little did I know at the time that this set off a string of phone calls between the parents of the *Mysfits* that turned this little friendly affair into an adult party to which children could come.

"I'll pass that along to Wales; he'll be happy to have that off his plate." I added.

"So, you guys do stuff like this a lot huh?" she asked.

"Yeah, we have an annual cookout in August, you know, before school starts. We do other stuff too when we can. We're pretty close, but you know that." I replied.

"I know. I really do. I guess I was just thinking out loud."

"Don't you, Saundra, and the rest of your friends hang out?" I questioned.

"Not so much. You'd probably be surprised. It's more like a business relationship. Our parents all know each other and stuff..."

The way that sentence trailed off left me feeling like she didn't want to say as much as she did. I didn't know what to make of that and I didn't want to push so I let it go.

"So um, I've been thinking about Thanksgiving, are there other things I should know about you?" I asked, feeling weird because this was out of the blue.

"Yes." she answered matter-of-factly.

"Siobhan... I'm serious." I said affectionately

"I'm serious too, Phil. I've been through some things that will come out as we go. I think that's best." She said that with an air of apology in her voice that sounded so sincere that I wasn't even curious anymore.

She added, "Can you trust me?"

"Yeah... I can."

Later that week we learned that us *Mysfits* and respective parents will be joined by Meghan's weird group of friends and their parents. "Oh, Joy..." I thought as a picture of that evening started to coalesce in my mind. It's not like they ever said or did anything that made me *not* like them, they just put off a weird vibe... Meghan most of all but, of course, that was kind of covered by different feelings. The *Mysfits* together with Saundra Wallace, Olympia Dupree, Destiny Daniels, Ivanah Dvorak and Meghan will be a weird mix. "Maybe it'll work out." I hoped. No sooner than that sprout of hope started to take root I closed my locker and was interrupted by Wales with something I was embarrassed to say I hadn't considered.

"Hey Joe..." He had sort of a haggard look on his face.

"Are you... OK?" I asked.

"Yeah, I was gonna do this thing for Leigh you know, for Christmas, and I just found out it's not gonna work out." He plopped against my locker with disappointment written all over his face.

"What do you mean you 'just found out'? It's the middle of a school day!" I said incredulously, I mean this was 1985 – not like we had cell phones or anything. I came to find out years later that Wales took calls in the school's office like it was his own – the secretary took messages for him and everything. Anyway, he muttered something about a horse and carriage dismissively, sobered up, looked me in the face and asked, "So what are you doing for Meghan?" There it was, the weight of a responsibility I didn't really know I had and I had two weeks to the day to pull off something I didn't know how to do.

"I can tell by the slack-jawed deer in the headlights look on your face that you haven't even thought about it." he said disapprovingly. "At least this is an easy one..."

"What... what do you mean 'easy'?" I hated the fact that this stuff came easily for seemingly everyone else but me.

"Look, she's always saying stuff about how you guys work well together, right?"

"Yeah, so..."

"Just get her something that says that and you'll be fine. Trust me." That was the other thing, it seemed like everybody wanted me to *trust* them.

"OK, sure. Easy. If you say so."

So now *that* was my thing to obsess about while I tried to navigate everything else.

The Friday before Christmas everybody seemed to have caught the "spirit" but me. So, as I was humbugging my way through the day, I learned that this season was not to be complete without lumps of coal from the *Country Boys...* joy. Gym class was in full swing, we were playing this weird indoor game that was like soccer played with a dodge-ball. The difference was that you had to use your hands, you couldn't kick the ball or move if you had it. If you had the ball, you could only pass it. Everything else was basically the same. Of course, being such a physical game, opportunities existed for violence under the guise of the game. I had to duck and spin out the way of Al Stonebridge's and Terry Elsmore's attempts at decapitation with the ball. Jake, however, got in a rather nasty body-check. Yeah, it hurt, but I wasn't gonna let that show and give him the satisfaction. The hit wasn't the bad thing it was what he said while we were both on the floor. You see, with them it's the same stuff over and over again, you kind of build up an immunity against it all. He left no doubt about what Terry said to Meghan only this time it didn't end with a punch, it ended with the two of us staring each other down and me simply saying, "Yeah, whatever..." and walking away. Something Meghan said about not giving anyone the power to make you feel a certain way made sense all of the sudden. Normally I would have cast the incident onto the internal bonfire that I used to deal with such things but this was easier somehow. As I walked away, I let him know that it was nice to know that he still cared.

Christmas morning was here and, as usual, I had the task of distributing the gifts to the family from under the tree. After I was done, there was one gift left, Meghan's. We knew she and her mother were not going to be in town that day so we agreed to meet up afterwards. No sooner than I took my eyes off the festively wrapped package under the tree, the doorbell rang. Venturing through the living room festooned with seasonal decorations and discarded wrapping paper I got to the door thinking an uncle or cousin decided to come over early. It's hard to describe the butterfly ridden shock I felt as I found myself face to face with "my girl" through the glass of the storm door. She and her mother were standing there on the porch, a surreal scene given I had no forewarning. I opened the door and we embraced without saying a word. Her mother chuckled as she made her way past us upon my parents' invitation.

"Hi." Sometimes simple words are best. We found ourselves in the living room alone where I dug her gift out from under the tree and she mine from a bag she held. As she began to unwrap the box, I began to explain it in that way people do when they want someone to like something. She was finally holding it in her hand, a turquoise geode. I'd learned during one of our conversations that turquoise was her favorite color. I told her it reminded me of her because there was so much beauty and mystery on the inside that only true friends would see. She stared at it for an uncomfortable amount of time, so much so that I began to feel that she didn't like it. Then she looked at me without saying a word and a single tear fell from her left eye. She put out her palm on which sat a small wrapped box. She had the most tender look on her face as I took it slowly. Unwrapping the box and opening it, I found that she remembered my favorite color was the golden-hour color of sunsets. I pulled out the burnt-orangish colored geode pendant on a leather necklace and sat there, stunned. We sat in silence for what felt like too long before I said, "Um… wow."

"Yeah… wow." she whispered.

I asked, "How could we have possibly…"

She answered, "We think so much alike it's just crazy!"

Her mother came in, took one look and what we each had and jerked her head back with a quizzical expression. She and Meghan exchanged looks that meant something to each other and began to laugh. I joined in just to be funny.

OK so *that* wasn't awkward at all. They had to get on the road so they wound up leaving about ten minutes later.

Being off from school for the next several days was a good – scratch that – a bad thing because it gave me time to think through all of this stuff. I was weirded out because we gave each other geodes and I would have to wait a few days before we could talk about it. On top of that, I had to look forward to the New Year's party… at her house no less. Anyway, that week was, surprise surprise, spent in my journal, in front of my computer, and enduring Gene's lectures on whatever it meant for someone that age to be a man… whatever. Don't get me wrong, he had some good points but it was getting old and I didn't want to be remade in the image of Gene Tucker – no offense.

THAT ONE NEW YEAR'S:

New Year's Eve fell on a Tuesday that year and it couldn't have come fast enough though at the same time it came too fast. I both wanted that night and didn't at the same time. My thoughts and feelings were going north, south, east, and west at the same time. If Gene were there, he'd probably have slapped me for being emotional and not taking charge, "owning" my situation as it were. Whatever it was, I had a couple of hours to deal with the fact that I wasn't going to work it out anytime soon. Meghan I could handle, her mother, her weird crew, and coach Gene all at the same time… not so much.

This thing kicked off at nine o'clock, my parents and I were there a few minutes early. Once again the walk up the driveway seemed to get longer the more I walked as if to prolong the agony of anticipation. It being really cold that night didn't help at all. The door opened and we were greeted by… Wales. How that happened I didn't know but I was grateful. As soon as I pulled off my coat to reveal my dorky shirt and tie, Wales pulled me aside in another room and loosened my tie in just the right way to make it look cool and unbuttoned my top button. He muttered something like "hopeless" and "never learn" as he walked away. I looked myself over in the mirror on the wall before joining everyone in the, I guess, living room or whatever that room was called. Quickly noticing there were no kids in the room, I knew I was out of place. I felt someone take my hand from behind and I turned to find Meghan, beaming her smile at me. I took a second before taking her up in my arms. We heard her mother and some others chuckle while we hugged.

"Oh good grief…" she whispered. "Let's get out of here."

I took a moment to admire the black dress with silver highlights… so choice!

She led me to the… the… I don't even know what you call a room like that. Whatever it was, it was where all of us kids were. Gene and Wes had yet to arrive.

The room was divided between the *Mysfits* and Meghan's friends, including the always beautiful Saundra. I found it interesting that I had no interest in Saundra at all. Only Meghan and I were standing together.

"Well, this seems right. It's not like they hang out with each other at school why should they now?" I said.

"I don't like it." Meghan had that look on her face as though she were thinking through the defense to some attack in a game of chess. "I know what to do, wait here." she said as she bounded up a staircase I didn't even realize was there. As I waited, Wales sidled up to me.

"Not what I had in mind." he said discretely.

"Me neither but Meghan has a plan, trust her."

Meghan came back down the steps with some cassette tapes in her hands. She held them out to me as if to say, "this is the answer" and walked over to a stereo system enclosed in a rather unassuming cabinet. Moments later the room was filled with music from what would turn out to be a mix tape of classics from the late seventies and early eighties. The Pointer Sister's "Slow Hand" was playing softly in the room as Meghan spoke up, "Everyone find somebody to dance with." This was met with a bit of hesitation.

"Please..." she said, looking at her crew, with a tone I wasn't sure I'd heard before.

Whatever it was, it did the trick. They walked over and one of them started dancing with Bruce. It was about that time when Gene and Wes walked in, they'd apparently rode together. Gene, without knowing what was going on, walked right into Saundra's waiting hands and began to dance. It was like it was choreographed. Of course, I danced with Meghan. Before too long she and I were doing what we liked to do best, sit on the side and watch people. We played the game where we tried to guess what someone was thinking...

"Okay, your turn. Gene, what's he thinking?" she asked.

Gene was still dancing with Saundra with no end in sight.

"Oh, something like... 'Wow, I must be the man, Saundra came to me!'" I said.

We laughed and just enjoyed each other's company. We laughed even harder when Lipps Inc's "Funky Town" played and people obviously didn't know how to dance to it. Everybody was having a really good time and I actually felt bad that I thought it wouldn't go well.

"Who are your favorite bands?" I asked not believing I hadn't asked this before.

Shalamar's "A Night to Remember" started to play.

"Well, Shalamar is one of them..." she said gesturing to the music playing, "...but there's Fleetwood Mac, but only because of Stevie Nicks, Parliament is fun, Pat Benatar – I love her. That's about it off the top of my head. What about you?"

"Well I..." I started, interrupted by her mother wheeling in a cake on a cart.

"Everybody get some cake and sparkling cider." her mother instructed as she pointed out that it was ten to midnight.

The adults joined us in the "whatever" room for the eventual count-down. Soon The Police's "Every Breath You Take" played as Meghan and I just sat there in each other's arms watching her night unfold. Finally the room started to chant the countdown from ten as midnight approached. When 1986 was born, parents kissed each other, Wales kissed Leigh, and Meghan and I stared into each other's eyes as though we held the world in our hands and knew that this new year would be *our* year somehow. What we shared in that moment was better than a kiss – besides we'd talked about it and knew we weren't ready for that. And so, with respect, adoration, and feelings that were getting to be bigger than me, we shared that most sincere moment and whispered, "Happy new year..."

CHAPTER 14:
"EVERY LITTLE THING SHE DOES IS MAGIC" – THE POLICE

For the rest of the Winter break, the first week of 1986, I was on cloud nine. I didn't know what that year held but the stark difference between that year and the previous was both frightening and exciting. Apparently, my light-heartedness was evident because while I was flying high that week I had to endure the constant ribbing of my family, "Did you talk to your *girlfriend* today?" and "Aww aren't you two just so cute!" "Good grief!" I would think, relating to how Charlie Brown would have felt at times like that. They liked Meghan well enough, actually they were quite impressed with her, but that didn't keep them from having their fun. Apparently, Meghan's mother was doing the same thing and she was just as embarrassed. However, she always seemed to have a matter-of-fact composure when it came to "us". As far as she was concerned, we were together and that was simply that.

"QUACK! QUACK! QUACK! QUACK!", that demented duck of an alarm clock screamed at 5:30 Monday morning and I was not happy. Determined to stay on vacation as long as I could, I'd somehow convinced Meghan to do the same so we stayed up late the night before watching TV together over the phone. We would change the channels, we only had four good ones, and catch bits and pieces of shows about which to comment in between whatever we were talking about. At the time the decision to stay up late sounded good, it wasn't – nope, bad idea. Like a zombie devoid of higher brain functions I performed my morning routine and only began to wake up standing in the brisk, no, butt-end of the earth cold air of the bus stop. I'd spent the majority of the break inside so the twenty-something degrees of that morning was, in a word, "uncomfortable". This was also the first I'd seen of Saundra since the party.

"Hey Joe..." Saundra called.

"She speaks!" is all I could think but what I actually said was, "Hey Saundra, what's up?"

"Cool party, huh?"

"Yeah, Meghan really worked it out." I said.

"That was the first time I'd really seen you two together. You really are good together. She told us that but seeing it was cool. You guys have really good energy. The two of you have such a beautiful aura." she complimented.

"Um... Thank you?" not knowing really what to say I continued, "You and Gene looked good on the dance floor."

"Gene, yeah, he's fun and all but not... I mean we don't like... blend... you know? Like you and Meghan." She seemed uneasy saying those things.

"OK, well I'm glad you had fun."

"I did, I think we all did." she stated.

Thankfully this awkward conversation was cut short by the arrival of the bus. Boarding the bus, I took a place somewhere in the middle. I'd reached some form of stable consciousness by the time Wales boarded. We'd talked briefly since the party but no real debriefing had taken place. I was prepared.

"So, why were you there so early?" I asked.

"Well, I wanted to get the lay of the land to see what I had to work with. I was pleasantly surprised; I mean I knew she lived in a nice house but wow – and just the two of them live there! Anyway, it was good that I was there because when you walked in it looked like your mom dressed you. I mean, no offense, but I did what I could." Wales had a smirk on his face as he let those words escape.

"Well, I appreciated it. I did look better after you got ahold of me." I said, begrudgingly.

He stretched and looked at me with kind of a "I might go too far with this question" face. "So um... Leigh and I were talking. You and Meghan look like you've known each other for years. I guess we saw it because it's like that for us. Is it *easy* for you like it is for us?"

"I don't know what it's really like for you but it is easy for us. I mean, man... we got each other basically the same gift for Christmas. It freaked us both out and her mom too. We get each other somehow... but... I don't know"

"But what? Does she still weird you out?"

"Yeah. I can't shake the feeling that something is waiting right around the corner or something. Maybe all of this is new for me and I just don't know how to feel so I make up stuff... I don't know."

"Maybe... I guess time will tell. So, uh... we noticed you didn't kiss her..."

I had to deal with Gene talking about this too so I was ready to speak to that observation, "That's right. We talked about that stuff a few months ago and agreed that kissing would only take our minds to places we don't want to go. We want to know each other and build on the fact that we just seem to 'fit' in ways we don't really understand. We didn't need words to say what we had to say."

"Aww... that's romantic"

Determined to shut down this conversation I took aim and let this go, "Wales, are you in love with Leigh?" I knew this would do the trick, and then this happened.

"Yes." he stated. I could tell he was sure about it.

"O...K... Um... Wow..."

"Yeah, I told her for the first time after we kissed. It had been there for a while now and I wanted her to know."

"What'd she say?"

"She said that she'd been waiting for me to get there, and she told me that she loved me too. Do you love Meghan?"

"Dude! Too soon!"

"It sure looked like it. That's all I'm saying."

The rest of the conversation consisted of the musings of the two teen-aged sages over the fact that we were both in seemingly solid relationships that neither of us wanted to ruin by doing something stupid. I thought to myself that if anyone was going to do something stupid it would probably be me because Wales is such a good planner and I couldn't even remember to get Meghan a gift for Christmas without prompting.

Walking through the halls we met up with Leigh who was getting a head start on the day, her enthusiasm should have been inspiring but it wasn't.

"Hi." she said as she swept Wales up in a hug. They embraced for a few seconds before she greeted me, "Good morning, Joe."

"Hi Leigh."

"Cool party, huh?" she asked.

"Sure was."

"So, um... Tommy and I were talking and we think you and..."

"Meghan go great together." I interrupted, "Wales told me."

Just then I was hugged from behind and I broke into an embar-rassingly sheepish smile. "Oh Joe, I'm so tired! Uhg! I though we said we wouldn't do this late phone call thing again!" Meghan said as she released me. I let her see my smile as I turned to look at her.

"Hey, you agreed..."

"I know... I know... and now I pay for it! Did I hear my name?"

"Uh, yeah... Leigh and Wales were saying that they think we're good together. They really liked the party, by the way."

"Thank you, I had a good time too." she said holding my hand and trying to stifle a yawn. "Joe and I have really strong energy and we're building on it." At this she bumped me and smiled coyly, "I've got to get to class, where I'll probably sleep." We hugged and she went off to class.

Bruce was late to lunch that day but when he did show he had a smile on his face and carried several manila envelopes. Without words he handed them to each of us except Leigh. We all looked at each other and then at the envelopes. Opening them we found copies of the pictures from October's dance two copies each of the pictures we took getting out of the limo and at the dance. "I thought we might want to share them with our dates." suggested Bruce. We all acknowledged this as a good idea and thanked him profusely.

"I pretty much forgot about these pictures!" Wes exclaimed.

"Yeah, I thought I'd just see them in the yearbook or something." Gene added.

"These are really good!" I said incredulously.

There we were, Meghan and me, well-dressed with the Ray-Bans. I reminisced on the night as I flipped to the picture of Meghan with her head on my chest as we slow-danced. This was the picture that made it into that year's yearbook. I thought about how everything changed since that night and how one night could make such a difference in someone's life. A lesson I would learn again in the future. I couldn't wait to give her a copy. I wondered if she'd frame and display the pictures like I was sure to do.

After last period, Meghan leaned back against her locker as she ran her hand over the first picture almost as though she could feel the texture of that captured moment through her fingertips. She then flipped to the second and let out a little gasp as she smiled and looked up at me. It's hard to describe how you can relive something through someone else's eyes, I was simply happy that she was happy.

"This was the moment." she almost whispered as she reviewed the picture once again.

"What moment?" I asked. A few seconds, which felt like minutes, passed.

"We'll have to talk about this later." she evaded, I thought, as she looked at her watch. I had to admit that it was late and I had to get to my bus as much as she had to meet her mom.

That night I got a phone call at like six o'clock. I was squarely in the middle of a good game of *Rescue Raiders* on my Apple 2e, high score and everything. Needless to say, I was annoyed by the disturbance until I realized the ring came from the "Bat-phone", that private phone on my computer line with the ringer set to low so I could take my calls privately.

"Hello?" I answered as if I didn't know who was calling me.

"Hi Phil, I know this is early but I have *got* to get some sleep tonight."

"Meghan, you know you liked staying up as much as I did."

"I did and I wish it didn't have such a price tag, because I want to talk some more but you know us, we'll look up and it'll be one-thirty or something."

"Yeah, you're right." I said, defeated.

"So, here's the thing..." she started. Now, I'd come to learn that whenever anybody started with this particular turn of phrase, it meant that something was about to happen that I was expected to take part in or I was plainly not going to like.

"OK..." I crept verbally, bracing myself.

"Mother would like you to come for dinner this weekend. She saw that I was so tired today and when she found out why she said she, 'had to really get the know the only person who can rob her daughter of her sleep', because she knows how much I like to sleep."

"Aww, that makes me feel good." I said in a teasing voice, toying with her.

"Whatever... so can you make it?"

"Gene and I have some much-needed hang time this Friday so is Saturday good?" I was already feeling awkward and had a sense of anxiety but I didn't want her to pick up on that.

"That would be perfect. I already told her about your food allergies, so don't worry about any of those."

Yeah, I've got food allergies, the kind that can be serious. This was another thing that I, as an awkward and often clueless teenager, had to deal with.

"Thank you, so Siobhan..." I'd come to enjoy using her special name every now and again because it kind of made a bond between us – exactly like she wanted. "What did you mean when you said..."

"You see, this is how you suck me in and I fall for it every time." she interrupted. "I've got about an hour of homework and then I sleep. I'm sorry but can we please talk about this another time?"

"Are you saying that I manipulate you?"

"No... It's like you know that I want you to understand... wait a minute, not funny!"

I laughed. "I get it... good night."

"Good night, Phil."

The rest of the week went by rather quickly. I've found this is often the case when you have some level of anxiety about an upcoming event, like Saturday's dinner. It had been arranged for me to go home with Gene on Friday after school so as to maximize our hang time. We ordered an extra-large "Baltimorioni pizza with a two-liter bottle of Coca-Cola (Classic, thank you very much - we'd abandoned the "New Coke").

"I've been thinking of a new word I learned, "Kavorka". Seeing my clueless blank stare he continued, "It has to do with a special magnetism that attracts the opposite sex."

"Why... What's this about?" I asked, knowing what his answer would be.

"Because that's what I had at the party remember? Saundra came up to me without having to be asked." he said with a cocky smirk as he took another bite.

I promised myself I'd hold my tongue and not tell him that Saundra and the others were all but ordered by Meghan to dance and he'd just come in at the right time.

"Hmm... that sure was something." I said agreeably.

He looked off for a bit and said, "It sure was..."

I almost laughed but held it.

We went on to talk about Wales and Leigh and whether or not they were moving too fast. Gene felt that people move at different speeds and mature differently. I had to agree but to drop the "L" word at thirteen was a bit much.

"Leigh is thirteen going on, like, forty-five or something and Wales, Wales could be dropped off on the north pole tonight and show up on your doorstep tomorrow morning wearing a sombrero and eating bread from a French bakery in Paris." he playfully mused.

We laughed because it was true.

"Yeah, I suppose they *are* a special couple." I admitted.

"Look, I asked you about this a few days ago but the way you and Meghan were cuddling on the couch by the window, watching everybody... I mean, the two of you looked like..."

"Like we were in love, I know... I know." Nobody else but maybe Meghan could get this kind of thing out of me so I just let it happen. "I don't know what I feel... thirteen, remember? I just know that life is better when we're together and even better when we're really clicking and we were really clicking that night."

"So... how *do* you feel?" he asked as though I didn't tell him six seconds prior.

"I feel... I feel like my feelings are too big for me and I have to grow into them. Like shoes or clothes that are bought too big expecting you'll grow. That and terrified that I'll mess this up somehow. It's funny, it's easy when we're together but scary when we're apart." It almost felt good to get that off my chest... almost.

"You got it bad man... bad!"

"Maybe so but I'm stuck in it now. Meghan and I will just have to see where this goes."

"I still can't believe that after all of this you're the one with the girlfriend."

"She's not... whatever. I'm sure you being single won't last long. I bet you'll get married first."

"The way it looks to me, you'll be the one getting married first. Tell you what, whoever gets married first gets a hundred dollars from the other."

"Sure, fine whatever." I don't know why I took the bet, just one of many crazy things teenaged guys do, I guess.

Later on in HQ, the movie *A Nightmare on Elm Street* was playing in the background as we both mindlessly focused on some video game.

"Serious dinner with the mom, big step."

"We've *all* met her mother, what's the big deal?" I retorted.

"What's the big deal. Dude, she wants to get to *know* you..." he said without taking his eyes off the screen. When a video game is involved, teenagers have a way of saying profound things dismissively.

"Well, I guess that's different. What the heck, man, just as I was getting good with this dinner thing!"

"I'm sorry but I don't want you to be blindsided. I think this is some next-level <expletive> and you need to be ready." he was still playing the game calmly, and well! "You need to think about what she's looking for. You said it yourself, we're thirteen, just kids. If that's true, why this serious dinner all of the sudden? It's not like she hasn't met you before - <expletive> she's been to your house and met your parents like twice. What more could she want? I don't know but I do know there's more to this than meets the eye."

Is it possible to both want to choke and hug someone at the same time. In that moment, I felt he'd just done me a great favor, the jerk! Now I had this stuff weighing on my mind and weigh it did – heavily. It weighed so heavily in fact that I didn't surrender to the advancing forces of slumber until two the next morning. In a few sentences Gene undid a sense of calm that took most of that week to build. At least in my restlessness I figured out some possible questions I might get making me feel at least somewhat prepared.

GUESS WHO CAME TO DINNER:

That Saturday night I was dropped off at the now familiar long driveway. My mother had already spoken with Ms. O'Neil by phone so pleasantries had already been exchanged. There was a car in the driveway that I did not recognize. As I passed the late model Toyota Corolla the front door opened and a familiar girl stepped out onto the porch, shut the door and paused a second as she looked at me. She seemed startled.

"Hi Stephanie." I said as she passed me on the driveway.

"Oh, hey." she said as though her mind was elsewhere. She seemed shook up about something.

Stephanie Anders was an eleventh grader I think, a band geek and the school's current Drum Majorette.

I got to the door and rang the bell. As I waited, I found myself feeling the geode pendant I got for Christmas through my shirt. I noticed I'd taken to doing this whenever I was nervous or just wanted to distract myself. I wore it next to my skin so I could feel it. I began to think about how... the door opened and in doing so brought my mind back to reality.

"Hi." Meghan said, letting the word hang in the air for a moment.

What is it about the smile of someone you care about that just disarms you?

"Hi." I said, letting myself enjoy the exciting insecurity of the moment. Emotions can set up the oddest paradoxes, juxtapositions, or whatever you want to call them. In this moment I was something like happy to not know what to expect and for me, that's weird.

She invited me in and we stepped through the door into the foyer. Yeah, odd, isn't it? I didn't mistype, I wrote "we" and meant it. Here's why. I could SWEAR that as I crossed the threshold it felt like there were two people in front of me and two behind me and I wasn't afraid. It felt like they were on "my side" whatever that meant. It was like I could see by feeling if that makes any sense. It felt like they were tall, like too tall. It felt like they would have had to stoop to walk through the doorway. There was something in the way Megan stepped back when I walked in that let me know she felt it too but this was impossible... wasn't it?

"What? What's wrong?" I asked.

"Um, nothing... it's nothing..." She looked around me a bit and then slowly found her way into my embrace. Chalk it up to just being a teenager or hormones or whatever, I couldn't think of anything else but how great she smelled and how soft she felt in my arms. She was wearing a maroon sweatshirt over blue jeans and matching maroon socks. I don't know why that's burned into my memory but it is for some reason.

"I saw Stephanie Anders outside; I didn't know you knew her."

"Mother is friends with her parents, she had to get something from her."

As we walked into the dining room, or whatever that room was called, I mean this house had so many rooms that this was probably "a" dining room rather than "the" dining room. Anyway, as we walked in, her mother was on the phone.

"That's not what she wants and you know it. Sure, it's hard, I know, but I think you need to do what she wants." Her mother looked in our direction for a moment and then went back to her conversation, "Angie... Angie... I've got to go, Meghan's boyfriend is here for dinner... OK.... You too... bye." her mother said as she ended the phone call.

I shot a quick look at Meghan who... hehe... who was trying with all her might to match the color of her sweatshirt and looking down and away from me.

Her mother turned after hanging up the phone and, beginning to take a step, stopped short while looking at me then looked around a bit like Meghan did at the door. A few seconds and she was back to normal. She looked at her daughter and shook her head. "Oh, get over it, embarrassing our children is the right of every mother!"

I fought the smirk, I really did, and lost. I reached for Meghan's hand and she jerked it away as she shot me a playful, "I'm still embarrassed" glare. I was gonna tease her with this for all it was worth and then wear it out and she knew it.

Her mother led us into the kitchen. I was fairly certain the house had only one of these. As we walked, somewhere in the back of my mind I knew my "friends" were still there. This was the oddest feeling. The kitchen was well decorated down to the brick motif and copper pots and pans hanging over a central marble-topped island. Funny thing was that everything was clean but the kitchen table was decked out with a full meal and set for three. "She didn't cook this meal. Did she?" was all I could think.

The three of us sat down at the wood-block table. Ms. O'Neil asked me to ask grace for the food, which I did. From there I noticed her strategy was to watch the way Meghan and I interacted. The funny thing was that Meghan watched me notice her mother's strategy and, if she was anything like me – and she was, she was working on how to give her mother what she wanted to hear. We talked about school, friends, the party, family… we just went on and on. Pretty soon it was time for desert and her mother excused herself from the table only to bring back from the refrigerator a chocolate fudge chocolate on chocolate cake.

"Wow… my favorite!" I said.

"I know." replied Ms. O'Neil.

I looked at Meghan and back at her mother, "I don't think I ever told Meghan that, how did you know?"

Meghan smiled and chuckled a bit as if she knew something.

"Because it's Meghan's favorite." she said with a smirk.

"Are you catching on now?" Meghan said leaning her head on one hand and smiling at me.

"This is just weird." I said looking at them as if they were crazy. They laughed.

Other than that, it was a pretty cool evening, filled with laughter and conversation… and then this happened…

"Meghan, can you please give us a few minutes? I'll send him up to you when we're finished." The emotionless deadpanned face said to the reddening, fearful face with the incredulous expression.

"Y- Yes Mother." sheepishly.

Meghan took my hand under the table and squeezed it a bit and then excused herself from the table. When she began to go up the stairs it began.

"Joe… as you know Meghan's father is not here anymore and that means I have to fill both roles. Does that make sense?"

"That makes sense." I replied as my mind began to plot a solution for the questions that would likely come next.

"Good. I hope you don't mind my being direct and I hope I don't make you too uncomfortable."

"OK."

"I know my daughter and I know how she feels about you. Because she feels that way I know you do too."

"How do..."

"Give me a minute... She would do anything for you. That would scare me if it were anyone else but because I know you would do the same, I'm not worried. I know you respect her and want what's best for her. I couldn't ask for anything more in a 'friend' for her. Because you're so similar in the way you think and feel, your relationship has grown very quickly and I don't want either of you to get hurt. You have a lot of time ahead of you, take it. She's been through a lot and we've had a lot of experiences that many people never get to have. We've learned things over the years, things she will share with you as time goes by."

When she said that, something shifted, I could feel a tension inside me that I didn't understand.

"I've learned a lot from her already, Ms. O'Neil. She's so mature and confident."

She laughed out loud. "Those are the exact words she said about you!"

"Really?"

"I'm impressed by the two of you, I really am. Thank you for sharing your evening with us. Now please, go ease her pain, she's just upstairs in the sitting room probably worrying that I'm embarrassing her."

"OK, thank you, Ms. O'Neil."

"Oh, and do me a favor... tell her I pulled out the baby pictures." she said whispering with a mischievous smile. "Tell her she has the cutest birthmark."

I laughed and shook my head as I walked to the steps.

I found Meghan sitting impatiently in what her mother called a "sitting room". When I got to the top of steps she stood up and put her arms around me.

"You..." I said as she looked up at me, "have the *cutest* birthmark."

She stared at me with one eye twitching and just as she was about to absolutely lose it I said, "just kidding, she told me say that"

"Mother!!!!" she yelled.

So much laughter from downstairs.

"I don't know if I like the fact that my mother likes you. Ganging up on me like that is not cool."

"Birthmark huh?"

"Shut up! I take it things went well."

"Yeah, she was really nice." I assured her.

I let a few seconds pass and then decided to play with her.

"So, um... am I your *boyfriend*?" I asked with a teasing voice.

Red-faced again she whispered, "So embarrassing..."

"It's OK." I said as I turned to take in the room, "If I'm not, I don't know what I am." I said this hoping to take her off guard like she did me on Thanksgiving.

"Are you OK with that?" she asked. With that I was just about knocked off balance when I retorted, "Only if you're OK with being my girlfriend."

"I think I am."

"Then so am I."

There was silence for a bit then...

"Siobhan, what did we just do?" I asked.

"I think we just teased each other into a new definition."

SURREALITY:

Monday morning Wales found me staring into space on the bus as if I was looking down a long tunnel. I think in that moment I understood the term "thousand-yard stare." I thought I could hear him talking but it was like he was speaking though a Schultz filter... you know, what adults sounded like on *Charlie Brown* cartoons - "Wah Wah Wamp Wah"... Anyway, I was brought to my senses as he passed his hand in front of my face.

"Meghan's my girlfriend." I said incredulously. That morning the events of Saturday night hit me again like a sack of bricks.

"Um.. what?" he asked, as if he didn't quite hear me.

"We decided that's where we are."

"OK... whoa. This is big for you guys, I mean, we all thought you were already there and..."

"I know. We just hadn't said those words." I interrupted. "Gene is all over this. He's acting like my coach or something." It was true, Gene was to me like a high school football coach who was living vicariously through his players and taking it much too seriously. It was like that when I was on the phone with Gene the day before.

"So I guess dinner went real well."

"Yeah, but Wales, this is all so fast. But you know, it's like her mother said, 'we have a lot of time and we should take it.'"

"That's... not bad." he said with a look of approval. "Look, you should do what Leigh and I did when we were starting out and nervous. Agree to enjoy the ride and see where it goes."

Right then a weight lifted off of my shoulders and I saw Wales in a new light for that was perhaps the most profound thing he'd ever said to me. He could physically see the change in my posture.

"Are you OK?"

"Yeah... Yeah, Wales, that actually helps – like a lot!"

"Yeah, it helped us too. We don't know where this is going but the ride is better than I could've imagined."

"Come on..." I said playfully. "You two will be one of those couples that'll say, 'I married my high-school sweetheart.'"

"I hope so." Wales replied beginning to have a bit of a thousand-yard stare himself.

Nothing made Monday mornings bearable like feeling Meghan's arms slip around my waist while I was at my locker. As she did this, she held tight and whispered, "Good morning, boyfriend."

"Good morning, girlfriend." I said as I turned to look her full in her smiling face. We were both smiling and getting used to our new definition.

"How are you doing?" I asked playfully.

"I feel light and happy. The kind of happy someone feels when they're excited about what they don't know, like opening a present."

"I kind of feel the same way but to be honest I'm worried because I don't know how to act in a relationship like this." I admitted.

"I've never had a boyfriend so I don't know either."

"Me too, I've never had a boyfriend."

"Ha... Ha..." she said shaking her head.

"Wales said we should just enjoy the ride and see where we go." I offered.

"I like that."

"Let's do that." I said.

That day as lunch got started Bruce and I found ourselves looking over at the Country *Boys'* table wondering about this new girl. She had stringy red hair, freckles, and piercing blue eyes. She was cute in some ways. Just then Leigh sat down and noticed where we were looking, "That's Margaret McCormack, she goes by 'Maisie', she just transferred here. To listen to her it makes sense that she would sit there, she has that southern drawl in her voice and everything."

"Is she in one of your classes?" Bruce asked.

"Two actually, Precalculus and Gym."

"Precalculus?" I asked rhetorically, sounding impressed. "Any addition to that group can't be a good thing."

The others began to join us with their trays, filling their usual seats at the table. "Maisie" was the talk of the table which only makes sense in an eighth-grade world. We all shared the same concern that a rival "gang" had just increased in strength. We sounded like something out of that 1979 movie, *The Warriors*. That lasted for just about all of a teenager's attention span and then we talked about any number of things for rest of lunch, including me and Meghan, annoyingly.

As the school-day came to a close I visited Meghan's locker since our tradition was to see each other before heading home. We caught up on the day and let each other know what we had planned that night... stuff like that. As we concluded we held each other and made each other laugh. I liked making her laugh. All was well and then I heard this unfamiliar voice...

"Hey look boys, I guess ebony and ivory really can live together in perfect harmony! Salt and Pepper over here should get a room." Maisie McCormack said in her southern drawl to the two Country *Boys* with her.

Amidst the laughter from Maisie's friends, Meghan broke our embrace and abruptly turned to the aggravating southern belle. I thought she might have been planning to "destroy" her like she mentioned doing to Terry Elsmore at Thanksgiving so I put my arms around her shoulders to hold her back and whispered, "Not now, no Krav ma-whatever." Her eyes were locked on Maisie as they walked away. She gave a dry chuckle and turned back to me.

"You know I wanted to. No one..."

"No one gets to make you feel that way again, I know. You know, you said you'd teach me some fighting stuff maybe I can teach you diplomacy."

"The way I feel now, maybe I do need some of that." she said wryly.

"Yup, she's a Country *Girl.*" I thought to myself. I was disappointed that our lunchtime suspicions had come true.

That Saturday saw the first Confirmation Class of the new year. We were discussing Peter's confession and Jesus' declaration that He would build His Church on that rock. It was an interesting discussion leading to musings on how the Church needs to function as one if we are to see Jesus' promise that "the gates of hell would not prevail against it." Afterwards, I had my customary time with Pastor Summerstone. I filled him in on everything that happened over the past month. Somehow surprisingly, he took all of this very seriously.

"So, a few things." he said leaning forward in his chair, looking at me over his desk.

When someone in authority says, "So, a few things." prepare for whatever you've submitted to be returned to you, no matter how lovingly, with red pen marks all over it. Believe me, I've had what I think is more than my fare share of papers returned to me like that at school.

"I can tell from the way you talk and your body language that you have deep feelings for her. That makes this next thing a bit more difficult for me to say."

"OK..." I said, gripping the seat of my chair to brace myself.

He continued, "I need you to prayerfully consider... that means you ask God to clarify and help you understand something as you seek His will. I need you to prayerfully consider why He wanted you to know that He'd assigned angels to go with you to that house. I mean, I know that angels being assigned to people for reasons we may or may not understand is normal, but what is not normal is when He wants us to be acutely aware of them. There has to be a reason for that."

He leaned back in his chair, steepled his fingers in front of his face and went on to say, "Since we've been talking, my interest in spiritual things like this has increased. I'm concerned that both Meghan and her mother were aware of them too. Joe, I think something's... wrong here. I want you to guard your heart. So many people your age get so blinded by feelings that they can't see straight. I wouldn't say these things if I didn't care. I also feel that maybe I've earned enough of your trust to 'get into your business' so to speak."

"Thank you, I appreciate it, really. I know something is weird but do you really think it's bad?" I said.

"I don't know but I have to wonder why you would almost see angels with you as you went into their house. Do me a favor, listen carefully to everything she and her mom say and watch what they do. Anything really wrong is bound to come out sooner or later."

I sat back in my chair resigned to the fact that he had to be right about this. "I will, and I'll let you know." I would have been upset but for the fact that I knew something was weird – off in a way.

That Tuesday was a normal day, relatively. People were going through the motions to get through the day like so many of us do as we go through life. This is a rather depressing thought actually but it was what it was. According to my journal nothing really happened that day... except the Space Shuttle exploding! We were freaked out when a teacher interrupted our science class with the news. This shuttle mission was notable in that NASA was putting a civilian teacher in space for the first time. The whole country had been looking forward to this mission and now the whole country was in shock and mourning. This was no less true for the school for the days that followed.

This had been kind of a big year for space-related things. Not too long after the Space Shuttle tragedy, we were disappointed to find that Halley's Comet could not be seen very well given the Earth's position and light pollution in the city. Those things notwithstanding, we all still craned our necks for a few nights trying to catch a glimpse of something we may only see once in our lives.

The following weeks were filled with school, *The Mysfits*, teenaged confusion, and oh yeah – that hazy euphoric cloud that covers you when you're that age and in a relationship. That cloud covered me like the "fog of war" they talk about in old war movies. It was a delightful combination of not knowing what to do and thinking you know what to do at the same time. By "delightful" I mean bad. Somehow, we made it through and we began to find our own groove. Her mother and my parents wisely decided to slow us down. They felt, and they were right, that we were too young for feelings this big coming so easily. So, these were the restrictions:

1. No unsupervised visits.

2. No visits except once a month because we already saw each other every day at school.

3. Phone calls end after 30 minutes and only two of those per week.

I called these the "Three Commandments". At first, we were offended but after discussing we realized they were right, we had the rest of our lives to work on "us" … oh to be that age and carefree. At some point I discussed this with Wales who promptly made me promise that my parents wouldn't talk to his mother anytime soon. We laughed.

When we weren't looking, time flew past us and Spring Break was but a week away. Huddled around our lunch table, we discussed plans for the upcoming reprieve from our daily slog through the halls of academia, even Leigh wanted a break – we were shocked, I know right?

"Well, Tommy is gonna be with me and my family out at the cabin in Deep Creek." Leigh said plainly.

Wales beamed in an awe-shucks kind of way.

"OK, that means no helicopters or first-class flights to Paris." Bruce said matter-of-factly. Bruce had a dry humor but it made us all laugh just the same.

Wes added, "Ohh... a week with the *Adams Family!*"

"Cut that crap!" Leigh snapped with a smile.

Because of schedules and all, we eventually agreed upon an outing to the harbor for anyone who could make it. The rest of that week was up to us. Our parents, in their benevolence, permitted Meghan and me to hang out for two days during Spring Break but only because her mother would be around. We took what we could get.

That week before the break seemed to stretch forever, like a kid feels when he's waiting for Christmas. Soon enough it was over. Being a Christian school, the week ended on Thursday as we were off on Good Friday. Easter weekend was fine but as a kid, the week afterwards is what held my attention. I spent that Monday doing exactly what I'd hoped, nothing. Well, not exactly nothing, video games, movies, and television – sometimes at the same time. Because Meghan and I could only have so many phone calls, we'd planned our hang times before the break at school. She asked me to bring a sweatsuit to her house on Tuesday when we were supposed to hang out. I had an idea what she was planning and I was right.

TRAINING DAY:

The next day, my mother dropped me off at Meghan's house in the morning on her way to work. I was greeted by my old friend, the driveway. I guess I began to like it actually because it gave me a chance to think about the day ahead of us. I got to the door and rang the bell. Nothing weird here, all was well, and then the door opened. When it did it was like a light was shown and I could see – without actually seeing with my eyes – the four friends of mine like I did before, that "seeing by feel" or something. "Oh boy." I thought as Meghan looked around the porch suspiciously for a second or two from inside the door. Her mother was behind her doing the same thing with the same pensive look on her face. It was definitely different, it was thicker, like the feeling was clearer somehow.

"May I come in?" I said partly to break the silence and partly because I felt that since I was with friends I should be invited. Interestingly enough, after that I began to ask for permission to enter every time I visited someone's house even to this day. Not that this happens every time but it just seems right.

"Of course… come in!" Meghan said, hugging me as I crossed the threshold. Her mother smirked and shook her head. "I'll be in my office" Ms. O'Neil said as she departed the foyer.

"Did you bring a sweat suit?" Meghan asked.

"Yes, but why?"

"You'll see."

We had a light breakfast, just fruit and bagels with cream cheese. Then she invited me to use a powder room to change. She was already dressed for the occasion, black sweatshirt, matching sweatpants, and white Converse shoes with pink laces. She was just too cute that day. Anyway, we went out into the back yard where a cooler filled with ice and water bottles sat.

"It's fight day, am I right?" I asked plainly.

"Fight? We never fight, have you noticed that?" she countered.

Actually, she was right, we have *never* fought. Like, we agreed so much that even our disagreements were acceptable. "Um… yeah, I guess I have."

"Good, we aren't going to fight, think of this as 'training day'." she said as she slowly maneuvered around me. BOOM! I was on the grass. I was going to hate this.

"I'm going to go slow with you at first, Phil, but I want you to attack me for real. Krav is an aggressive art. I will hit you and you just might hit me and it will hurt but we'll get a lot out of it. Are you OK with that?" she gave these instructions as she helped me to my feet.

"Yeah, in for a penny in for a pound and all that." I said, trying to hide the fact that I was catching my breath.

"In for a pounding is more like it for your first day. I got beat up on my first day too."

She looked me in the eyes and stepped close. She tilted her head just right and closed her eyes half-way just inches from my face. I actually thought she was going to kiss me despite our self-imposed rule. BOOM! She hip-tossed me like I was a crash dummy (I sure felt like one too).

"I can pull you off your guard any time I want, we both know this; you have to be watching at all times."

Right then I rushed her like we were in a fight. I did not like the taste of grass but that's what I tasted because I was once again on the ground, this time face down.

"OK, we've made it clear that my girlfriend can beat my tail. Is that what this is about?" I said as I made my way to the cooler thinking all along that I would feel this beating for like the rest of my life!

"Think of it as learning that your girlfriend can protect her boy-friend." she said with her megawatt smile. I was watching because she knew I loved her smile and I suspected she was trying to catch me off-guard again. She edged closer.

"No… beware of beautiful women smiling, back off." I said with force. Now I was trying to catch her off guard. Seeing as how she was blushing, I just waited for her to look down and away – her nervous move. See I knew her too. As soon as she did that, I threw the water bottle in her direction, wrapped her up and took her to the ground. We struggled for a moment, just a moment, and then I realized I was in the most devious arm-lock I'd ever seen and grunting in pain. Yeah, it hurt. Only when I tapped the ground repeatedly and hard did she let me go.

"That's the spirit!" she said.

"You have GOT to be kidding me!" I yelled as I struggled to get up. Then I did it. While I was bent over away from her, I waited for her to approach me and I spun and threw a punch. I was praying I wouldn't connect but part of me wanted the punch to land. If it had, she would have been out for sure because all of my weight and leverage went into it. In a blink it was deflected by her arm and her instinct and training took over and her elbow connected with my face. I dropped. She just stood there with her hands to her face. Tears were streaming down her face like she was the one who'd been hit.

"I'm so sorry! Please forgive me! Please! I just reacted!"

I got up silently and took off my sweatshirt to reveal my tank-top undershirt. It was over 70 degrees by then and I was over-heating. I silently sat on the ground and said, "I'm fine… it didn't hurt." I paused and then, "April fools, yeah it did… and bad!" True, it was April fools day but this was no joke.

She put her hand on my face where she'd hit me with her elbow and left it there for a minute. I was disarmed. She could've wrecked me right then and I couldn't have stopped her.

"Let's sit for a minute." she motioned for a set of patio chairs as she spoke.

My vicious, humiliating beat-down by a girl easily fifty-pounds lighter continued for another hour before I started to get the hang of some of the techniques. I actually put her on the ground a few times and she admitted that I really got her – at least, that's what she said. Everything was cool, and then this happened… I'd just launched a surprise take-down that worked and we were wrestling on the ground again. Of course, again, she had the upper hand and then we heard, "Meghan!" It was her mother on the balcony overlooking the back yard. She was standing there with what must have been five Baltimore City Police Officers.

"You see Officer? It is as I said, my daughter and her boyfriend practicing martial arts." Ms. O'Neil said.

"Her *boyfriend*?" One of the Police Officers asked out loud.

"Yes Officer, and I'm quite fond of him too! It's 1986 for God's sake! Will that be all?" she asked angrily.

"What's all this about, Mother?" Meghan asked as we both got to our feet.

"Oh, just one of our *neighbors* saw you fighting a… guy in the back yard and got concerned. They were just being neighborly." she said with every bit of sarcasm she could muster.

"Oh to be black in Roland Park!" I thought to myself.

The three of us decided for the sake of peace that we should call it a day. My body agreed. Meghan showed me to a guest room upstairs. I used the adjoining bathroom to shower and change back into my non-crash-dummy clothes. We met up again downstairs in the basement rec room where we promptly fell asleep leaning on each other while watching television.

We both woke up to the flash of a camera and my mother and hers standing in front of us, grinning. They gave us the courtesy of saying good-bye to each other, alone.

"You'll be there on Friday, at the Harbor?" I asked hopefully.

"I sure will…" she said with a smile. "Listen, I'm sorry about the cops and all."

"Believe me, it's not your fault. No worries."

This was one of those things I elected to leave out of the story when I told my parents about my day. My mother would have worried for sure.

I spent the rest of the week until Friday bathing twice per day in a cold bath. You see, I was trying to get my body to stop yelling at me. I thought I could drown out the pain. It only partially worked. By Thursday I'd come to live with the pain. On top of that, my ego had its butt handed to it and it just had to accept it. I couldn't even enjoy *The Cosby Show* that night. I found the time and strength to record the week's events in my journal and poured myself into the bed.

THAT DAY AT THE HARBOR:

Amazingly, the parents were fine with a bunch of early teenagers hanging out at the harbor for the day. After taking a couple buses, I found myself on Pratt Street by ten-thirty that morning looking up at the *World Trade Center* where Meghan and I had that first real talk. As it was Spring Break, not a few people had the same idea. The atmosphere was festive with crowds of people gathering around any number of street vendors. In those years, the McCormick Spice company had a factory not too far from the Inner Harbor and the scent of nutmeg and other spices wafted throughout that part of downtown. That scent is one of my fondest memories of visiting the harbor. It was kind of a cool day weather-wise so I was wearing a denim jacket over a white sweatshirt and acid washed jeans – an eighties look, believe me. It was a bright day and I had the good sense to bring the Ray-bans we got from Wales. I slowly made my way through the crowds, taking in the day. I had to be at the meeting place, *The U.S.S. Constellation*, at eleven so I had roughly thirty minutes. I was elected to be the one who had to think of stuff to do that day since both Wales and Leigh were away. To be honest, until this moment, I hadn't given it a second thought. I figured we'd all get down there and fun would just happen. As I walked the promenade, I noticed that B-104, a prominent top 40 hits radio station, was setting up a Spring Break themed stage. As interesting as this was, in my eyes it couldn't beat the funnel cake stand next to it because I hadn't had breakfast. By the time I got through the line and had my none-too-good for me confection in hand, covered with baked apples and powdered sugar, it was about five minutes to 11.

I got to the meeting point just about on time. I found Meghan, Gene, Wes, and Bruce waiting for me.

"Look at this guy, he's already gotten something to eat, just couldn't wait for us." Gene accused. "Maybe you should kick his <expletive> again, Meghan."

Blushing and shooting Gene a wry smile, "Correction, *we've* already gotten something to eat!" my girlfriend said as she greeted me by taking my funnel cake. They all shook their heads and so did I, defeated.

"Whumt?" Meghan asked with a full mouth, looking around from face to face.

"Nothing." I said. I put my arm around her shoulders and we all began to walk.

By the time Meghan finished off my funnel cake we were half-way to the Science Center. I don't know why we were walking in that direction. It was like the captain of the ship was asleep... oh yeah, that was supposed to be me! There was a Jet-ski demonstration near there and I played it off as though I meant to go there. I fooled no one but they really didn't care. Just the light atmosphere and everybody joking with each other is why we were there.

I suppose Meghan was in the mood for taking things from me that day. She wasn't wearing any kind of jacket, just a tee shirt – pastel pink over blue jeans and those converse with the pink laces. She went to hug me, or so I thought, I soon realized she was peeling off my jacket. It was chilly with the breeze coming off of the water.

"You'll be alright in that sweatshirt." she stated, justifying her purloining.

She slipped on my obviously too big for her jacket and then she rolled sleeves and did whatever else women do to look cute. Now my look was incomplete unless I was going for "eighties dork". Whatever. At least she was happy, right?

We got lunch at this one sub place in the Pratt Street Pavilion. The funny thing was that with the exception of Meghan, we all sat in our normal places as though we were in the school's cafeteria. We all laughed when we realized what we'd done. Then we explained it to Meghan. Meghan and I led the group in a round of "What are people thinking", our little game where we give voice to what we think a stranger out of earshot is thinking. Everybody was rolling when they caught on.

We hit the *Six Flags Power Plant* indoor amusement park at about 1:30. That experience was, for lack of a better word, odd. We all knew it was an experimental thing with a movie theater that let you smell the scenes in addition to seeing it in 3D. We had fun nonetheless and I think that was just it, we could have fun doing just about anything. We spent a couple of hours in there and each got foot-long hot dogs on the way out of that part of the harbor. We were about to go paddle boating when Wes caught a glimpse of the B-104 stage. Turns out it was a massive karaoke event. It was actually free. They were just doing it as a publicity stunt. We walked over there and found a crowd of people just enjoying the obviously paid backup singers (wearing B-104 swag) and the poor, brave, and possibly drunk, souls who ventured to the stage to be heckled by their friends. We stayed there for a few songs and found it funny enough… and then this happened…

"Phil?" Meghan whispered in my ear.

Looking around to make sure no one heard her use my name, lest they think it was cute and tease me, "Yeah, what's up?"

"Remember when you asked if there were things you didn't know about me?"

"Yes… why yes I do." I said in an accusatory tone more playful than not.

"Do you want to learn something?"

"Um… sure." I could feel the icy finger of trepidation dragging itself up my spine.

"Come on guys." Meghan said to the group of us.

We thought she was going to lead us to some other activity or something… but no! She led us right up to the stage where she hugged me hard, whispered "Trust me.", and grabbed my hands as she let me go and then made her way to the Disc Jockey at the booth.

All I could do was shake my head in disbelief while cries of, "Noooo!" rose from Wes and the others.

The DJ and Meghan exchanged a few words, he nodded and she was given a microphone and waited for the lady on the stage to finish. Looking at her, I didn't know this girl. She had such a clear look of confidence on her face as she waited, no blushing, no nothing! It was like the stage was her home and she was going to the fridge. No, the girl I'd known was gone and there sat every bit of a woman as though she'd aged beyond her years in the space of a few minutes!

The music stopped; it was a somewhat brave version of Cyndi Lauper's *Time after Time*. Meghan stepped to the center of the stage and waited for the music to start. It was Pat Benatar's We *Belong*. She began to sing and if I didn't think I knew this girl before, I most certainly didn't know her now. I mean, she nailed it! She was into the song and looking at me during the chorus. The crowd grew as people began to think it was some kind of concert. As much as it went over with the crowd, it went over with me all the more. She simply slew me singing that song to me. She effortlessly pushed through the power stanzas of the song like it was written for her. The four of us were simply stunned as we watched her sway and own that performance.

When she was finished, the crowd went ba-na-nas! Do you read me? After that she started to walk off the stage when the DJ's voice boomed over the speakers, "Wait, Wait, young lady. You can't just leave us all hanging like that. What do you say crowd, do you want…" he looked at the notebook he had, "uh… Meghan to sing another song?" The crowd started to chant her name. She blushed, looked down and away, but when her head came back, she was oddly confident again. She strode over to the DJ and exchanged some words. Whatever she said made the DJ's expression change as though he was really impressed. She walked over to the center of the stage and waited for the music. She looked me dead in the eyes as Pat Benatar's *Love is a Battlefield* began to play. She slowly raised the microphone to her lips with hands barely emerging from the sleeves of my jacket and began to vocalize along with the song. OK, if you're not familiar with these two songs, I highly recommend you stop reading and go to the Internet. You will not be disappointed. Anyway, she ROCKED THAT SONG OUT. It was like Pat Benatar was on stage. Meghan matched Benatar note for note and power note for power note – to me it was better (I was probably biased). In the space of a moment, I knew why people pass out and why they do weird things at concerts. The way she was dancing and singing, I was entranced! I was brought back to reality by Gene. He was looking up at the stage like everybody else but slapping me on the back while doing so, "That's your girl man! Wow, look at her go!"

Gene insists that I let him interject here:

Look, when he says that she sang that song better than Pat Benatar, he wasn't kidding. That girl got up there and sang those songs like they were hers and she meant it. The way she rocked that crowd... I just don't know... mind-blowing! The way she was looking at my man here said it all, she was head over heels for him. Hell, *I* wanted to date her after that.

When she was done with the song, she went over to the DJ who spoke with her for a while – like a long while. When they were done, she came down the steps where I snatched her up in a big hug lifting her off her feet from the last step. She laughed hysterically. I set her down, threw my arm around her shoulders and kissed her as hard as I could on the top of her head. We shared a glance as we walked away side by side, arms around each other. People were slapping me and her on the back as if both of us had sung. I had the biggest "This is *my* girlfriend!" smile on my face. The others were hero-walking behind us as we led the way. I didn't even know what to think. Apparently, the DJ offered her a job singing with his band at weddings and parties. When he learned her age, he told her to get her parents. She took his business card but didn't plan to take him up on his offer.

That night I sat down at my desk with the two now framed pictures of me and Meghan on opposite corners. Needless to say, I lit my journal up with the happenings of the day. It was about eleven when my phone rang. We'd already used up our allotted phone calls but I didn't care either.

"Hello?"

"Hi, Phil. We don't have much time."

"I am so… so… impressed with you. What *are* you?"

"<laughing> I'm glad I could share that with you. I was only singing for you. You know that right?"

"I think I do."

"Well, be sure of it. I can't wait to see you again."

"Me too, but I have a mirror so…"

"<laughing> Alright, good night."

"Good night."

She kept my jacket!

CHAPTER 15:
"CRUEL SUMMER"
- BANANARAMA

"Man, I wish we'd been there to see that!" Wales exclaimed as I told him about that day at the harbor.

"Well, it was certainly better than food poisoning." I responded. Apparently the first day of their week at the Adams' Deep Creek cabin, Wales thought it would be a good idea for him to cook dinner. It was not a good idea. The next day had been, well… unpleasant. None of them felt right until Thursday afternoon.

"Tell me about it!" Wales said despondently. "So, she's a ninja... and a rock star? Someone hit the lottery!"

"Something like that, I guess."

"Joe, there is one more thing that maybe she hasn't told you. You know I seem to find things out sometimes..."

"What is it?" I asked as I gave him my complete attention.

"She's from another planet." he replied with a deadpanned face.

We both laughed hysterically.

Meghan and I respected the *Three Commandments* to the letter and even decided that sometimes not seeing each other at school except for chance encounters in the hallways would be a good thing. We agreed that we would be better off for it and amazingly it was true. We were stronger than ever but we did have schoolwork and other friends to think about. Well, we did make exceptions for the occasional morning greeting.

As time progressed, the thoughts of the student body turned more and more to Summer, that seemingly endless expanse of days filled with nothing but carefree living. This would have been true for *The Mysfits* but for the fact that we were eighth-graders and for us that meant there was one more thing this year to think about, the eighth-grade lock-in. It loomed on the horizon and as this was a rite of passage for eighth-graders only, we didn't know what to expect. Bruce was on the planning committee and assured us that it was nothing to be afraid of except that it was to be the singular event through which soon-to-be ninth-graders would jockey for position on the social ladder. It was to be a night filled with sporting events, a dance, a dinner, a chapel, and breakfast. Truly a time to leave one's mark – a yearbook defining event if ever there was one, which meant there had to be some thought put into it. So, because this thing was a week away now, we were all huddled around Wales at lunch as he led us through the checklist he devised. For some reason we thought we were just too cool to be normal, so we had a dress code and a common list of supplies so we would always look good throughout that night. My only regret was that Meghan couldn't be there because she and her mother had plans in New Jersey that weekend. I was never too clear on what went on in New Jersey that required them to be there so often. I would later learn... well, that's for later.

"I just don't understand why we have to have a dress code for ourselves." Wes stated.

"Trust the process." was all Wales could offer.

Shaking her head, Leigh added, "It's important that we stick together as we go into high school and not get pulled apart. I know it sounds weird but everything we can do to stay 'us' is somehow important."

"Can't say that I get it but, whatever." Wes said, surrendering.

It's not like the dress code was a bad thing. I mean the color combinations were cool and we would all look sharp.

THE LOCK-IN:

Somehow the day came sooner than expected. We all came to school that day with duffel bags filled with the various attire and sundries required for the Lock-In. This night would see the eighth-graders take over the CAB from dusk til dawn. Of course, Wales had a place for our stuff provided by the Janitors. Leigh and Wales had been sad the past few days because *The Pride of Baltimore* got caught in a storm and sank north of Puerto Rico. They knew some of the people who served on that ship where they'd had their first date. We all hoped the Lock-In would cheer them up. As a group we decided to simply stay at school until the start of the event. The six of us found one of the few picnic tables between the classroom buildings and the CAB. Leigh produced a *Monopoly* game that we wound up playing for almost the whole time we had to wait. I have to say there was some shady playing going on in that game. It was all in good fun even if the rules were trampled a bit.

"So, what do you guys think about high school? What do you think will be different?" Leigh asked the group.

"I think it's exciting, something new. New people come in at ninth-grade so that'll be different at least." Bruce said optimistically. Bruce, the guy on the yearbook committee and just about every other planning committee he could find, always seemed to sound like a commercial for the school. This was just as well seeing as he was so involved in school events that he felt like they somehow belonged to him.

"You know, we start at the bottom again. I mean, when we were seventh-graders it made sense but we've been here two years and back to the bottom." Gene added. Back then "middle School" was comprised of grades seven and eight – the way it should be.

"Some people will see that as a way to start over." I offered.

"Yeah, but not me." Gene replied with a shrug.

"Whatever..." Wes inserted, "Harder classes, everything counts now – like for college and what not."

Leigh was beaming... nerd.

"I just think of how epic everything will be when we start driving." Wales pondered out loud.

"...and the jobs that will have to go with that, right? Gotta pay for outings, gotta pay for gas." Leigh reminded us, reducing the epic-ness by that much.

Gene leaned over to me, "You alright?"

"Yeah? What's up?"

"Just checking in, I know it stinks not having Meghan here. I think we got used to having her around."

"I'm doing alright, and it does stink. Thanks for asking." I was truly touched because I knew that was his way of saying that he missed her too, that she was accepted. I felt good for her.

Just before dinner was to start in the cafeteria, we went to our respective gym locker rooms to change. When we emerged, we found ourselves wearing matching maroon shirts over black pants – Wales' dinner attire. I thought this was a bit much but I rolled with it anyway. I must say, though, we did look sharp as we filed into the cafeteria.

To our surprise, the cafeteria was well-decorated for the night. The tables were decked with white tablecloths and votive candles. The lights were dimmed (I didn't even know they could do that) and silverware set beside real plates awaited each student. It took us a minute to adjust to this now weird place that we thought we knew so well. Once we did, we figured we would go to "our table" since this would be one of the last times we would eat there because ninth-grade and above had lunch in the senior high cafeteria. As it turned out, seems like everybody else had the same idea.

Dinner was provided by the faculty. It was comprised of their own homemade specialties. The menu ranged from meatloaf to mac and cheese. It was actually quite good. During dinner, a slideshow developed by the yearbook committee provided entertainment. Whoops and wails went up as pictures from sporting events and such graced the screen. We paid special attention to the section on October's dance where a certain overly well-dressed group in Ray-Ban sunglasses were prominently featured. I was personally embarrassed as the last picture from the dance, the one on which they chose to fade to black, was of Meghan and me slow-dancing with her head on my chest. Oh, the "Awww" from the crowd didn't seem to stop. I could hear the word "cute" being said way too many times. However, the *Country Boys* brought me back to reality, especially Jake Thompkins' red-faced angry expression.

A small chapel service occurred after dinner. It was neat because it sort of tied everything back to God and His Word. Mr. Tidewater spoke a bit on legacy and what it meant for us as students. Kind of different having chapel in the cafeteria but I suppose this whole night was about change and different experiences. Since Faculty were there before us and would be there long after we were gone, we expected that they would not be so affected by students moving through school from grade to grade but apparently the talk on legacy really got to them. Throughout the night we would overhear them reminisce about former students and lives they'd played a part in changing.

For about an hour or so after chapel, we had a dance in the gym. It was reminiscent of October in that the same decorations were used. As the dance progressed, we, or maybe just I, got the point that it brought us full circle as far as the year was concerned. As there were no outside dates for the dance or anything, people danced with people they would have never expected. It was actually a great way to mix, mingle, and break down some of the social barriers that were constructed in the seventh-grade. I got a change to dance with Jasmine C. of the *Sidity Committee*, she had an impressive sense of humor and even dared to try to recreate the picture of me and Meghan during the slow dance. We all got a kick out of that.

After the dance we quickly changed into our sports attire, a green sweatshirt with gray sweatpants. This was also in line with the school's color scheme. Anyway, team volleyball was up first. We didn't have to worry about picking teams because we decided a long time ago that the *Mysfits* were a team. Sad to say we only got third place but those we crushed, we *crushed*. We didn't fare nearly as well in basketball, which followed. However, we did take the cake when it came to what was called "midnight softball". Though it wasn't yet midnight, it was the thought that counted. The three-inning softball games were played under the lights of the Varsity field. We joined with the *Band Geeks* to form our team and discovered that Leigh was a really good pitcher. She had that underhanded wind-your-arm fast pitch down to a science. Come to think of it, she probably did use science somehow to help her game... nerd. Come on, she *was* (and is) a nerd but we all loved her for it and secretly wanted to be her at times – like during exams and whatnot.

After softball we got a chance to just hang out. Some of us joined other games that were happening, some of us slept for a while. I mingled with a few classmates and eventually ran into Petra Taylor. We talked school and summer plans and then she added...

"You know Joe, I was hoping you'd ask me to the dance. I thought it would have been cool and since we've known each other for like all of our lives it would have been easy."

"I'm sorry I didn't think of it. My mind was all over the place and I wasn't thinking straight the whole time, believe me." I confessed.

"Well, it all worked out for the best, I guess. Tim Barnes asked me and we had a really good time. We're going slow but it's good. Also, look at you and Meghan. You two seem good together. So everything worked out for the best I guess."

"Yeah, I guess so but that doesn't mean that we should forget about our friendship." I suggested.

We went on to reminisce for a while and enjoy a friendship years in the making.

At about 3:30, we were all wide awake and decided to step out of the gym for some air and to see the stars. Because it is so dark at night in that part of Baltimore County, the night sky can be a spectacle. We'd been out there for ten minutes or so and everything was fine, or so we thought, and then this happened... We heard a noise coming from the opposite side of the building, around the corner. It was a door opening and closing. The gym had several doors that led outside and we thought nothing of it until we turned to find the *Country Boys* lurking around the corner. Just as we were about to go back inside because we didn't feel like talking to them, we heard a voice behind us.

"Hold on, just where are you going?" Maisie said with her particular brand of southern drawl.

We looked at each other and all of us knew this was probably not going to end well. This was something that had been simmering between our two groups for two years and it was about to come to a boil. We started squaring off. Two things became apparent rather quickly, Terry Elsmore wanted to finish his "conversation" with Gene and Jake Thompkins was not there. I quickly realized that Jake must have sent them because he knew if he got caught he could get expelled. So without Jake, the remaining Country *Boys*, Terry, Maisie, Al Stonebridge, Parker Wilson, and Milton Edwards made their moves. They probably wanted to scare us more than anything and didn't expect us to fight back, because fight is exactly what we did – and viciously. One second we were sizing each other up, the next we were all on the ground rolling and punching. This went on for about an hour, or so it felt, before Mr. Philmore came through the door, yelling. Turned out it lasted less than a minute. The teachers quickly split us up into two rooms and ~~interrogated~~ asked us what took place. Because the teachers knew the *Country Boys*, it didn't take long for them to put the pieces together. The *Country* Boys were put in the equipment room while we had to stay in the weight room behind the bleachers. After the questioning, we stayed in the room for a while to cool down.

"So *that* happened!" I said.

"I wish it had been longer!" Gene added, vehemently.

"This is my first fight." Leigh said into space, "...and I'm not worried about getting into trouble!"

"I don't think we are." Wes responded.

"Thank God for that!" added Bruce.

"Um… Leigh, what's that in your hand?" I asked.

"Oh..." she said, examining the strawberry strands with a wide-eyed expression, "Some of Maisie's hair, I guess?"

We all sat there for a moment looking at each other and then we laughed uproariously. Six dirty and disheveled teenagers as happy as we could have been. Bruce put his hands on his head, leaned back on his chair's hind legs and exclaimed, "I *love* being a *Mysfit*!" What the *Country Boys (and Girl)* didn't know, couldn't have known, is that if there was any doubt that we would stick together come high school, college, or life after school, they helped put it away. They intended to intimidate and hurt us and it only made us stronger.

After a few minutes of cooling down, we were invited to join the rest of the students in the main gym. We did so only for the few seconds it took us to get to the locker rooms where we took quick showers. Wales preparedness proved prophetic in that we had clothes to change into, albeit the dinner attire again.

The rest of the event went well. There were whispers about our "gang turf war" in such exaggerated terms that only early teenagers could devise. Our rivals had to stay in the equipment room, a makeshift detention hall, for the rest of the event - all but Jake Thompkins. Because he was not involved, he was allowed to stay with the rest of the students basically alone as he didn't have his "crew" anymore. We didn't pay him any attention.

Breakfast was the responsibility of the faculty and a few volunteers. Making pancakes with Mr. Philmore at five-thirty in the morning was a strange experience but one I would come to cherish. Mr. Tidewater had been right about legacy and I began to see the shape of it as I thought about the friendships I'd made and how profound it had been for all of us. Mr. Philmore and I got a chance to catch up. He was particularly interested in how Meghan and I were getting along. Oddly enough, just like Pastor Summerstone, he had his reservations – I didn't know from where because I didn't tell him nearly as much. I never expected that much later in life he and I would be in touch and would reflect on how God used the relationships formed and events at our school to shape our lives.

As morning dawned everyone cleaned up and packed up. I think having that experience really underscored the way we would relate to and watch out for each other throughout high-school and beyond. It's funny how you don't really understand how important a small gesture or a seemingly normal event can be until much later.

As I came to expect, Meghan was aghast at what happened and then quickly settled into wishing she'd been there. I was of two minds about that. On the one hand, she'd have dealt a serious blow to whoever came for her, on the other, we may have gotten into trouble for her breaking someone's bones. I let it go. I wasn't too sure if she ever did.

The school year that once had weeks left now only had days and we were well within the home stretch. We were all excited and looking forward to relaxing from what turned out to be a rather trying year.

"Do you think you can come over this weekend sometime for an end of the year celebration?" Meghan asked with pretty-please eyes.

"Sure, I'll see who else can..." I began before being interrupted.

"I was thinking just us... and Mother, of course – '*Three Commandments*' and all..." she said.

"OK, how about Monday morning. I think I may have figured out that arm-lock of yours." I all but asked for another beating.

"You're on!" she said as though challenging me.

I invited her to my Confirmation Service which would happen two Sundays from then. She smiled, nodded, and gave me a big hug.

REFLECTIONS:

That Friday night, Wales, Gene, and I were sitting in Gene's *Headquarters*. The three of us didn't get together as often outside of school as we would have liked. Well, Wales had Leigh and now I had Meghan but Gene and I were able to make it work and tonight Wales did too. We had a ball, eating pizza, making fun of each other, and playing video games. Things kind of got serious as we recapped the year. We were all surprised at how much each of us had grown over the year.

"Yeah, I mean, look at me... I was scared about the dance and it feels like I've been stretched every time I turned around since then." I said.

"You're wel-come!" Gene replied obnoxiously. I knew where he was going with that and in some kind of way he was right in that he played a part (rather was used by God to play a part) in helping me grow.

"Yeah, OK..." I gave it to him...

"Let's not forget who masterminded the events." Wales said, pretending to examine his fingernails in a high-society kind of way.

"That is true, man. I just don't know how you do it time after time but you do come through for your people." Gene complimented.

"Why thank you, thank you very much." Wales' Elvis impersonation was um… lacking.

"But for real though… and I'm just saying… how different would things be if the six of us didn't get together." I asked.

The three of us sat there in silence as we each drank some Coke Classic. We slowly shook our heads.

"Yeah, man, that's it right there." Gene thought out loud and then looked at us.

We sat in silence until I broke it.

"I'm hanging out with Meghan at her house on Monday. Probably gonna get my butt kicked again."

"Yo, you gotta get me in on some of that training!" Gene insisted.

"Naw man, ain't gonna have you rollin' around on the grass with my girl!" I insisted. Funny how my grammar would slip sometimes around Gene.

"Wait a second!" Wales exclaimed, "You guys study with Leigh sometimes!"

We all laughed.

"Wait up, didn't she say something about taking Summer classes?" Gene asked.

"Yup! That's my girl! She wants to take advanced whatever math. She told me but I don't remember." Wales, like the rest of us, thought that school was mostly a Winter sport and that the Summer was best left for fun.

"Well, more power to her." I said, "If anyone can handle it, it's Leigh."

AN INTRODUCTION, OF SORTS:

I woke up Monday morning at six-thirty, a full hour past normal time and you know what? There was no alarm! Yeah, I disabled that sleep-killing electro-demon for the Summer and I pumped my fist as I got up. I looked at the picture of me and Meghan slow-dancing and thought about the day we were going to have. Sure, I was bound to get hurt but at least we would be together. I thought about how strange it was that spending time with her had gotten to be so easy. Heck, it was even easy being around her mom – go figure!

The quick breakfast I had was still settling as I walked up the now friendly driveway. As I drew closer and closer to the door I wondered if my "friends" would join me. My finger sunk into the doorbell housing and I heard the melodic sound inside. "OK, no friends here so I guess everything is cool, great!" I thought. When the door opened it was like a camera flash went off but not really. How can I explain it? It was like a flash of light without light. It let me see without seeing that my four friends were indeed standing right there like before – two in front and two in back. OK, there was now NO WAY this was my imagination. I mean I saw what I thought were Meghan's and her mom's reactions before but that could've been anything, right? Sure enough Meghan opens the door and stops, pausing to look around for a few seconds with a strange expression. OK, I'm all over this now.

"Meghan, what's wrong?"

"Nothing… It's just that… no, it's nothing."

"OK… weird, but OK…" I knew her pretty well by then and knew she was holding a lot back for some reason. "May I come in?"

"Um… sure! Of course!"

Looking back, I now realize how monumentally stupid this was. Look, If God lets you know that you need angelic protection, the most dominant warriors in existence, do yourself a favor and take it seriously.

My teenaged butt didn't and I just walked my happy tail into a situation that must have been dangerous somehow for the third time! Oh what teenage hormones and emotions do to a brain. This reminds me of that "Frying Pan" TV commercial, "This is Your Brain on Drugs". OK, time for a commercial break, go look that up on the Internet. Don't worry, I'll wait. OK, so I chose to walk in anyway, and why? Because my girlfriend stood on the other side of the threshold. I have to chalk that one up to a lack of good sense and a fried egg.

Meghan's mother was in the adjacent sitting room staring at me. This made me uncomfortable.

"Hi Ms. O'Neil!" I greeted her cheerfully.

"Hello Joe, I trust you and yours are well?" Ms. O'Neil said. OK, this was weird, this was the Ms. O'Neil from the mall a few years ago, not the fun-loving lady who helped me tease her daughter. Something was wrong.

"So Meghan, should we get started?"

Meghan looked at her mother who gave a nod of some sort. "Um… sure, but before that, Mother wants me to talk to you."

"Uh… sure, we can talk." I said this but as any guy will tell you, when a girl says they "need to" or "want to" talk, it's a great big red flag and my Spidey sense was a-tingling!

"Come with me…"

As she led me by the hand up the stairs, I noticed her mother's head tracking us… like a machine of some kind – eyes fixed on us. We made it to that "sitting room" where we shared a moment after dinner that night and then through it to a door off of the second-floor hallway. She opened the door and there was her bedroom.

"Uh… Siobhan, Three Commandments, remember? I don't think…"

"Trust me." she interrupted as she pulled me in and closed the door. "I need to be where I'm most comfortable to talk about this."

"Alright, dude, you're weirding me out like seriously right now!"

"Trust me, you'll see."

The bedroom was big like the other rooms in this mansion, I mean like easily four times the size of mine. She had a four-poster-bed complete with the veil and next to it an ornate wooden night stand upon which sat our framed slow-dance picture along with the Ray-Ban sunglasses and the geode I'd given her for Christmas. There was a wardrobe, the C.S. Lewis kind, an adjoined bathroom and other ornate (expensive) furniture. A large television that made me feel like it was watching us like some one-eyed monster sat on a chest of drawers. There were a few posters on the walls, Pat Benetar - as expected, Stevie Nicks posing in a black dress, and one of Queen. Everything sat upon a big oval oriental rug, maroon in color, with a pattern running throughout. As this was a corner room, there were windows on the two furthest walls from the door and sunlight shown through the windows on the one side and cast window-pane shadows on the floor.

"Let's sit on the floor." she said as she sat cross-legged on the rug. I joined, facing her.

Nervous, I began rub my geode necklace through my shirt.

"It's cute that you do that."

"Do what?" I asked.

"Touch your necklace, I've seen you do it a few times and you didn't even know you were doing it." she replied, smiling a soft admiring smile.

"What do we need to talk about?" I asked as though the proverbial "other shoe" were about to drop.

"OK..." she started. The pause after that was not a good sign – it never is. "You invited me to your Confirmation Service and I'm honored, I really am, but we need to talk about it."

My mind spun as I was trying to think of what we could possibly need to talk about. I was brought back to focus as she continued...

"Mother and I, we're um... Christians... plus"

"Uh... plus what?" I asked, fear creeping up my spine.

"Plus some things we've learned that I need to share with you."

"Meghan, I'm not gonna lie, I am VERY concerned right now."

"I get it but you'll understand when I introduce you."

"OK, introduce... OK, to who!" I was worried.

"Wouldn't you say that life is a journey?"

"OK, I guess." I answered.

"Alright, good, every good journey needs a guide, right?"

"Maybe, I don't know."

"The answer is 'yes' and we *do* know."

"OK, alright, Jesus is my guide." I said.

"OK, sure, but what if you could have another one, like in addition?"

"What. Are. You. Talking. About?"

"I know how you feel about me, and I feel the same way about you, do you trust me?"

"You're starting to make me wonder but, yes."

"Will you trust me just a little bit further?"

"Yes."

"Phil, there's a reason we're so in sync with each other, why we feel such a strong connection. Mother and I think we knew each other before. How, why, and how well we knew each other we'll have to find out."

"What in the world are you..."

"Just do this for me... This one thing..." she interrupted, putting out her hands, palms facing up. "OK, put your palms on mine and close your eyes and do what I say. OK?"

Not proud of this but I did it.

"Do you feel my hands underneath yours?"

"Yes." I replied, her palms were soft and uncharacteristically moist, as if she were sweating nervously.

"OK, you know that place between our hands where you end and I begin, erase that, let that line fade from your mind. There's just us now, not the two of us."

Something changed. I don't know what but it did.

There was a long pause and I could hear her breathing heavily. The pause was so long and awkward that I was just about to open my eyes when she spoke.

"Come with me..." she said in a soft almost sleep-like whispered voice.

Then we were... there. It was like dreaming but I was fully awake... I mean more awake than I had been. The sky was somewhat cloudy and contained the brightest moon I'd ever seen in my life. It was shining like a mini-sun between banks of clouds - it was so beautiful. We were standing in a meadow flanked with groves of trees. On one side I could see the ocean in the far distance, its expanse illuminated by the moon just enough to see the distinction between the sea and the sky. The grass was tall, up to our knees, and seemed to sway in a breeze that wasn't there. The ground was soft and warm, the air was still and smelled as sweet as the best of Spring days. As beautiful as this place was, it didn't feel right somehow. I could feel it somehow pleading with me as if it were saying, "Be at peace, this is where you belong." The sensation was so intoxicating that I sort of lost myself as I watched the moonlight play of the leaves of the trees, and twinkle on the distant surface of the water and then I saw Meghan. She was dressed in a white gown of sorts but she was radiant, almost glowing. She was beautiful as if the moonlight washed away any imperfections. The way the light danced on her hair and face made me think she was made of the same substance as the unbelievable moon in the sky. I regarded myself only to find I too was awash in moonlight, dressed in white, and physically "perfected" like she was.

We were alone here and we walked together in this private Eden as I suppose Adam and Eve once did in theirs. We held hands as we walked a distance toward the ocean and it finally dawned on me to ask, "Wow, where are we?"

She smiled back at me and said, "This is the meeting place. It's somewhere between where we are and where she is."

"Who?" I asked.

"Let me introduce you to my Guide, The High Evolutionary, Lady Siobhan of the Gaels." She motioned for me to turn around. I did so and there, kind of floating several inches off of the ground was the most devastatingly beautiful woman I'd ever seen. She too was dressed in white but her gown was flowing in that breeze that wasn't there. Her face kept morphing from one strikingly beautiful face to another every few seconds.

"Why... why is her face changing?" I asked.

"She shows the faces of all the women she's been throughout history. She's a high-elevated person, Phil. She's dedicated to helping us get to where she is."

Then she spoke.

"Welcome, Phil... We have much to discuss." Her voice, if you could call it that, sounded like a chorus of women speaking at once.

AT LEAST... that's what Meghan *wanted* to happen. I would later learn that this is how their "Introduction Ceremony" is *supposed* to go.

HERE'S WHAT ACTUALLY HAPPENED...

"Phil, there's a reason we're so in sync with each other, why we feel such a strong connection. Mother and I think we knew each other before. How, why, and how well we knew each other we'll have to find out."

"What in the world are you..."

"Just do this for me... This one thing..." she interrupted, putting out her hands, palms facing up. "OK, put your palms on mine and close your eyes and do what I say. OK?"

Not proud of this but I did it.

"Do you feel my hands underneath yours?"

"Yes." I replied, her palms were soft and uncharacteristically moist, as if she were sweating nervously.

"OK, you know that place between our hands where you end and I begin, erase that, let that line fade from your mind. There's just us now, not the two of us."

Something changed. I don't know what but it did.

There was a long pause and I could hear her breathing heavily. The pause was so long and awkward that I was just about to open my eyes when she spoke.

"Come with me..." she said in a soft almost sleep-like whispered voice.

All at once the atmosphere, that spiritual awareness that allowed me to sense my 'friends' and feel the Voice on the field, SHIFTED and I knew in my spirit that I was in danger somehow. The Voice that I felt, not heard, on the upper field at school came back as clear as it had been that day.

"Stand up!" the Voice said. I did so immediately and when I did, Meghan scurried to the far wall in fear.

I could feel my four friends but they weren't just standing there anymore. I could feel that they were somehow closer and protecting me. I could feel that they had swords of some kind and they were poised for battle somehow.

"Recite the poem you wrote." I felt the Voice say. After reading the book of poetry Pastor Summerstone had given me, I'd written some of my own. One in particular came to mind and it just flowed from the top of my head...

The Light, it shines in the darkness and the darkness flees.

This is something that those mired in darkness, they cannot seize.

Though ten-thousand fallen angels stand before me with wings unfurled,

I fear not.

For greater is He that is in me than he that is in the world!

Ten thousand demons before me stand

All are swept by His command!

So let it be known throughout the land,

that Jesus the Christ sits at the Father's right hand.

For upon Whom shall I call in my day of dread

But the One Who shall judge both the quick and the dead.

This is He who's held me since the day of my birth

The LORD the God who made the heavens and the Earth.

Meghan began to cry and I mean weep.

"Do not turn around, back out of the room slowly." I felt the Voice say. The five of us began to back out slowly without turning. When we got to the hallway, Ms. O'Neil had her back up to the wall, arms spread wide and flat against the wall, as though she were pinned somehow.

"Get out of my house!" Ms. O'Neil struggled to scream as best she could as though in pain.

Saying nothing, I continued to back down the hallway through the "sitting room" and then down the steps. My friends were not playing. I knew that they were ready to strike when and if they had to for somehow I knew they were still poised for battle like in the bedroom.

Once I was off the property entirely, the tension in my spirit began to subside. Dazed, confused, and somewhat horrified, I began walking through Roland Park. I guess I made it several blocks when suddenly an ambulance with sirens tore out of a driveway just a few feet in front of me. The hedges obscured the driveway such that I couldn't see it coming. Just as I was about to start walking again, a tan Volvo tore out of the driveway and followed the ambulance. Adrenalin pumping at max I paused, looked around the corner of the hedges to make sure there were no other cars and walked the rest of the way through Roland Park making my way to Falls Road where I caught the bus and found myself at home within the hour. I called my mother at work and told her I wasn't feeling well so I came home early, this was somewhat true.

"MAD WORLD" - TEARS FOR FEARS:

Exhausted somehow on so many levels I slept well into the night with few interruptions from concerned parents. It was 3:35 the next morning when I sat at my desk and at least tried to begin to chronicle what happened at Meghan's house. I remember the time because of the clock's angry red numbers biting through the darkness of my room as I awoke as if they were red-hot and burning themselves into my memory like a branding iron. I tried and tried and then I cried and cried. I was DEVASTATED. I cried for profound loneliness. I cried for Meghan's friendship. I cried for Meghan's soul. And then I slept.

In the following days it became rather apparent that Meghan and I were no longer together. This was a bit more than a shock to my parents who were rather seriously "pro-Meghan". To their credit and my sincere respect, they respected my process. They gave me space. They let me grieve. Then they worried. They worried because I was despondent, there were no signs of progress. I mean, granted, only a few days had passed but how long could I really lay on my bed staring at my ceiling before someone would think I needed help... which they sought in the form of Pastor Summerstone who paid a visit. They let us have some one-on-one time wherein I told him everything that had taken place. My parents opened the door to check in on us only to find both of us sitting in the room staring off into space with blank expressions, his eyes wide as saucers. They gently closed the door without saying a word.

"We are WELL outside my experience here; I will not lie." he said incredulously.

"Join the club." I responded. Neither one of us looking at each other directly.

"I know confirmation classes are over and the service is this Sunday but I need to see you often." he said.

"I agree."

"Here, this is my home number. You call me anytime, day or night, if... well... if something happens." he said as he scribbled something on the back of what looked like a business card.

"I will but Pastor Summerstone, what do you think I should do in the meantime?"

"Well, for starters, I don't think you need to be seeing Meghan or her mother."

My voice broke as I said, "I hadn't planned too."

"Secondly, I want you praying. I can only imagine that it will be hard and you are very sad right now but I need you praying."

After we spoke some more about God's grace and we prayed for Meghan and her mom, he left me in the solitude of my room. Let me say something here, and I didn't know it at the time, teenagers aren't the best people to leave alone to figure things out for themselves. Remember the brain on hormones and emotions – don't think that goes away so easily. So, in the coming paragraphs I hope you can hang with me as I try to describe for you what it's like for a teenager dealing with life issues for which they have no framework to process. The first thing that happens is that a teenager will blow things WAY out of proportion, words like "never" and "always" creep into their vocabularies. They say things like, "I will NEVER meet someone like her again!" and, "I will ALWAYS be alone." Think about it, they've never had these experiences before so how do they know how to deal with them? That's why they need adults when this stuff happens. They need their parents and other trusted adults to help them gain the right perspective. They may also get oddly particular about the weirdest things but neglect other things. For instance, they may start to count days but neglect showering or eating. Like I did, they may become very clean, cleaning themselves, their rooms, etc. and neglect people. I was pretty textbook when it came to my descent into depression and despair. There was a word for what I was going through but I just couldn't find it. It seemed as though the world had lost its color and there was no more fascination about anything. My life during that period was a complex masterpiece painting of distorted swirls of the color gray. Everything, food, entertainment, computer stuff, all tasted gray and sounded blah.

Like some demented version of the *Twelve Days of Christmas* I began to count days. So on day four since the incident, the Friday, I declined the opportunity to hang out with Gene who I'd been talking to on the phone the whole week. He was shocked and I could tell he was, in his own way, hurting for me. No, I chose to lay there on my bed and stay in my own headspace. I would later learn that my situation had caused concern among the other *Mysfits*. Even if I'd known that, it wouldn't have made a difference. You see, depression and despair are like pain in that they become the only things you can think about. I put on slow music and laid on my bed as much as I could. I was ordered to dinner and chores but that was all I intended to do. I got pretty good at counting and making shapes out of the cracks and brush strokes in the paint on my bedroom ceiling, like faces in the clouds. I had a long way to go.

Day five was like day four, pretty much more of the same except it was Saturday and my parents were home so that meant they forced me to interact. I was made to go grocery shopping and I had to eat with them as was the custom every day. My brother called. He was sorry for me but could offer little comfort as he was to be in Delaware for the Summer due to school stuff. I thought about the next day and the Confirmation Service in which I would have to participate. Somehow, I just didn't feel like it. Boy, listen to that! I'd had experiences with and from God Himself and I took them for granted, see, I told you depression and despair can make you look inward and neglect things.

Day six was here and it was time to get up and get ready. I did so with relative ease although robotically because life tasted gray, sounded dark, and looked like a dull hum. In a suit and tie now, looking quite dapper for a robot programmed to go through the motions, all I could think about was getting back to my nice bed and brush strokes on the ceiling. There is something comforting in lying about and not doing anything that appeals to the depressed teenager. It's too much like not having to deal with things anymore, not having the weight of life on your shoulders, it's peaceful and restful when you know you will ALWAYS NEVER have peace and rest again. It's like being dead to the world. Death… hmm…

MAUERBAUERTRAURIGKEIT:

I would normally have been delighted to see the other *Mysfits* attending my Church service but today it was just "meh…" I was sitting up front and to the side facing the center aisle with my confirmation class. As the service progressed, I could feel the eyes of my friends finding me and sizing me up. They were concerned, I knew it but I just didn't care. All I cared about was trying to ease this pain, this dull ache that no one in the world had EVER felt and that I would NEVER be free of because I would ALWAYS feel it.

One by one we stepped to the microphone, read selected passages of Scripture, and answered challenge questions and made vows confirming our prior baptisms and our faith in Jesus Christ as our Lord and Savior. I knew Him to be so in many ways… but the loneliness, my God the loneliness and the emotional ache. This experience, one which should have been a joyous occasion, an important memory filled with friends, family, fellowship, and cake, was slathered in the grayest of paints by my bleak outlook. Afterwards, during the reception that followed in the fellowship hall, I saw Leigh and my mother talking for a long time. I just knew mom was filling her in on my new lifestyle and that I'd probably get a phone call later in the week… whoopee!

That night, as I lay on my bed of peace and despair, my mother entered the room.

"Phil, honey?"

"Yes, ma'am?"

"I got a chance to talk to Leigh today. I've always liked that Leigh." Of course she did, all the parents did. Let me tell you something about Leigh Winter Adams... Leigh could call your parents at 3:34 in the morning on any given day and say, "Uh... hi... I need to come over to your house now and rob the place then burn it down with you in it, is that OK?" and they would think to themselves, "Leigh must have a good reason..." and be all like, "Well I guess you have a good reason... do you need a ride?" I'm serious, she'd built that kind of trust.

"She starts Summer school for advanced math tomorrow." Mom added.

"Yeah, I heard..." I said dismissively.

"School ends at eleven and she needs a place to study so she asked if she could come here." Now she had my attention. "She will be coming here every day from twelve to six or when I get home so I can take her home."

"What... Why?" I emoted as though I were being punished.

"You will let her in every day for the six weeks and make or order lunch for her, I prefer you order it. Do you understand?"

Normally a friend coming over would be nice but not now. "Alright, I get it..." I mumbled something about Leigh and heard...

"What did you say?"

"Sorry..." Apparently bad-mouthing Leigh was not allowable.

On day seven, sure enough, "ding-dong" yelled the doorbell. There was Leigh, on the porch fresh off the bus or something. So help me, if she had someone drop her off here and not at her own house...

Opening the door, "Hi Leigh, please come in."

"Hi to you too. how are you, Joey?" she meant that from her heart, like really, so I couldn't be rude.

"Everything kind of sucks..." best I could do.

She put her arms around me and told me things would get better. She knew I'd heard that cliché a lot recently so she didn't belabor the point. We made our way to the basement where she set up shop at the bar sitting on a barstool and dove right into whatever it was they'd gone over that day in class. I'd ordered sandwiches from *Steamboat Angela's* before she got to my house so they'd be on time. She enjoyed it as much as I usually did. Mine tasted... gray. Leigh was one of my best friends in life and by day eleven I realized that I'd never spent that much time with her, like just us. Sure, I was watching re-runs of *Get Smart*, *I Dream of Jeannie*, and *Gidget* every day before she joined me for *Star Trek* but I saw pretty quickly what Wales sees in her. I have only known a few of what I consider to be genuinely selfless people in my life and Leigh is one of them. Speaking of Wales, he managed to come over for the afternoon every now and then. That too would have been nice but you know... gray and all.

The following days were more of the same, gray and blah. Leigh (and sometimes Wales) just wouldn't let me be. Gene's birthday was on the 15th of July and the *Mysfits* had gone to see *Labyrinth* and hang out. We wound up catching *Ferris Beuhler's Day Off* too. "They made a movie about Wales!" Bruce exclaimed when it was over. My birthday was the 20th, just a few days away so we made plans to go see *Aliens*. I wasn't up to it and was trying to find a way to break that news. I was spiraling down into a deceitful type of despair, the worst kind, so it should be no surprise that by day 37 I was annoyed and on top of that it was a "Wales Day" too. So there the three of us were, in the basement as usual. Having just finished lunch, Wales and I were trying to get smart by watching an episode of it while Leigh was getting smart the old-fashioned way.

"Why do you guys do it?" I asked out loud as I continued to look at the TV.

"Do what?" Wales asked.

"It's been over a month and you guys keep coming here when you and I both know you could just go home."

"Because you're here..." Leigh said. I heard her get off of the stool.

"Why don't you just let me be by myself like I want to be!" I said as I got up to face her.

Knowing something was up, Wales turned off the TV and stood up too.

Walking towards me she said, "You can't be alone, you need people."

"Really! What makes you think I need you!" I yelled.

"Hey, man..." Wales said gently as he put his hand on my shoulder.

Knocking it off me, I replied, "No! Answer the question! I don't need anyone! I don't need you here! Why don't you just LEAVE!" My frustration had been building all this time and I was bound to blow up at somebody.

Without saying a word, she closed the distance between us and wrapped her arms around me. I actually tried to break free but she held on and then pulled Wales in. They were holding me tight.

"Get off me and just go! Why don't you just leave!" I yelled, my voice breaking.

She put her face next to my ear and said, without raising her voice, "We're not gonna let you drown, Joey."

"Drown..." That word sunk in for a moment. It was the word I'd been searching for this whole time. I broke, just sobbing and I dropped to my knees. They went down with me, just holding me as tight as they could. Then they started to cry and then to weep just like me. The three of us were a sobbing mess and then Leigh started to pray through her tears the most gentle and delicate appeal to her Father on my behalf. I would write some of it but it's too delicate to sit on paper. I wept all the more that such an innocent plea could be made for me. We were weeping as she continued to pray and then she pulled both of us in tight and let go of English as she took hold of the language the Spirit gave her to speak with God her Father in private. At the same time Wales began to quote Scripture, like with authority. I'd never known him to quote Scripture, let alone to do so with such precision. It was like he was a biblical sniper shooting each of my issues like so many tin cans at target practice. He started with the 23rd Psalm, went some other places, and then repeated several "The Lord is my..." statements. "The Lord is my provider... my Healer... my Protector... my Comforter..." he continued to say repeatedly. OK, I must admit that I wasn't the swiftest horse in the race so it took me a minute to realize that as he was repeating his phrases, Leigh was repeating hers as well, though not in English. I could feel the atmosphere shifting and we wept as a weight I could not begin to explain came up off my shoulders. Leigh felt it too because, tears streaming down her face, she began to thank God for the work He'd done and how He'd answered her prayers. It was the most powerful experience I'd ever had with someone up to that point. We didn't want to let go of each other so we didn't for a long time. When we did, the sheer sight of each other made us weep from our hearts. I'd never been moved so deeply. Until then I'd never cared for and been cared for so deeply by my friends. It was so strong that we had to sit back-to-back to keep from crying. Through tears I apologized profusely for what I'd put them through.

"It's OK Joey, we love you and when you hurt, we do too." Leigh said as they turned to look at me.

When our eyes met, they again glazed, then dripped, then ran with tears of appreciation. God had done a profound thing and we knew it. From then on whenever things got gray I would remember those tears and be encouraged.

Eventually the tears that came at the sight of each other subsided and we sat there encouraging each other for the rest of the afternoon. We spoke of what happened while Leigh was praying. I knew she was a member of a different denomination than me and that Wales and his family joined her church.

"In our church, we're encouraged to believe God for the miraculous." she said. "As I spoke, Tommy was apparently moved to interpret."

"Yeah, that was new to me but I'm glad He did that." Wales added.

I felt comfortable somehow telling them everything that happened, like I shared with Gene and Pastor Summerstone. With wide eyes they listened to me tell them about my "friends" each time at Meghan's house. I went on to tell Leigh about the upper field, something Wales already knew about.

"Why didn't you tell all of us about this before?" Leigh asked with an almost hurt tone in her voice.

"I guess I thought you guys would think I was crazy."

"Oh, Joey, we're all in this together..." she said in that one tone that makes you feel both ashamed and loved all at once.

"Yeah man, together from now on... OK?"

"Alright... all in then..." I said.

We were all in agreement but I knew something was up because Leigh kept looking away nervously. I was just about to ask her about it when she started to speak.

"And, I guess... since we're all in this together, I need you guys to help me."

Both Wales and I agreed with curious looks on our faces.

"Well... oh my gosh this is really hard..." Leigh said putting her hand over her mouth.

"Whatever it is, you know we're here for you, Leigh." Wales offered.

"OK, you know how I get stressed out about school and stuff? Especially exams and whatnot?"

"Sure, but you always do well, right?" I asked.

"Ha... yeah... I do but that's the thing. What you guys don't know is the pressure in my family that my sister and I have had to go through. The pressure to do well in everything is really high and stressful. When Laurel saw how hard it was on me, she taught me how to deal with it like she does… by smoking marijuana."

With the slightest nudge from a feather Wales and I would have fallen over.

"It was a little at first but now it's hard for me to get by without it. I hide it pretty well but I'm struggling with it. Laurel gives it to me whenever she comes home."

I took one look at Wales and if I wasn't proud of him before I sure was now. The look of dogged and tearful determination on his face let me know that in some way he'd grown over the past few seconds. He put his hands on Leigh's shoulders and looked her straight in the eyes.

"We will beat this. If you're struggling then I'm struggling too."

She nodded and accepted his hug.

My mind was swimming. The perfect image of Leigh's family that I'd envisioned dissolved in an instant and all I could think about was how I could help Leigh. We agreed that we would do whatever it took and somehow at the time that seemed to be enough.

When we heard my mother come through the door, we were amazed that it was after 5:00 - that time had flown by so quickly. Leigh packed up her stuff and we went upstairs to meet her. She put her arms around my mother and said as she found a few more tears, "We had a good day! A really good day!" Right then I was added to the list of people whose houses she could burn down in the middle of the night with them inside and I didn't mind at all.

The weight of despair was gone and though my time of dealing with depression was long from over, a corner had been turned, I was equipped for the battle. The oppressive gloom was gone, color began to creep back into the world and with it that sense of wonder as if all things were new. Hope began to grow like so many flowers in a field in Spring. Taste returned to food and the melody of life that is the hallmark of the young hung softly on the wind of the four corners of my world. A few days later as I turned fourteen, I realized I'd received in the form of powerful life lessons and friends the best gifts for which I could have ever hoped.

WESLEY:

As had become our custom after a movie, we went to the pizza place near the arcade in the Golden Ring Mall. I was still reeling from the experiences of earlier that week and told the rest of the *Mysfits* that I would fill them in after the movie. So, as promised, in a somewhat secluded corner booth I told the rest of my best friends the story from top to bottom – upper field to Meghan's bedroom. I left out the details of what happened in my basement because I thought that was a personal thing between Wales, Leigh, and myself. Leigh and Wales seemed to feel the same way. However, I should note that as I relayed the details of that experience during a working session with Gene, he was none too pleased that we'd kept the more spiritual part of that to ourselves all these years. I suppose we still have some work to do on being totally transparent... maybe. I still feel that some things are personal and should remain so. Anyway, after relaying the details of those events, A few of us noticed that Wes wasn't quite himself. He seemed disengaged and preoccupied and since game recognizes game so to speak, I knew he was depressed.

"What's got you down, Wes?" I asked with a knowing look on my face. The thing is, I didn't know where he was in the process. He could have blown up and caused a terrible scene or he could have cried and spilled the beans. Thankfully it was the latter. Wes folded his hands on the table and looked at me for a second then everyone else, their faces becoming more pensive as they realized there was something really wrong.

"He hit her." Wes said, voice cracking and not due to puberty. He then gained a bit more control and continued, "He hit her and knocked her down!" he grunted that last statement with rage.

"Whoa… whoa..." I said, "Who hit who?"

He looked at me with a wry look as if to say that I knew very well who hit who and I just didn't want to admit it. He was bouncing his leg absent-mindedly and started to fidget in his seat. "His company lost a contract so they let him go, they fired him! He got mad and hit her when they got into it over money. <Expletive>, <expletive>, <expletive>, what the <expletive> am I gonna do!" Tears started to flow. So, side note here about Wes… he'd never been like this around us and by that I mean vulnerable. Sure, he hung out with us but this was the first time we'd seen him really open up. He must have been in a lot of pain. Anyway, just when I thought I couldn't have been more impressed with our group of friends, Leigh reached out and took his hands and, on that cue, we all did.

"I don't know. Wes, we don't know what to do but you're not alone in this." she said. She had that way of saying something you expected everyone to say but in a way that made you know she really meant it. I'd experienced this first-hand a month before. We all expressed the same sentiment and went on to discuss what we would do while Wes sat there and let us help him make decisions. I later learned that sitting there and letting us not only into his business but suggest and decide what would happen was the hardest thing he'd ever done in his life. Even as the only child of a rather strict father and somewhat compliant mother, he turned out to be independent and very self-confident. It was hard for him to swallow his pride like that but it was a testament to how much he trusted us.

We decided to bring our parents into it and have them as gently as possible reach out to his mother. We knew this would be hard and Wes thought there would be consequences but the alternative scared him more, and rightly so. Just as we'd planned outings and events, we planned this thing out methodically. We each knew how we thought each of our parents would react so we decided that we would tell them in order of most to least cautionary and have them call each other in that sequence to make sure no one would fly off the handle. This way they could approach Mrs. Moon as a united front. It actually worked much better than we could have hoped because the parents, much like their children, decided to get together and discuss what they were going to do. A few days after that, the mothers had a dinner to which they invited Mrs. Moon. I was told it took a lot of doing but Mrs. Moon agreed to a plan for she, Wes, and their dog, Tango, to leave the house with the help of the other parents. Not only did our parents bond over this but something about this reinforced all the more how much we needed each other. The plan had them moving sometime in October so we all had to play it cool for the months of August and September, even during the end of summer cookout at Bruce's house.

That August, we saw a lot of Wes and his presence was very much welcomed. Not only could we keep an eye on him, it made sure he didn't have a confrontation with his dad that could put the plan in jeopardy. It turned out to be good for him too; the more we hung out and just took it easy, the more relaxed he seemed to get. Heck, we even got him to laugh a few times like at the cookout when Wales got up and sang a karaoke version of Michael Jackson's *Beat It*. He beat it to death alright but that was good. That all worked just as Wales intended, he knew the tension would be high so he brought a karaoke machine and everyone's attempts to do what Meghan had done so well several months prior made everyone laugh – even Mr. Moon. It's funny, even with all of that going on, my mind still wandered to Meghan and that one shining day at the Harbor during Spring break. Dag! Being a teenager was hard.

MR. TIDEWATER:

The following is not something I experienced first-hand, rather it is something we all pieced together over the coming year. This is our best guess of what happened and exactly why. Understandably, we weren't able to ask specifics but as far as the rumor-mill went, this is the absolute cream of the crop that could be verified. I, of course, applied a bit of artistic license.

Lyle Tidewater, beloved music teacher and storied legend of the school in terms of what he meant to the community as a whole, sat alone in his spare bedroom turned office in his craftsman home. His wife and son were away at a birthday party for one of his son's friends. In picture frames, the walls held many memories of band competitions and students whose lives he'd touched over the years – many of whom dropped him a line from time to time. He regarded the pictures from his chair behind his desk. In each corner of the room stood a stand upon which a musical instrument gleamed in the light. He was meticulous in the polishing of these prized possessions and displayed them prominently. His gaze fell upon the single picture frame on his desk which held a photo capturing a happy moment in time when his wife was holding their three-year old son, now ten, at a community pool. It had been his son's first time in a pool and they'd found the parents' joy of experiencing old things afresh through the eyes of a child. He remembered his wife as being beauty-queen material before their son's birth but never quite so after. In fact, she'd rather let herself go just a few years after that picture. He ran his fingers over the picture for a moment before his eyes found the letter on his desk. He read the opening sentences again, hoping they'd changed in the intervening minutes since he'd last read them.

Mr. Tidewater, it has come to our attention that several acts of impropriety may have occurred concerning you and a female student whom we decline to name in this letter. We have chosen to contact you in this manner as we feel it to be the least disruptive method at our disposal. Please make yourself available for an emergency meeting of the school's board this coming Monday night at 7:00.

"One mistake, one, and so many years down the drain." he muttered to himself. He knew what happened. He knew because although he urged her to think of her reputation and his career, she was scared... and pregnant. He knew that she'd told someone - her parents, another teacher, it didn't matter who, the effect was still the same. It was all over, his career and almost certainly his marriage.

Mr. Tidewater kept in pretty impressive shape. Even still, his hair grew white and the years shown on his face in ways that disturbed him. The thought of being able to turn the head of an attractive young girl was exciting to him. He thought it ironic that he minded his figure more than his wife. He tried to justify what he'd done because he didn't find his wife attractive anymore but even he couldn't believe that. He did what he did because he wanted to and that was the end of it. He even tried to blame the girl for telling someone. "Stephanie, why did you have to say something!" he yelled. He knew that this too was wrong. She was a pregnant teenager, what was she going to do but tell someone. At the beginning of the past school year, he'd entered into a relationship with Stephanie Anders, the school's Drum Majorette. He'd somehow found the exhilaration and taboo to be so intoxicating that the mere thought of it made him feel young and vital again.

He ran his hands though his hair and leaned back in his seat. He held this position for a few minutes as he contemplated his next move. Having precious few choices, he sat forward in his chair, placed his palms flat on his desk and nodded his head as if to agree with a line of reasoning only he could hear. He then got up and put on a record of his favorite symphony. He stood there for a minute reflecting on the beauty of the music. Giving a nod to the record player, he retired to the bathroom where he took off his clothes, folded them, then lay in the tub where he relieved his veins of their burden with his straight razor.

Lyle Tidewater, beloved music teacher and storied legend of the school in terms of what he meant to the community as a whole... was gone.

If you or someone you know is struggling with thoughts of suicide, please, please call

The 988 Suicide and Crisis Lifeline

(National Suicide Prevention Lifeline)

Dial the three-digit dialing code **988**

or

1-800-273-8255

There is no shame in reaching out for help!

Literally EVERYONE in your life will thank you for it!

			Music References				
Artist's Last Name	Artist's First Name	Song Title	*Name of album in which the song first appeared*	Production Company	Year Released	Medium	Ref. in Chapter
Hill	Patty and Mildred J.	"Happy Birthday to You"	*N/A*	Clayton F. Summy	1893.	Sheet.	5
Fishman,	Paul. (Re-Flex)	"The Politics of Dancing."	*The Politics of Dancing.*	EMI, Capitol Records,	1983.	Record.	10
Hart,	Corey.	"Sunglasses at Night."	*First Offense.*	EMI,	1983.	Record.	11
	Tears for Fears.	"Everybody Wants to Rule the World."	*Songs from the Big Chair.*	Phonogram, Mercury,	1985.	Record.	11
Michael	George. (Wham!)	"Careless Whisper."	*Make It Big.*	Columbia,	1984.	Record.	11
	Foreigner.	"I Want To Know What Love Is."	*Agent Provocateur.*	Atlantic,	1984.	Record.	11
	Pointer Sisters.	"Slow Hand."	*Black & White.*	Planet Records,	1981.	Record.	13
	Lipps Inc.	"Funky Town."	*Mouth to Mouth.*	Cassablanca Records,	1979.	Record.	13
	Shalamar.	"A Night to Remember."	*Friends.*	SOLAR,	1982.	Record.	13
Collins,	Phil (The Police).	"Every Breath You Take."	*Synchronicity.*	A&M,	1983.	Record.	13
Benatar,	Pat.	"Love Is a Battlefield."	*Live From Earth.*	Chrysalis,	1983.	Record.	14
Benatar,	Pat.	"We Belong."	*Tropico.*	Chrysalis,	1984.	Record.	14
	The Police	"Every Little Thing She Does is Magic."	*Ghost in the Machine.*	Atlantic,	1981.	Record.	14
Stevie Wonder	Paul McCartney	"Ebony and Ivory"	*"Tug of War"*	Columbia,	1981.	Record.	14
Lauper,	Cyndi.	"Time After Time."	*She's So Unusual.*	Portrait,	1983.	Record.	14
Smith,	Curt (Tears for Fears).	"Mad World."	*The Hurting.*	Phonogram, Mercury,	1983.	Record.	15
Jackson,	Michael.	"Beat It."	*Thriller.*	Epic,	1982.	Record.	15
	Bananarama.	"Cruel Summer."	*Bananarama.*	London,	1984.	Record.	15

Movie References						
Film Title	**Director First Name**	**Director Last Name**	**Distributor**	**Year Released**	**Medium**	**Ref. in Chapter**
The Right Stuff.	Philip	Kaufman.	Warner Bros.	1983.	Film.	3
Star Trek III: The Search for Spock.	Leonard	Nimoy.	Paramount Pictures,	1984.	Film.	6
The Terminator.	James	Cameron.	Orion Pictures,	1984.	Film.	6
Back to the Future.	Robert	Zemeckis.	Universal Pictures,	1985.	Film.	8
A Nightmare on Elm Street 2: Freddy's Revenge.	Jack	Sholder.	New Line Cinema,	1985.	Film.	13
A Nightmare on Elm Street.	Wes	Craven.	New Line Cinema,	1984.	Film.	14
The Warriors.	Walter	Hill.	Paramount Pictures,	1979.	Film.	14
Labyrinth.	Jim	Henson	TriStar Pictures,	1986.	Film.	15
Ferris Beuhler's Day Off.	John	Hughes.	Paramount Pictures,	1986.	Film.	15
Aliens.	James	Cameron.	20th Century Fox,	1986.	Film.	15

Television References							
Episode Title	***Show Title***	**Studio**	**Broadcast Station**	**City**	**Date**	**Medium**	**Ref. in Chapter**
(Various)	*Who's the Boss*	Embassy Television	WJZ-TV,	Baltimore, Maryland	1984-1992	Television	9
(Various)	*The Cosby Show*	Carsey-Werner Productions	WMAR-TV,	Baltimore, Maryland	1984-1992	Television	10, 11, 14

			Television References				
Episode Title	Show Title	Studio	Broadcast Station	City	Date	Medium	Ref. in Chapter
(Various)	Peanuts animated specials	CBS	WMAR-TV,	Baltimore, Maryland	1971-1976	Television	14
"Frying Pan" (aka "Fried Egg" and "Any Questions?")	Public Service Announcement	Partnership for a Drug-Free America	Various	Baltimore, Maryland	1987	Television	15
(Various)	Get Smart	Talent Associates	WBAL-TV, WMAR-TV,	Baltimore, Maryland	1965 – 1970	Television	15
(Various)	I Dream of Jeannie	Sidney Sheldon Productions, Screen Gems	WBAL-TV,	Baltimore, Maryland	1965 – 1970	Television	15
(Various)	Gidget	Screen Gems	WJZ-TV,	Baltimore, Maryland	1965 – 1966	Television	15
(Various)	Star Trek	Desilu Productions, Norway Corporation, Paramount Television	WBAL-TV,	Baltimore, Maryland	1966 – 1969	Television	15

		Book References			
Author Last Name,	Author First Name	Title	Publisher,	Year	Ref in Chapter
Andersen	Hans Christian	The Princess and the Pea	C A Reitzel	1835	1
Clancy,	Tom	The Hunt for Red October	Naval Institute Press,	1984	4
Carroll	Lewis	Alice's Adventures in Wonderland	Macmillan	1865	12
Schultz,	Charles	Peanuts	United Feature Syndicate,	1950	14
Addams,	Charles	The Addams Family	The New Yorker	1938	14
Elohim	YHWH	Bible	King James Version	Various years BC and AD This translation: 1611 AD	Various

Video Game References						
Title	Version Number	Contributors	Company	Date of Version	Medium	Ref in Chapter
Karate Champ	1	Technōs Japan	Data East	1984	Video Game	6

Board Game References					
Designer	Date	Title of Game	City:	Publisher.	Ref. in Chapter
Lizzie Magie, Charles Darrow	(1935)	Monopoly		Parker Brothers	15